W9-BFO-231

Praise for Beth Webb Hart

"Like a Charleston garden in a Southern storm,
Love, Charleston exposes the tangled, tenuous roots
of Family in the ebb and flow of Faith and Love.
Hart's new novel is lush and gripping—
you won't want to put it down."
—Nicole Seitz, author of *Saving Cicadas*

"If you love Charleston, you will *Love, Charleston.*
Beth Webb Hart writes with flair and insight
about fascinating people and beautiful places."
—Robert Whitlow, bestselling author of *Deeper Water*

"*Love, Charleston* brims with heart-tugging emotion,
rich Southern details, and the hope
that's birthed through faith. Well done!"
—Rachel Hauck, author of *Dining with Joy*

"Taking the reader to the captivating and idyllic city
of Charleston, SC, Beth Webb Hart reminds readers
in that beautiful, poetic, Southern way she has,
that life is still flawed, people are still human,
dreams can still be delayed, but God's grace
casts a wide enough net to catch us all."
—Denise Hildreth, author of *Hurricanes in Paradise* and
Savannah from Savannah, regarding *Love, Charleston*

"Hart's writing is lovely, her characters endearing,
and humor leavens the darker moments."
—*Publishers Weekly* review of *The Wedding Machine*

BETH WEBB HART

Love, Charleston

Love Inspired

Recycling programs
for this product may
not exist in your area.

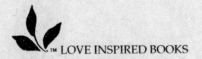 ™ LOVE INSPIRED BOOKS

ISBN-13: 978-0-373-78712-8

LOVE, CHARLESTON

Copyright © 2010 by Beth Webb Hart

This book was previously published by Thomas Nelson, Inc.

Scripture quotations are taken from the HOLY BIBLE:
NEW INTERNATIONAL VERSION® NIV®. Copyright © 1973, 1978, 1984
by Biblica, Inc.™ Used by permission of Zondervan. All rights reserved
worldwide.

www.LoveInspiredBooks.com

Printed in U.S.A.

Lovingly dedicated to my sisters,
Peggy and Libby

He restores my soul.
—Psalm 23:3

Chapter One

The Reverend Roy Jessup Summerall Jr.
April 3, 2008

Roy's right eyelid began to twitch when he sat down in the small antique chair across from Bishop Boatwright. He pulled at his stiff white collar. It was an XXL, but it fit his thick neck snugly, and he often undid the metal tab toward the end of the day to give himself a little relief. He repositioned his broad frame, and the small chair creaked. Then he rubbed his wide, sweaty palms on his khaki pants and looked up to meet the bishop's gaze.

"Church of the Good Shepherd is thriving, isn't it?"

Roy nodded his head. "I can't tell you what a blessing it is to serve in my hometown, Bishop. It couldn't be better for me and Little Rose." Roy had a thick South Carolina sandhills accent, very different from the slow, round tidewater drawl of Charleston. The sandhills accent was clipped and most of Roy's *e* and *a* vowels made the short *i* sound so that the word *heck* or *hack* both sounded like *hick*. It was the kind of accent folks in the metropolitan areas of the state called country or redneck, and he tried to temper it when he met with the bishop, whose office was at The Cathedral of St. Luke and St. Paul in the center of downtown Charleston.

"Why do you think it's going so well?" The bishop's question seemed more directed to the stack of papers on his desk than to Roy. The old man tugged at his white muttonchops before looking up.

The young priest cleared his throat and puffed up his broad chest. "Well, we keep it simple, I guess. I stick to the Gospel in the pulpit every Sunday, and we pour all that we have into our Alpha Course, which folks have attended from as far afoot as Darlington, Hartsville, and even Florence."

The bishop patted the left pocket of his pressed purple shirt. He wore a large and ornate gold cross around his neck that he kept tucked in his pocket when he wasn't decked out in his heavy robe and ruffles.

Roy looked out of the thick glass panes of the third-floor corner office. It was a Holy City view if he ever saw one, with the largest, most historic steeples in the country dominating the skyline— St. Philip's on Church Street, St. Michael's on the corner of Meeting and Broad, St. Matthew's on upper King, St. John's on Archdale, and the Unitarian church right next door which he had forgotten the name of.

He smiled when he thought of his simple red brick sanctuary, circa 1967, back in Ellijay, with the lettered marquee in the front. This month it read, *Distressed? Try This Address! (Every Sunday at 10 a.m.)*

He turned back to the bishop, who watched him steadily as if he wanted him to say more. "It's my kind of people at Good Shepherd, sir. The kind I grew up with, and we speak the same language, you know?" He tugged at his collar and smiled. "They trust me, and I know just where they're coming from. Then it's not long before one or another brings in a friend or a neighbor or coworkers…" The chair creaked as he sat back. "And that's why we've grown, I reckon. 'Cause we know and understand each other."

Bishop Boatwright made a steeple with the tips of his fingers, then he raised his white bushy eyebrows, forming two symmetrical arches. "I called you here because I have a new position I'd like to recommend you for, Reverend."

The twitch in Roy's right eye turned into a flut-

ter. He reached up and rubbed it, then he leaned
forward, resting his elbows on his wide knees.
"Bishop, you know it's been a tough few years
for me personally."

"Of course I do." The bishop squinted. His pale
blue eyes shot a sharp look that Roy recognized
as a complicated blend of love, concern, and most
striking of all, appraisal.

He kept on. "And now Rose and I are hun-
kered down in Ellijay. She loves her school, and
my mama sold the farm and bought a house just
down the road from us. Plus, my brother is only
ten miles away over in Robbin's Neck." Roy bit
his bottom lip hard. "It's been real good for me to
be back in my old stomping grounds after losing
Jean Lee." He patted the left side of his chest. "I
feel like the Lord's had his hand on my heart, and
he's been binding it up."

"Undoubtedly." The bishop balled his right
hand into a fist, his large, gold ecclesiastical ring
catching the afternoon light. Roy had been a
second-string offensive guard for Clemson University before he became an Episcopal priest, and
the bishop's gold band always reminded him of a
Super Bowl ring. This made him chuckle a little,
imagining Bishop Boatwright at the ten-yard line
giving some defender the Heisman before running
toward the goal.

Bishop Boatwright held out his fist and leaned

forward. "You know what happens after you receive healing, son?"

Roy wasn't sure how to answer this. Was it a theological question or a personal one? He wasn't bookish like the bishop; he just knew the Holy Spirit and felt its daily presence like the air his lungs inhaled or the soft light that fell on his face on his morning walk to work.

"Sir?" he said.

"It's been my experience these short seventy-six years"—the bishop pounded his fist twice on the arm of his chair—"that after you receive healing, the Lord calls you *out* to a new frontier." He pursed his pink lips and leaned forward. "He takes that fresh strength and puts it to a new test."

Roy tilted his square chin. He was a big, handsome fellow with a head full of thick brown hair and dark brown eyes to match. Bishop Boatwright had confirmed him when he was twelve years old. And he'd ordained him the same year his wife died some fifteen years later. Both times he had laid his stubby hands on Roy's head full of hair, his gold ring rubbing against the boy's scalp, blessing the holy ceremony with the presence of the Almighty One he represented. The truth was, this man was in authority over Roy, and like Saul on the road to Damascus, there was no use kicking against the goads. He exhaled and uttered a prayer of mercy. "What did you have in mind, sir?"

"Phil Rainey is retiring this spring."

Phil Rainey, Phil Rainey, Phil Rainey. Roy ran the vaguely familiar name through his mind as he thought about the other churches in the middle part of the state. The only Phil Rainey he knew was the rector of St. Michael's in the center of downtown Charleston. The fancy old church on the corner of Meeting and Broad where his Aunt Elfrieda used to drag him during his miserable summer visits.

Roy reached up to steady his right eyelid again. "I'm…you don't mean…?"

Bishop Boatwright nodded. "Yes. St. Michael's here in Charleston. I'd like to recommend you to their search committee." He looked toward his desk as if his mind had already concerned itself with his next appointment. "I think you could be the man for the job, Reverend Summerall."

Roy felt the burn of perspiration beneath his arms. He blinked several times and set his jaw. "With all due respect, Bishop, I'm not the kind of fellow that can lead a Charleston church, especially a South of Broad one." He looked around the room at the shelves and shelves of books as if to find proof. Then he pointed to his mouth. "Just listen to my accent."

The bishop turned back and cocked his head in curiosity.

"Or this." Now that Roy had the bishop's attention, he smiled and pushed a little bit of his tongue through the gap between his two front teeth. "I need braces."

The bishop furrowed his bushy brows and Roy continued, counting off the examples like a verdict.

"I drive an all-terrain vehicle on the weekends, I go to the races for fun, I wear gold jewelry. Heck, I even vacation at Myrtle Beach by my own choice." Then Roy said with a firm whisper, "Bishop, did you know that I have a *tattoo* of a Clemson tiger paw on my right shoulder?" He rolled his shoulder forward at the mention of it. He had dislocated it his junior year, and his senior year he had torn so many tendons that he had to have an operation. It still gave him a fit. "Sir, I wouldn't know the first thing about ministering to those 'mind your manners' and 'just where do *your* people come from?' folks."

The bishop took his time standing up, then ambled over to his desk where he thumbed through his stack of papers. "You spent your boyhood summers in Charleston, as I recall." He glanced toward Roy, who was peering out of the window at St. Michael's massive white steeple with its clock tower and weather vane and one-ton bells that had called the city to worship since before the Revolutionary War. He remembered reading about how the steeple was painted black during those days so the British ships wouldn't spot it. Only it backfired.

The black made the church all the more noticeable from the harbor, and the troops were quick to ransack it.

"They were the worst summers of my life." Roy rotated his right shoulder again. "My brother, Chick, and I were treated pretty harshly by the local kids." Roy could still hear Heyward Rutledge calling him a "Neanderthal" when he asked the fellow's crush to dance at one of the Friday night parties at East Bay Playground. He'd had to go home and look that word up in Aunt Elfrieda's encyclopedia, and then he had to take the scientific definition and translate it into the slang.

The bishop chuckled. He sniffed the air and scratched his muttonchops.

Then he looked down at Roy and whole seconds passed before he nodded once. "You might be just the man for the job, Reverend. I want you to be open and trust me in this. I'm going to recommend you to the search committee and the vestry, and you'll be hearing from them."

Roy sat back in his chair as though he had been hit by a three-hundred-pound nose guard. The chair seemed to waver, and for a moment, he thought it might collapse under his weight. He pictured Rose, his five-year-old daughter, curled up in Mama's lap on the front porch this morning. Charleston was the last place he wanted to raise her. Jean Lee was gone. Why in the world would the bishop, why would the Lord even, want him to entertain this outlandish idea?

The bishop bowed his head and started to pray, but Roy didn't hear the words. When he heard the old man say, "Amen," he stood and firmly shook the bishop's hand. Then he got back in his pickup and drove quickly down Interstate 26 toward Interstate 95 where the live oaks and palmettos gave way to the scrub pines and the flat lands of the only place, this side of heaven, he ever wanted to call home.

"What did high-and-mighty have to say?" His mama was sporting her new rhinestone-encrusted flip-flop heels and white shorts too short for a sixty-five-year-old woman. She was flipping pancakes on his griddle while her new husband, Donny, and Roy's office manager, Skeeter, sipped coffee at the kitchen counter.

"Breakfast for dinner, Daddy!" Little Rose abandoned her piano-playing in the den and ran into his arms. He picked her up and squeezed her tight, overcome as he often was by how her little embrace soothed his very soul like the balm of Gilead.

Mama turned down the eye of the stove and stacked three fluffy pancakes on a plastic Dora the Explorer plate. She coated each one with a thick pat of butter and set them on the little round table in the corner of the room.

"Enjoy 'em while they're warm, Rosebud," she said. "This is a one-plate-at-a-time meal, and I'll do your daddy's next so y'all can overlap."

"What's news around the church house?" Roy massaged his bum shoulder and looked to Skeeter, who blew a bubble with the pink gum she always seemed to be gnawing on. He watched the bubble deflate as she pulled four white slips from her Day-Timer. "Here are the messages, but the most pressing matter is Brother Jackson."

Roy winced, his dark brown eyes narrowing. "He looked real good a couple of days ago."

"Well, hospice told Mrs. Jackson that they figured that was a last burst of energy. They think the end is near."

Roy nodded and looked at his watch. "I'll take him the Eucharist tonight."

"Can I go too?" Rose said. She was dipping a fork-full into a pool of syrup she had poured right on Dora's oversized head.

Rose loved Mr. and Mrs. Jackson, who used to sing in the choir until they found cancer in his pancreas. And she often made sick visits with Roy. She was no stranger to Ellijay Memorial and the Darlington County Hospice Center or the Robbins Neck Funeral Home for that matter, and the nurses and caretakers usually set aside a lollipop or some other little trinket from the dollar store in anticipation of her next pastoral visit.

He nodded yes as Mama handed him a stack of pancakes.

"What did Bishop Boatwright want, son?"

"He wants to recommend me for a job…" Roy shook his head in disbelief as his kitchen got real still. "In downtown Charleston, of all places."

Mama's eyes widened. "The Holy City!" She clicked her long, silver fingernails together and winked at Rose. "Now wouldn't that be something!"

"Charleston?" Rose's eyes lit up. Her granny had taken her there once and bought her a pair of red, glittery shoes. "Oh, that's my dream city, Daddy!"

Roy pushed his pancakes aside. He turned to Donny. "Why do all females go ga-ga at the mere mention of Charleston?"

Donny shrugged his shoulders and smiled.

Jean Lee used to love Charleston, too, Roy now recalled. She'd begged him to take her to some historic bed-and-breakfast on their first anniversary, and he had complied, though he didn't care much at all for the squeaky old bed or the ridiculously high rate or the bathroom down the hall that they had to *share* with four other guests.

"Don't get too excited, gals," he said. "I don't think the bishop has really thought this thing through. And if it was up to me, we'd *never* leave Ellijay." He gently laid his paper napkin over his plate. "I'm going to run over to the church to get what we need for Brother Jackson's Communion."

"Well, who is it up to?" Rose said. Skeeter popped her bubble gum and Mama cocked her head, her big, amply-sprayed hair shifting in one cohesive clump.

Roy shook his head like an exasperated teacher and pointed upward with his index finger. "Now who do y'all think?"

Late that evening after administering the Eucharist to Mr. Jackson, who the hospice folks predicted would meet his Maker within the next forty-eight hours, Roy lifted Rose out of the pickup and tucked her into bed.

Then he went to the hall closet where he kept Jean Lee's stuff. He often came in here late at night and took comfort in the touch of her shimmery blouses, her cowboy boots, and the sweaters folded neatly on the shelf above that still contained just the faintest hint of her sweet and powdery scent.

He thought about Bishop Boatwright and his surprising request to submit his name to the search committee of what was arguably one of the oldest, stuffiest, most affluent churches in the whole diocese. He didn't want to minister in some historic monument where the parishioners might shudder with disdain at his country accent or shoo him out with the business end of the broom the way Aunt Elfrieda did when he forgot to put the napkin in his lap during one of her Sunday afternoon dinners. Truth was, he couldn't even imagine relating to those folks. It was a ridiculous idea. Maybe Bishop Boatwright was slipping as he tilted toward retirement. Maybe he was downright delusional.

Roy tucked his hands into the satin-lined pockets of the pink leather jacket Jean Lee bought on a vacation they took to Six Flags in Atlanta. She had stood in front of the three-sided mirror at one of those strip malls on the outskirts of the city and said, "Tell the truth now, Roy. Is this too much for a future priest's wife?"

"Nah," he said. "It's you, baby." And it was. It fit her in all the right spots, and he knew in his heart that God wanted her to be herself—lipstick, teased bangs, and all—like the first day he laid eyes on her in the parking lot of Ellijay High just days after his sixteenth birthday.

It had taken years to get used to life without her. And he was just beginning to feel (after much urging from his mama and daughter) that he could maybe meet someone one of these days. He had even thought about asking Skeeter out but the bubble gum bothered him, and he just never seemed to get around to it. Maybe now was the time. Or maybe now he was ready to meet some of those daughters and nieces the ladies at church kept trying to introduce him to.

Roy's unspoken hopes were becoming clearer in his heart and mind. And they were these: that he might love again and expand his family right here in Ellijay with his mama down the street and his brother, Chick, and their lively brood just a few miles away.

"My life is here, Lord," Roy said as he buried his face in the pink leather jacket. "Don't allow this to be taken away too."

Chapter Two

Mrs. Della Logan Limehouse
July 12, 2008

Della sat in the corner booth next to her cousin, Anne, smacking one of her gold gladiator sandals on the floor. They were at Earthfare, a whole-foods grocery store and café just over the Ashley River where they met to catch up every other Saturday along with Anne's sister, Alisha, whom everyone called Lish.

"Wonder where she is?" Della glanced at the clock on the wall, then reached across the table to squeeze Anne's wrist. "I don't want to ask you how you're doing because you'll just have to repeat it when she gets here."

Anne grimaced and repositioned her remarkably long frame. "Don't I wish I had something new to tell you?"

Della's eyes softened and she rubbed the top of

her cousin's long, freckled hand. "Remember what Nana used to say?" Anne wrinkled her brow and shook her head no.

Della took a bite of her tabouleh and pointed with the prongs of her fork. "Sometimes no news is good news."

Just as they relaxed into a chuckle, Della spotted Lish and her family in the bakery section. "Well, looky here." She peered beyond Anne's shoulder. "If it isn't the Doctors Sublime."

Lish's tall husband was somehow both sporty and distinguished-looking as he pushed the grocery cart with their three-year-old daughter gnawing the handle and their five-year-old son riding on the back, reaching for a sample of a vegan oatmeal cookie.

Lish was seven months pregnant with her third, a subject she'd written about all spring in her "Dr. Sutton Comments" newspaper column. She'd covered morning sickness, prenatal nutrition, heartburn, genetic testing, leg cramps, mood swings, gestational diabetes, and Braxton Hicks contractions.

The handsome, fertile duo were both in scrubs, ready for the morning they would spend at the Holy Cross Free Health Clinic where they volunteered on weekend afternoons.

As Lish turned and tousled her son's brown locks, Della watched Anne gape.

"Yeah." Della leaned in to whisper. "I know what you're thinking. It's hard to believe she still has seven weeks to go. Is it me, or does she seem almost *twice* as big this time?"

"C'mon, Del," Anne muttered. "She's not *that* big."

Little Andrew spotted his aunt and cousin in the corner booth of the café and ran over to embrace Della, who tickled him hard beneath the arms before kissing his rosy cheeks.

"Cousin Del," he said. "Will you get me a cookie?"

Della scrounged around the bottom of her pocketbook. She pulled up four pennies, half of an old Cheerio, and a ball of lint.

Anne waved a five-dollar bill and Andrew snatched it.

Then he looked up through his long, dark lashes and smiled at Della. *What a knockout*, she thought.

"Thanks, Aunt Anne!" he said in the direction of the baked goods. He ran over to his daddy, who shook his head in surrender and opened the cookie bin.

Della felt Anne turn to her. "Why doesn't he embrace me like that?"

"I've seen him hug you lots of times."

"When his mama tells him to." Anne rested her narrow chin on the palm of her long, thin hand. "I suppose it's my height. It probably scares him as much as it does all the other men in Charleston."

"Anne." Della groaned before gently punching her cousin's shoulder. "I want you to stop waiting around and get out there and take hold of what you want." Della, who was more than a foot shorter than Anne, had been ordering her cousin around since they were children, and it was hard to stop now. The three had spent their childhood summers together at their grandmother's house in downtown Charleston, roaming the streets until dark. They'd climbed trees at White Point Gardens and reenacted duels in Stoll's Alley. On allowance days they'd snuck down to the old market for a praline or a sliver of fudge, which they devoured quickly before pestering the boys who fished treasures out of the restaurant trash bins, or spying on the longshoremen who stumbled out of the local bars and down the cobblestone alleyways singing songs.

Lish waddled toward them, then turned back to wave good-bye to Drew, who usually walked the kids over to the public library to pick out a book so she could have her girl time.

Della stood to give her a hug.

"Cute shoes," Lish said.

"Goodwill." Della did a few steps of the foxtrot they learned at Cotillion when they were kids. "I've made friends with a gal who works there, and she calls me whenever some South of Broad size 5½ drops off a shoebox."

"Savvy," Lish said. She heaved herself into the booth next to Della. "So what did I miss?"

Della fished for a tomato in the corner of her to-go container. "Well, Anne was just about to tell us about her secret life as a dancing bartender at the Harley-Davidson Pub in North Charleston."

Anne spit out a mouthful of her peach protein blast, and Lish laughed.

"You know, maybe I've missed my calling." Anne stood up for a moment to grab a napkin from a neighboring table, and it seemed as if the whole café turned to examine her striking height. She was six foot two with thick, wavy red hair that added at least another inch, and she had the longest, most narrow hands and feet Della had ever seen. "Maybe God didn't say, 'Stay and wait' that day in the bell tower." Anne winked at Lish. "Maybe he said, 'Buy a leather mini and learn to mix a drink.'"

Della cut her eyes at Lish. From time to time since they were kids, Anne claimed to have *heard from God*, but Della was skeptical. Her most recent claim was that one winter afternoon a few years ago in the bell tower of St. Michael's, where she served as the cocaptain of the bell ringer band, she'd heard from God regarding her desire to find a mate. She said that just after she took hold of the rope and called out, "Treble's going. She's gone!" to her team of eight, who stood in a circle ready to practice their rounds and change ringing, she had asked God if she would ever marry. He said as clear as the copper tongue of the treble clanging against the bell's side, "Stay here and wait." In fact, she had even stayed in the drafty tower until midnight that night, hours after all the bell ringers had departed, until she remembered that verse about a thousand days being the blink of an eye for God. She decided "Stay here and wait" could be a little longer than that very day.

Della often reminded her thirty-six-year-old cousin that "Stay here and wait" was not a clear-cut "Yes." And as for Della, she couldn't imagine God *speaking*. The thought of it kind of disturbed her because, in truth, she wasn't sure that he existed.

Couldn't it have just been the sound of the bells? And if he did actually *speak*, wouldn't we humans (Anne included) be apt to misunderstand whatever he was trying to communicate? And c'mon now, if God did actually exist, would he really be upset if Anne, say, went out on one of the set-ups Della had tried to arrange with the tallest men she could find? Or would he be disappointed if the single accountant/bell tower cocaptain (who was getting way too obsessed with her tabby cat for

Della's comfort level) signed up for one of those Internet dating services?

"You know, Anne"—Della bit her lip—"we're not getting any younger. Don't you think—"

Anne held up her hand. "Don't say it today, Del." She swallowed hard. "Yes, I've thought about it. Maybe I didn't hear it right." She put her head in her hands for a moment. "You know, the Central Council of Church Bell Ringers outside of London has invited me to apply for a six-month training program where they'd place me in a few English churches for method ringing training in order to prepare me for the full peal we hope to attempt next year at St. Mike's." She shrugged her shoulder. "I was thinking maybe I should apply."

"Are you kidding?" Della said. "I think you should absolutely go for it."

Anne grinned and straightened her shoulders. "Remember how much I loved that semester in London when I was in college?"

"Yeah, I do." Della and Lish said in unison. Then Della pounded the table once. "You know, the truth is, you're not in that bad of a place, Anne." She reached out and put her hands firmly on top of her cousin's. "You can start over. Your whole adult life. Do you realize how many people wish they could do that?"

Anne pulled back into the cushion of her booth. "Yes, I know what you're saying." She gently crossed her thin arms. "I'm lucky not to have married the wrong guy or anything. But I can't say I agree with you that I'm in a good place, Del. I'd give anything to have what you and Lish have. You know that."

"Yes, we know." Lish stretched out her swollen hands. "But your life's not over yet, Anne. You're probably not even halfway there, so maybe Della's just saying that going off to England with a clean slate is pretty exciting…provided you don't stay over there too long."

Della swallowed hard. "Thank you for putting it so diplomatically, Lish." She turned to Anne and winked. "That's what I'm saying. And I'm also saying that I bet there are some pretty tall chaps on the other side of the pond, and maybe you can swipe one and bring him back."

Anne smiled. "We'll see."

"Good," Della said as she felt both sets of eyes turn to her.

"Your turn to spill it," Lish said.

Della shrugged her little shoulders. "Well, in my case no news is *bad* news."

"Hard times?" Lish tucked a piece of Della's thin, dirty-blonde hair behind her ear.

"Yeah." Della scoffed. "Peter hasn't had a commission in five months, so we're pretty much surviving on my teacher salary, and we've got to come up with a big chunk of change next month to pay a portion of Cozy's tuition."

"What about the new novel?"

"I'm cranking it out as fast as I can, but it will be a good six months before I get my advance. And you know it's not that much."

"You'll ask for help if you need it, right?" said Lish.

Della looked down at Lish's belly. "Yeah." She thought she could almost see the baby kicking beneath the taut blue scrubs. She met Lish right in the center of her bright blue eyes and pointed to her abdomen. And just as she was about to say, "And you know I'm dying for another one of those," Lish jerked forward and opened her eyes wide.

"You okay?" Della jumped.

Lish grabbed her belly. "Just a Braxton Hicks." She squinted her eyes. "I've been having them a lot this week."

"That one looked like it hurt." Anne wrung her hands.

"It kind of did." Lish raised her shoulders as if to shake it off. She looked at her watch. "Okay. I've got fifteen minutes before the kids get bored at the library. Give me the rest of the lowdown."

After Anne grumbled about a coworker who sent her a nasty e-mail, and then told a lengthy and detailed story about her heroic cat who saved her from a bat who flew into her kitchen last week while she was eating a bowl of Special K at the sink, Della turned to Lish and said: "So what about you, Dr. Sublime?"

Lish sucked her teeth and blushed. She looked back and forth at Della and Anne, then said, "The CDC is still courting Drew even though he turned them down last month. He knows how I feel about leaving Charleston, and he says he'll turn them down again." She gently patted her belly button, the outline of which could be seen through her scrubs. "And I'm not at all ready for this baby, y'all. Mary Jane is still in the crib *and* she's refusing to potty train. I haven't washed the infant clothes in Dreft yet. I'm not even sure where my breast pump is. The room's not set up. And worst of all, Drew and I can't agree on a name. "

"Wait." Della leaned in toward Lish. "Are you telling us that you are human?" She tapped Anne's foot under the table. "If this is true, I can stop fantasizing about finding an off button in the back of her head."

Anne smirked and Della squeezed Lish's shoulder. "You've still got seven weeks. It'll come together. You're a pro at this whole thing."

Lish nodded. "Yeah, I guess so."

Just then Drew knocked on the window and pointed to his thick, black waterproof watch at the end of his tan and muscular forearm.

Lish held up her index finger and mouthed, "One more minute." She turned back to Della. "Guess who I ran into yesterday?"

"Who?" Della fished at a piece of parsley in the back of her mouth.

"Todd Jervey," she said. "He just moved back to town, and he was all asking me about you. Do you know he's read all of your novels?"

Della had been engaged to Todd before she met Peter, her husband. Todd went on to be a successful psychiatrist, and she read in the paper a few months ago about how the Medical University of South Carolina just hired him to be the chair of the Psychiatry Department.

"He's never married?" Anne asked.

"Nope," Lish said.

Della tapped her fingers on the rust-colored Formica table. It wobbled.

This time Drew rapped on the window with both fists while the kids clung to his legs.

"Gotta go," Lish said. She leaned forward and kissed them both on the forehead.

"Todd Jervey." Anne shook her head in disbelief. "Back in Charleston."

Della shrugged her shoulders. "Yep."

Anne bit her bottom lip for a moment. "I wonder if he ever got over you, Del."

"It was seven years ago." Della readjusted the

table to correct the wobble. Then Anne recounted a story of Todd getting his johnboat stuck on a mud bank one day when he had taken all the gals out for a boat ride just off of Edisto Island. They'd had to wait six hours for the tide to go all the way out and back in again before they could get home.

Just then Della looked down and noticed a pool of blood on the seat beside her.

"Oh no!" Anne shouted, pointing out the window. Della stood and stared out into the parking lot. A crowd was gathered around her cousin, who had collapsed and was lying on her side on the hot, black asphalt.

Chapter Three

Roy
July 12, 2008

"Hi, there." A trim, clean-cut man in a light blue seersucker suit and bow tie met Roy at the door of the St. Michael's parish hall. The man shot out his hand. "I'm Heyward Rutledge, senior warden."

"I think we met as kids." Roy held out his hand and returned the firm handshake. "My brother, Chick, and I spent our summers on Legare Street with our aunt, Elfrieda Summerall."

Heyward cocked his head and Roy thought he could detect a sudden recognition in the man's pale green eyes. "Yeah." The man nodded. "Maybe so." He gestured toward the large meeting room just off of the kitchen. "Well, come on in. The search committee has a little lunch prepared, and we can grab a bite and get right into the interview process."

Roy met the five members of the search com-

mittee, which included two other men who could
be Heyward's clones, give or take ten years. They
were both fresh-shaven, dapper attorneys with
boyish faces, clean hands, and freshly clipped fingernails. There was an old and decorated naval
commander with a black patch over his eye; and
the smallest, most regal little lady Roy had ever
seen. She sort of reminded him of a miniature
Queen of England dressed just so for a high-tea
party.

"I'm Eliza Belser." She smiled and took his
hand. "But everyone calls me Ms. B. And I knew
your Aunt Elfrieda." Ms. B.'s hand was cold and
soft, and he imagined it smelled both sweet and
clean, like the miniature hand soaps his aunt used
to display in a gold-rimmed china dish in her guest
bathroom.

"Let me show you to the buffet." Ms. B. led him
over to a long antique table full of food. "Everything here is from *Faithfully Charleston*, our St.
Michael's cookbook."

"What a feast." Roy's mouth, which had been
dry during his nervous drive down I-26, literally watered when he took a gander at the spread.
There was a tomato pie, a sweet onion pie, pickled
shrimp, and pimento cheese finger sandwiches.
And there were ham biscuits and cheese straws,
a blue crab dip with little white round crackers,
and a hummingbird cake with cinnamon and pine-

apple and pecans like his Aunt Elfrieda used to make for their Sunday dinner. (It was the only day of the week during his stay with her that he could remember looking forward to.)

He thought back to his interview at Church of the Good Shepherd five years ago. The search committee consisted of Bubba Jones, Brother Jackson, and Skeeter's mama, Donna Mead. They'd taken him over to the Quincy's by the highway exit, and he'd ordered a hamburger steak that was burnt to a crisp. He'd had to douse it with a lot of Heinz 57 to get it down.

"Did you make all this?" he asked the miniature lady. She tugged at her beige suit jacket and corrected her posture.

"Yes, she did." Heyward came over and patted him on the back. "The first thing you need to know about St. Mike's, Roy, is that Ms. B. runs the show. She's got more power than the vestry and the rector combined. I bet she'd even put the archangel in his place if need be."

"Oh, stop." The lady nudged him in the side. "Don't listen to that. I'm just here to help. I lost my husband fourteen years ago, and my children said to me, 'Mama, pour yourself into something you love,' and I've been helping out a little at the church ever since."

"Helping out a little?" Heyward said. "I don't think I've ever been in this building when this

lady wasn't cooking up something or running a
meeting or folding and addressing the newsletter."

Roy smiled. He had a lady like Ms. B. back at
the Church of the Good Shepherd. Her name was
Candy Mills and she was always organizing the
kitchen and sprucing up the after-church coffee
hour with sweet rolls or brightly colored cupcakes
that the kids devoured. Candy Mills was short, too,
but she was as wide as she was short and she had
these little gray whiskers on the tip of her chin.
Roy glanced at the narrow swinging door that led
to the St. Michael's kitchen. Candy Mills might not
be able to make it through that entryway.

After everyone helped themselves, Ms. B. gave
a brief and impressive history of the church, and
Heyward laid out their current status: 1,658 reg-
istered members, 450 of whom were active volun-
teers and financial contributors, a capital campaign
project for the new office and bookstore on Broad
Street that was in its final stages, and a need to
reach out to the younger families who came in for
a few months or years and then tapered off.

The room was dark and cool with burgundy
walls and a dark Oriental rug, and on the walls
there were ornately framed paintings and sketches
of the sanctuary by various artists over the last
three centuries. Roy pushed up the sleeves of the
navy blue blazer his mama had driven him to the
Marshall's in Darlington to purchase last week. He

had not had time to get the arms of the jacket taken up, and his right cuff kept brushing the crab dip on his plate every time he reached for his iced tea.

"Reverend Summerall," the one-eyed commander asked, "what is your vision for a church like ours?"

Roy cleared his throat and rotated his right shoulder. After three months of prayer, mostly of the "Let this cup pass from me" type, he had no desire to impress these folks. Of course he wished the best for this body of worshippers, but in his heart he felt that a church with such privilege and history wasn't the kind that he was built to lead. He suspected that a place like this wasn't desperate enough to *cling* to the Gospel as if its life depended on it. Was he judging on appearances? Yes, he was. Was he judging because of his own miserable Sundays here, with his aunt clucking at him and Chick if they so much as repositioned themselves in the hard wooden box pews? It was a strong possibility. *Forgive me*, he prayed as the Lord convicted his heart. Judging was a particularly toxic sin, and he knew it.

Then as the table stared him down, he opened his mouth and the words came spilling out in a way they did sometimes when his sermon took a Spirit-led detour. It was moments like those that he laid aside his notes and became a vessel, empty enough to be spoken through, if for just a little while.

"We can't assume folks know the Gospel." Roy sat up and let it come. "Even folks that have been coming here for decades. Or generations, for that matter." He rubbed his hands together. "So I think it would be wise to offer the Alpha Course. It's sort of a Christianity 101 that came out of this really fired-up church in London, and it breaks the whole thing down with real basic questions like 'Who is Jesus?' and 'What does his death have to do with me?' You know, that kind of thing."

"Ah," the group seemed to say. These Charleston folks were all Anglophiles, he reckoned. In fact, this church was formed thanks to the support of England when Carolina was still a British colony. He hadn't intended to hit a sweet spot. He felt the Spirit again and kept on.

"Anyhow, I would want to make sure everyone here knew the Gospel, first. That Christ died for their sins and that all they have to do is repent and believe in order to be saved. I want them to have a genuine faith and be able to tell others about it. I want it to burn in their guts and in their hearts." He patted his thick, dark brow. "That's my prayer for Church of the Good Shepherd, and that would be my prayer for wherever I was called."

Heyward sat back in his chair and narrowed his eyes. The naval commander nodded sternly, and two of the other lawyers gave one another a knowing look.

Too heavy-handed? Roy wondered. *Heck, this was the crux of the call on his life, and he wasn't going to soft-pedal it.*

"Go on, Reverend Summerall," Ms. B. said. She wasn't smiling, but her eyes were warm, and they caught the soft lights of a brass chandelier overhead.

So he did. "As for the young families, well, they need support. I'm a single parent, and it's tough out there. And while I was only married four years before my wife passed, I know married life can be a challenge. I guess I'd try to teach about how to stick by one another and how to raise kids up in the knowledge and love of the Lord." He pointed his thick finger on the table. "Kids can come to church here, but it's what's happening at home that counts the most. Our homes need to be a haven of blessing and peace. I'd drive that message home right from the pulpit, and I'd try to find ways to support couples as they create these havens of ministry for each other, for their children, and for the needy people the Lord puts in their path."

One of the attorneys raised his eyebrows, and Roy didn't know whether to take the look as astonishment or consideration.

Roy took a sip of his iced tea. It wasn't as sweet as the kind that Jean Lee or Mama made, but his

mouth was dry and it was refreshing. Plus, Ms. B.
had put fresh mint in there and that made all the
difference. He was a little warm so he took off his
jacket, and the thick gold bracelet Jean Lee had
bought for him at the Costco in Florence tumbled
down from beneath his black shirt. He shrugged
his shoulders and thought of one of the sermon
critiques he'd received from Dr. von Hasellyn in
seminary. The critique had blasted his grammar—
specifically the improper use of prepositions at
the end of sentences, but it had concluded on an
up-note with a list of positives about the shape
and meaning of his teaching, and a truism Roy
thought of quite often: *One must be oneself.* And
so he smiled at his chain and thought of the gap
between his teeth and kept on.

"You know the people at my home church are
hurting right now. Ellijay is an old mill town that's
been dying a slow death ever since the textile in-
dustry uprooted itself when I was a kid, and this
new recession is going to set us back even further.
I know Charleston has the two extremes in terms
of wealth and poverty. And I can't think of a better
mission, beyond teaching the Gospel to the ones
that are already coming through our doors, than
to reach out to those on the other side of the community's spectrum."

Ms. B. dabbed at the corner of her mouth with
a linen napkin, and the commander rubbed at his

eye patch. It must get awfully itchy beneath there, Roy thought. He sent up a prayer of comfort for the man.

"Well,"—Heyward bit the inside of his cheek— "who do you mean exactly?"

Roy thought of his descent into the Holy City from the highway ramp. He had noticed the crumbling houses by the highway and the face of a coal-skinned man staring him down from a doorway as he turned toward the tip of the peninsula.

"How about those folks who live on the other side of the crosstown? Are we directly ministering to them?"

Heyward looked to Ms. B.

"A little," she said. "Some of our parishioners volunteer at the homeless shelter. But we could do more."

The group took a collective sigh, and after a few moments Heyward stood up straight and stuck out his hand. "I think we know where you're coming from, Reverend Summerall." He reached across the table and waited for Roy to stand and meet his shake. "We've got two more gentlemen to interview, and we'll let you know where we stand."

Roy stood and smiled and accepted the firm grasp of each member of the St. Michael's search committee. Had he dodged this bullet? He supposed so. And he hadn't had to do anything but speak from his heart. Simple enough.

He grabbed his navy blue blazer, and just as he was about to turn and head for the car, Ms. B. grabbed his elbow. "Now for the sanctuary tour!" He looked down at her expectant face and nodded in defeat, and the lady led him out of the meeting room and closed the door with a gentle click; he could almost feel the committee observing his exit.

Ms. B. led him with all the authority of a colonial historian around the outside of the white, stately sanctuary that had been built in the traditional 18th-century English design, with a grand four-columned portico and a massively proportioned 186-foot-high steeple, a clock tower, bells, and a seven-foot-wide weathervane. According to Ms. B., the building had survived hurricanes, wars, fires, an earthquake, and even a cyclone with very little damage. Roy was impressed (in the way you would be impressed by a tour of Mount Vernon or the Biltmore House) by the beauty and history of the oldest church building in Charleston, not to mention one of the finest colonial churches in America.

The inside of the sanctuary was just as he remembered, dark with a three-sided second-story gallery and cedar box-pews that were available for purchase by the local gentry when the church first opened its doors in 1761. Ms. B. pointed out (as his Aunt Elfrieda had done when he was a boy) pew

number 43 in the north center aisle where both
George Washington (in 1791) and General Robert
E. Lee (in 1861) had worshipped. And then there
was the colossal handcrafted pulpit, near the foot
of the south central aisle that had a heavy-looking
top supported by two Corinthian columns. The
top was adorned with a large, hand-carved pine-
apple that Ms. B. reminded him was the symbol
for welcome and hospitality.

"How did that not topple over in the earthquake?" He pointed to the precarious top that
would surely crush a priest's head in mid-sermon
if another quake hit on a Sunday morning.

Ms. B. had just finished telling him about the
church roof and how it had not only been melted
down to make bullets in the war against the British, but the earthquake of 1886 had ripped it right
off.

"God's grace, I suppose." She nodded and then
took him down the center aisle to the Victorian-
style altar where the Tiffany stained-glass window designed after Raphael's own painting of St.
Michael served as the focal point.

Roy took a good look at the Almighty's archangel—the warrior, Michael, who in this image was
casting out the dragon, Lucifer. At first glance,
Michael looked a little too angelic for Roy's taste
with his pink skirt and his gold scarf billowing
in the breeze. But all you had to do was take one

good look at his biceps and the way he gripped the spear and pointed it at the weaselly beast to know this angel was not to be messed with. Raphael got it and so did Roy.

When the bells started to ring, Ms. B. clapped her hands and looked up at him. "Oh! They must be practicing. You must see the bells." She brought her little clasped hands toward her pointed chin. "They are one of the city's most beloved treasures, Father Summerall. Do you know what they've been through?"

Roy had to give Ms. B. an A in the enthusiasm department. He'd never seen a person love a building so much. He tugged at his collar. "Well, they went through two wars, right? But I'm ashamed to say I don't know the specifics, Ms. B."

"Let me tell you then." Her little gray eyes gleamed, and she puffed up her chest like a mourning dove. "The bells were imported from England in 1764. During the Revolutionary War, they were seized by the British as a war prize and shipped back across the Atlantic. Then a sympathetic London merchant—a good Samaritan of sorts—recognized them. And he purchased them and returned them to Charleston."

Roy nodded. It was a pretty amazing story. He watched Ms. B. raise her finger, and he figured there must be more to it.

"Then," she said, "during the Civil War, the

bells were sent to Columbia, but they cracked in a terrible fire there in 1865." She looked at the marble floor beneath her and shook her head, then she lifted it back up in triumph and met his gaze.

"So then what happened?" Roy couldn't help but be hooked now.

"Well," she said, "the metal fragments were salvaged from the fire and sent to England to be re-cast in their original molds and rehung. And that's what you're hearing right now."

"Wow," he said. "There's a resilient spirit here, I have to say."

"That's it," she said, and she pointed him down the aisle toward the front doors of the church. "But a church isn't really the building, is it?" She squeezed his elbows with a strength she didn't look like she could muster. "No matter how impressive the history."

"Not to me, Ms. B.," he said.

"Well, what would you say it is, Father Summerall?"

He smiled and gently patted her tiny bird-like shoulder. "The people."

After a tour of the clock tower where he met a few of the ringers as they trickled in, Ms. B. led him through the bookstore, bought him a Coca-Cola, and bid him farewell on the slate sidewalk of Broad Street.

It was a hot summer day, like the kind he remembered when he was a kid, with the syrupy smell of wisteria and overripe loquats hanging in the air. He was feeling a little nostalgic after Ms. B.'s history lesson and he decided to amble down Meeting Street, hanging a right on Lamboll as he made his way to the corner of Little Lamboll and Legare where Aunt Elfrieda's former home still stood, a pale yellow single house with a little lean despite the obviously major renovation job. He couldn't get over the polished quality of the place—the crisp new driveway with bricks and oyster shells where he used to park his bike, and the piazza with freshly painted floorboards that looked too new to creak or buckle or gather love bugs in its cracks the way they did when he was a child. How many times did he and Chick have to navigate those floorboards as they crept out in the afternoon to run their paper routes during Aunt Elfrieda's daily snooze?

When a peppy woman suddenly popped out of the front door and hopped in her BMW convertible with Pennsylvania plates, he thought he could hear Aunt Elfrieda rolling over in her grave on the edge of Magnolia Cemetery. She didn't hold people "from off" in the highest of regard, and the only thing that unnerved her more than two adolescents from a podunk midlands town she had to house and attempt to cultivate for three months out of every year was an ostentatious Yankee.

Roy chuckled, took a sip of his warm, flat Coca-Cola, then headed up Legare toward Tradd, where he recalled the rough-and-tumble Campbell boys at #27, who threw water balloons at cars from behind their gates, and then the three pretty girls at #18, who he could hear giggling and talking as they picked loquats and lounged beneath the shade of their grandmother's leafy tree. He remembered watching one of them slip over the rail at The Battery when he was on his paper route one hot afternoon. She'd sliced her shin pretty bad on the oyster banks, and he and Chick pulled her up, took off their shirts, and fastened them around her leg with some rubber bands to stop the bleeding. The girl's grandmother was so thankful when Roy delivered her home in the front basket of his bike that she gave them a bucket of ripe loquats that he and Chick delivered to Aunt Elfrieda, who said, "Well, good." She clucked her tongue. "I suppose Cozy Brumley will spread the word that you two aren't complete hooligans like those Campbell boys." She put her hand on her hip and smiled thinly. "Stay out of trouble this week, and I'll make you a chocolate chess pie for Sunday dinner." (He felt guilty for thinking it, but he couldn't say he missed Aunt Elfrieda.)

After a good stroll down Tradd, he headed back

over to St. Michael's alley where he hopped in his pickup and pulled out onto Meeting Street. He pulled over for a moment in front of the sweetgrass basket weavers on the corner to utter a prayer.

When he looked up a few moments later, he heard one lone bell sound, and he examined the grand portico of St. Michael's where he pictured Ms. B. pointing out yet another reason why the sanctuary had become a city landmark.

"Robert Ripley came through here in the 1930s," she'd said. "He took a look at this intersection, with St. Michael's here on the southeast corner, City Hall on the northeast corner, the County Courthouse on the northwest corner, and the Federal Court on the southwest corner, and he coined a new phrase—"

"The Four Corners of Law," a carriage tour guide had stolen her thunder as he pulled the reins of his horse in front of the portico and pointed out the corners of the intersection—"municipal law, state law, federal law," and then right to Roy's white collar, "God's law, all represented on four corners. Now isn't that something?" The tourists had smiled at Roy and waved. Ms. B. had waved back.

Now as Roy bade farewell to the church before pulling back out onto Meeting Street, one of the large wooden side doors of the sanctuary opened, and a striking woman in a long white vestment stepped out gently and loosened her red, wavy hair from its twist. She was the tallest, most lovely woman he thought he had ever seen, and as she rounded the opposite corner, the sun illuminating her hair before she disappeared behind the huge, white edifice, he thought of Mr. Jackson who had held on longer than anyone expected, passing only ten days ago.

The second time Roy and Rose had delivered the Eucharist, the man had pulled Roy close and said: "I saw some angels pacing around here last night. They looked a lot like us only taller, much taller. And more pleasing to the eye."

That night after returning from the Holy City, Mama and Rose asked him a million questions with an excitement he tried to deflate. Later he fell asleep in an uncomfortable position in Rose's lavender Barbie bed where he had been reading her *Heidi* for the third time that summer.

With his neck at an awkward angle against the Formica headboard, he dreamed in a way he had only dreamed a few times before. In his sleep, he was flying over an urban area. He eventually recognized the steeples and slate roofs as belonging to Charleston, and he was headed from upper Meeting Street toward the High Battery. The bells were ringing loudly, but there was no movement in the streets. It was dusk or maybe sunrise, and while the lights were turning on in the windows North of Broad, the neighborhoods surrounding the St. Michael's parish were completely still. When he looked down to the windows below, he saw only a blackness, as if everyone had vacated the neighborhood. The darkened panes of the tall windows reminded him of loneliness. And suddenly he found himself standing on a third-floor piazza where he peered into one of the large black rectangles only to find the shadowy figures of a man and a woman, fully dressed and lying down on top of a made-up bed. They were still as stones.

He woke up in a cold sweat with a sharp crick in his neck. Rose was facing him, curled up like a satisfied kitten, her lids gently shut, her little chest lifting up and down with each slow, deep breath. She looked like a smaller version of Jean Lee, the Peter Rabbit bedside lamp shining on her black hair, her red lips like a doll's as if they were painted on her face. He stood, leaned over to kiss her, and turned off the light as he rubbed his neck, then turned toward his room.

After dressing for bed, he couldn't shake the dream and he sat on his den sofa for several hours, wide-eyed, picturing those long dark rectangles. Roy Summerall had a feeling he was stiff-necked in more than just the literal sense, but he didn't dare let his mind or his heart acknowledge the sign that the dream seemed to be.

Chapter Four

Della

Della pulled into her dirt driveway in the twenty-year-old Honda Prelude her father had given her eighteen years ago on the eve of her high school graduation. She lived with her husband and six-year-old daughter on the corner of Radcliffe and Smith Street, three blocks north of Calhoun in the middle of the peninsula. Their place was the first floor of a rundown single house that leaned a good fifteen degrees to the left from the wear and tear of more than one hundred years of heat, humidity, and flooding from the storms that hit at high tide. The house was painted a reddish purple that must have been a fun and flamboyant choice in the late '70s. But today the place looked like a rotting plum, the dirty strips of paint peeling off in jagged strips across the clapboards. They had bought the house with Della's portion of Nana's inheritance in hopes that the neighborhood was on its way up, but eight years later she could still spot the guy who sold pot to the college kids on the northwest corner leaning against the Cash and Carry convenience store with a bulge beneath the left side of his baggy jean jacket. Though she had never seen a gun, she'd heard a shot more than once in the middle of the night, echoing down the corridors of the disheveled streets of her neighborhood.

When she opened the front door, the steamy air from her un-air-conditioned house smothered her. The thermometer read ninety-four degrees just inside the door. She took a slow, hot breath as if she was pacing herself for an hour in a sauna. A muffled laughter came from behind the closed door of her daughter's room—the one place in the house where they had broken down and bought a window unit.

Peter and their daughter, Cozy, were playing a game. They had built a tent by draping a fitted sheet over her bedposts, and they had brought in food from the kitchen and sticks from the backyard to simulate a campout. Peter, dressed in a black T-shirt and jeans, was wearing the gorilla mask he had bought last Halloween. He was crouched in a make-believe bush behind the bed. Cozy squealed with joy. She loved the element of surprise—that the gorilla was hiding, waiting to lurch at her when the moment was right.

Through the window, Della saw the heap of scrap metal and the blowtorch and face mask, resting on top of a headless shrimp who squatted slightly, his front legs playing a copper cello. Peter was a metal sculptor whose medium was crunched copper treated with a blue-green patina. The shrimp had sort of become his signature—he had a knack for giving each crustacean a kind of human personality just in the way they curled their tails or positioned their bulbous eyes. But he'd been known to sculpt frogs, sea turtles, palmetto bugs, mosquitoes, pelicans, and herons as well. In fact, the South Carolina Aquarium had two of his creations greeting every tourist who walked in the door, a six-foot toad holding a lantern and a ten-foot sea turtle in mid-flap with what almost seemed like a smile at the bottom of his round, prehistoric skull.

You could also see his work at the Children's Museum in Columbia and the Governor's School for the Arts in Greenville, and even farther afoot at the Bronx Botanical Gardens and the Peabody School of Education at Vanderbilt University. But commissions had been dwindling for the last couple of years. Art and books were the last expenses folks with means considered incurring when the economy turned south, and Peter and

Della were both feeling the beginning of the re-cession. They had always scraped by more or less with the meager advances from Della's publisher, her occasional teaching gigs, the periodic grants, and the sculpture commissions that seemed to al-ways materialize just when it looked like one of them would have to forsake their craft and start selling insurance or something.

Della had suffered a change of heart about their lifestyle ever since Cozy was born. A woman can change when she has a child. Her whole notion of what life ought to be can be altered. The conven-tions and lifestyles she used to disdain become the ones she desires most. Oh, she wanted so much for her child. Not necessarily material things, but the rudimentary basics of a decent life—safety, com-fort, a clean home, and a solid education. A woman can read one of those desperate-housewife novels like *Revolutionary Road* and say, "What is April's problem? Does she know how lucky she is to have a husband who brings home a decent paycheck? What's so evil about being a salesman? What's so philosophically wrong about making a steady living?" Della, even though she would have never predicted it, was becoming one of those women.

Then Peter lunged at Cozy, and she gave the requisite shriek before he hurled her onto the bed, where she bounced and shouted with delight. He lifted his mask so that the gorilla was face-up on the top of his head. "How's Lish?"

Della turned the window unit up a notch and said over its mechanical drone, "They're trying to stop the contractions. We may have to go over to Legare Street and stay with the kids."

"Why not bring them here?" Peter lifted his large hands, palms up as if he was making an offering.

Della was frequently taken aback by how fantastic-looking Peter was: six-five and absolutely chiseled with broad shoulders, a sharp jaw line, a tan that accentuated it all, and pale green eyes beneath dark, bushy brows. Once at a cocktail party, a flamboyant art dealer told her she'd married an Adonis. She'd blushed and nodded. But what was even stranger than Peter's Greek-god looks and their ability to stun her, even now after eight years of marriage, was her lack of desire for him—her utter lack of passion or attraction in the face of the undisputable fact that he was an eyeful.

Della could hardly stand the deep hum of the air-conditioning unit, but she walked over to it and let the cool air lift her hair off of her neck as her daughter came over and leaned in toward her. She rubbed Cozy's back as the sun caught the golden crown of her small, perfectly round head. Della turned back to her husband. "We can't bring them here because we have one bathroom and it's under construction, and our backyard is full of shards of metal and electrical wires and rusted nails."

Cozy turned to him and added, "And we don't have Rosetta who cooks and cleans, right, Mama?" Della nodded.

"All right. All right." Peter held out the heel of his right hand. "Don't you two gang up on me now."

Cozy grabbed the gorilla mask and put it on. "Me hungry," she called, then she ran back toward her mother, and all Della could see was a blur of black fur, tan little arms, and the flap of a yellow sun dress with white polka dots.

"I've got you, Mama!"

Then Della picked her up and spun her around and gently dropped her on the unmade bed where she kissed each pad of her soft little fingers. She gazed into her daughter's deep brown eyes. Next week she'd start first grade at The Pinckney School for Girls, an old and prestigious single-gender school where Della, her mother, and her grandmother had graduated from. The public schools in their district were failing, and while they tried for the magnet option, they received the last number in the lottery; they never even had the opportunity to test. The Pinckney School tuition far exceeded their budget, so Della had put her writing career on hold to serve as a full-time teacher in the middle school in order to make the payments.

"How would you like to spend the night with Andrew and Mary Jane?" Cozy's eyes widened and she tossed back her golden hair and sat up straight. She cupped Della's face in her delicate hands. "I would love it, Mama!"

Peter wrapped his arms around his wife and child. "Let's get packing, girls."

At the hospital Della spotted Drew in the hall, chuckling with two other doctors. They looked familiar and the closer she got, she realized that they were the infectious-disease fellows who rented the carriage house at 18 Legare. There was Rob, a stubby guy who started an herb garden beside Nana's old loquat tree, and Melanie, a towering blonde who could almost give Anne a run for her money in the height department.

"Things must not be too bad." Anne intercepted Della in the hallway. She nodded toward Drew and took a deep breath. "I mean, if he has time to shoot the breeze with his apprentices."

"True." Della reached up high and put her arm around her cousin.

Drew seemed to catch them out of the corner of his eye. He stepped away from the fellows and turned to them.

"What's the status, Dr. Sublime?" Della said.

"We're in a 'wait and see' mode." He raked his fingers through the thick curls of his salt-and-pepper hair. "They're going to stop the contractions long enough to do an amnio to gauge lung development. If it comes back strong, we may deliver as early as tomorrow night."

"How's she doing?" Anne whispered.

"A little anxious." He rubbed his stubbled chin. "You know how she likes to plan these things out."

"We know." Della grinned. "Maybe her next column in the paper can be 'Expect the Unexpected.'" They all chuckled, then she knocked his elbow. "Peter and I would be happy to stay with the kids tonight, and we'll get the nursery ready."

"That would be great, Della." Drew rubbed his hands together. "Rosetta's with them now, and she'll be back first thing in the morning to take over."

Della nodded and looked at the closed door where someone had scrawled the name Sutton with a black Sharpie.

"Can we see her?" Anne said.

When they entered, Lish sat up without fully taking her eye away from the baby's heartbeat on the screen. She was sitting on top of the bed in a hospital gown, and Della noticed—as she did every time she saw Lish's bare leg—the scar that ran down her shin from the time she fell off The Battery rail and into the oyster beds.

Della and Anne took their places on either side

of her bed and Lish patted both of their knees as if to reassure them. "Drew give you the update?"

"Yeah," Anne said.

"Not exactly what I had planned for today." She turned to Della. "You okay to keep the kids?"

"We're already packed and Cozy's about to do backflips, she's so excited."

Lish reached for a notebook on her bedside table and handed it to Della. "Here's the bedtime routine and the church schedule as well as their day camp that starts on Monday in case I'm here for a while. Rosetta will get their outfits ready."

Della showed the thorough notes to Anne. "Are you believing this?"

Anne turned to Lish. "Put me to work, too, okay?"

Lish scanned her list.

"I've got tomorrow off." Anne gently pulled the notebook from Lish's hands. "Give me an assignment."

She quickly read the list and handed it back to Lish. "I'll make the trip to Babies R Us. How hard can it be to pick out a car seat and a few pacifiers?"

"You don't mind?" Lish leaned forward and picked at her plastic hospital bracelet.

Anne nodded emphatically. "I can handle it. And I can do more. So call me when you think of something else."

"Thank you." Lish smiled. "I will."

Della bit at the tip of her index finger. "So what are the doctors saying?"

Lish tucked a strand of her thick brown hair behind her ears. "If all goes well for forty-eight hours, then I can go back home and stay on bed rest for a week or so. If the contractions continue, they may have to deliver early."

"Well, you're in good hands," Drew said as he entered the room. He stood at the foot of the bed and crossed his arms. "As far as I can tell, our biggest problem is settling on a name."

"Here." Lish handed them a list of girl names. "We've picked the boy name, but we don't have one for a girl, and I just heard the nurse slip and say, 'How's *she* doing?' when she examined the monitor."

"Oh." Anne took the list and glanced at the names. "You just want an opinion?"

Lish nodded. "Yeah, I'm just not drawn to one the way I usually am." Della looked over Anne's shoulder. The list read:

Emma Louise Sutton

Jane Brumley Sutton

Cecilia Elizabeth Sutton

"They're all beautiful," Anne said. She handed the list to Della. "I couldn't possibly choose—"

"Cecilia." Della nodded her pointed chin once. "How can you not hear that name and think of dancing at two a.m. at the frat house of your choice with Paul Simon's voice belting through the speakers, 'Ce-cil-ia, you're breaking my heart. You're shaking my confidence lately...' It's a completely upbeat name."

They all chuckled and Della leaned in to peck her cousin on the forehead. She sensed Lish's desire to have more time to flesh out her list. "We'll take care of everything!" Della took Anne by the arm. "Just rest and tell Cecilia to take a chill pill."

On the way to the parking garage, a voice called behind them, "Della? Anne? Y'all wait up!"

Della turned to see a tall, thin, bearded man in tortoiseshell glasses and a white physician's coat walking toward them. "I think that's Todd," Anne said. "Todd Jervey." He pressed a button on his key chain and one of those snappy little BMW convertibles lit up and beeped behind him.

"Della!" He waved his arm and slowed down when he got close. He stretched up and kissed Anne on the cheek and then leaned down and did the same to Della before stepping back to take her in. Della was in the thin gauzy white sundress she wore when the temperatures topped ninety degrees and her gold designer gladiator sandals care of Jodie at Goodwill.

"You look fantastic," he said. "How are you?"

"All right," she said. "Welcome back to town."

"It's great to see you." He grinned and shook his

head as if he was trying to fight off a chill. "I've read your novels. All four of them. My mom sent me the first one, then I tracked down the others."

"Good for you," she said. "You're in a very small fan club. You and twenty of my closest family and friends."

"Not true," Anne interrupted. "She's been nominated for an award, and thousands of people have read her books."

He grimaced. "Your voice is unmistakable, and your descriptions are dead on. They really bring me back to Charleston. Kind of make me homesick, even."

Della grinned. "Well, good. We need a decent shrink around here."

"So you've settled down. Have a child, right? I read that in your bio."

"Yes. A daughter. Cozy."

He smiled. "After your grandmother. Nice."

Della scanned his left hand. No ring in sight. He always wanted a boatload of kids.

"You?"

"Nah," he said. "This medical research thing has kind of sucked me in for the last ten years." He bit his lip, then readjusted his glasses. "So what are you two doing here?"

"Lish is in the hospital."

"What for?" The lines formed above his fair forehead.

"She's pregnant, and she started going into labor this morning."

"How far along is she?"

"Seven and a half months," Della said.

"Mmm." He narrowed his eyes and nodded. "I'll check in on her."

"No need," Della said. "Drew's got her surrounded by the top doctors in the state. But she'd probably love to see you."

He smiled and nodded. He leaned forward as if to give a good-bye kiss, but he stopped and took a side step toward the elevator.

"Well," he said, "I'm glad I ran into you two. It's been too long."

Anne grinned and waved. "Take care, Todd."

Della nodded and before she decided on what to say, he had turned and was heading toward the exit.

A sharp rush of brisk central air-conditioning greeted Della and her family as they walked through the front door of 18 Legare Street and into the grand home of her childhood. It must have cost a fortune to cool down the three-story home with its tall ceilings and wide, creaky floorboards.

Installing the central air system was only the beginning of the changes the Suttons had made to the place, and Della couldn't help but be taken aback when she discovered each new attempt to modernize the old home in which her grandmother had raised her. Last year it was the skylights and the hot tub on the third floor, this year it was the refurbished kitchen—the large stainless steel appliances and dark granite countertops whose surface shimmered like asphalt on a hot day.

The oven and fridge seemed like they took up too much room in the long, narrow galley kitchen where Della still pictured Nana beating eggs, frying fish, and canning loquats by the screened door. How many hours had Della and her cousins harvested the Japanese plums for Nana? They'd play a game called "Who's he gonna be?" where they'd twist the stem and count how many times it took for the loquat to release. With each twist, they ran down the alphabet. A, B, C, D and wherever it finally popped, that would be the initial of the man they would marry. Once they thought of a boy's name with the corresponding letter, they'd paint a vivid word picture of a beautiful life with the lucky boy that involved many children, a swimming pool, a trampoline, and some sort of red or white sports car.

Della sniffed the air and closed her eyes. The one thing the Doctors Sublime couldn't get rid of was the unmistakable smell of the old house. Despite the refinished floors and the fresh coats of paint and the new furniture their pricey decorator had brought in, the house still retained the faint scent of mothballs, mud, mold, and what Della could only describe as history. Age. Like Papa's pillow on a hot summer day when she snuck up to his nook on the third floor and lay down to read a book before he came home from work.

Now she took a look at Peter and Cozy and had to laugh. They looked like three hobos from significantly north of Broad Street with their mismatched bags full of clothes and toiletries: a dusty tennis bag meant to hold a racket and balls, an old canvas boat bag of Nana's that she used to pack Della's girlhood picnics in, a My Little Pony backpack, and soaps and toothbrushes in plastic Food Lion sacks.

Cozy opened wide her arms. "Wow, it feels good in here."

Andrew ran out from the kitchen with his face smattered with ketchup. He nearly toppled Cozy over with his big hug.

"You're spending the night!" he said.

"Yep," she said, grinning back at her parents. "I am."

After Rosetta served a delicious Cuban meal of seasoned pork tenderloin, fried plantains, beans and rice, and a tomato salad, Peter took the kids in the back garden where they played hide-and-seek, climbed the loquat tree, ate the plums, and had a pit-spitting contest just like Della and her cousins had done when she was a child. Then she hosed them off one by one on the piazza and sent them to their rooms to put on their pajamas. Mary Jane was having a hard time going to sleep after Peter read them *Paddington at the Circus* three times. When Della went to tuck her in, she whispered, "My mommy lies down with me sometimes."

Della grinned and wiped a strand of hair out of her mouth. "Does she?" she said. Then she lay down beside her and pulled the little girl close, relishing the crisp, clean, all-cotton sheets and the cool air from the vent above as it quietly poured down on them.

An hour later Peter gently woke her by massaging her shoulders. Her neck was stiff from squeezing into Mary Jane's little bed. When she stepped into the lighted hallway, she saw that he had two small fluted cordial glasses of Madeira on the window sill he must have poured from the wet bar in Drew and Lish's bedroom. He offered her one and nodded toward the third-floor piazza.

Della rubbed her eyes, accepted the glass, and followed him up another flight of stairs onto the porch where she leaned against the rail, surveying the familiar rooftops, chimneys, and gardens of their neighbors. The after-dinner drink was thick and sweet and tasted almost chilled from the cool house. "Mmm," she said. "Thanks."

He came quietly up behind her and softly kissed

her earlobe. His stubble tickled her neck. "Wanna fool around?"

In the historic beauty and new creature comforts of her grandmother's refurbished home, Della felt the contrast between her life and her cousin's. On paper she had what she thought she always wanted—an artist husband who loved her and their child. A truly great man. An inspired and devoted one. And a magnificent-looking guy to boot.

But this eking out a life as a writer and an artist was getting to her. She thought it would be romantic and meaningful and exhilarating, but it had actually turned out to be the opposite. She'd be thirty-eight in a few weeks, and she wanted more children, a house full. And she envisioned her brood attending above-average schools and dwelling in a clean, safe place with bedrooms like Mary Jane's—coordinated sheets and pillows, Madame Alexander dolls, and that crisp, cool air preserving it all.

Peter, on the other hand, could live this way forever. He loved their life. Their home. The way they made their little living. From the moment she met him, he had not changed. *She* was the one who had. She didn't set out to, but it happened, and she couldn't reverse it now.

When he pecked her shoulder, she froze. He let out a deep breath and cleared his throat. "Worried about your cousin?"

She fibbed with a nod and a "Mmm-hmm." Della used to tell Peter exactly what was on her mind. He used to be her confidante until she started to wish for another life for her daughter. Now what was on her mind would wound him. Maybe for good. And she couldn't stop the resentment or the fantasy of what could have been had she not broken things off with Todd to pursue a degree in creative writing. Had she not eyed Peter a year later across the Wells Gallery at the "art walk" while he shook hands with art collectors and posed for pictures for the style section of the paper beneath the beak of one of his enormous copper pelicans. She'd walked right up to the artist and flashed the broad smile that had cost Nana and Papa thousands of dollars at the orthodontist's to perfect. "Hi," she'd said, cocking her head. She had eyed the pelican and then the tall handsome man. "Stupefying."

He had grinned and given her a quick once-over. "Now that's an adjective you don't hear every day."

Now as she felt her husband's warm breath on the back of her neck, she couldn't help but think of Todd Jervey, stable and as predictable as the tide. And could she admit it to herself? Yes, financially sound. Why was that such a bad thing to want?

It was wrong to think this way. It was dangerous. But it was difficult to stop.

Peter squeezed her shoulders. "Drew called while you were napping and said everything looks good. He predicts she'll be home tomorrow." He gently kissed the crown of her head and stepped back. Della looked out into the night. She was sure there were stars to be seen above, but the humidity kept the sky a kind of thick ash gray.

"I woke up," a groggy little voice behind them called. Della turned to see Mary Jane standing at the top of the stairs in her monogrammed nightgown, rubbing her eyes.

"Coming," Della handed Peter her half-empty glass and walked Mary Jane down to the second floor, relieved to curl up beside the little girl beneath her pink striped sheets for the rest of the night.

Chapter Five

Dr. Alisha Brumley Sutton

The monitor felt tight on Lish's belly. Her doctor suspected a mild placental abruption, a slight pulling away of the placenta from the uterine wall. Sometimes blood could pool in the space between the two and that was why she was bleeding yesterday. It had been almost twenty-four hours and the baby's heart seemed steady and strong, but Lish could still feel her abdomen tighten every few minutes, and she had a localized pain on her left side that must be where the abruption was.

She knew enough about obstetrics from her medical school rounds on these very halls to know that if the baby continued to look strong and the pain subsided, she'd be able to go home late today. If the baby fluctuated too much, she'd be here until the fetus was strong enough to be delivered. Of course if the child went into distress, that was another story altogether. One she didn't want to think about.

The steady sound of the baby's heart rate as it moved across the monitor reassured her. Each child she had delivered had been strong and fully developed—able to hold on her chest, skin to skin, and nurse within minutes after their routine deliveries. In fact, she had practiced her Kegels so much with Mary Jane that she didn't even need an episiotomy. What a relief. She was jogging around The Battery within two weeks after that delivery, and she could wear her size four jeans by the end of the first month. As a pediatrician who had treated many sick babies, Lish understood how fortunate she was. With both Andrew and Mary Jane, her milk production was plentiful and her children seemed to thrive from the moment they left the womb.

Stronger than the contractions and the localized pain was the emptiness in her belly. With the exception of half of the last third of Mary Jane's waffle, she hadn't eaten anything in almost twenty-four hours.

"Darla," she said to the nurse who came in every hour or so to check the monitor and take her temperature. Lish made it a point to learn the nurse's names right away. They are the ones who are on the ground doing most of the work; they are the ones who are around to save your life at a moment's notice. "I'm starving."

Darla gently cocked her head to the side. "You know you can't eat anything until we've observed the baby for twenty-four hours." She checked her watch. "You've got six to go."

"I know," she said. "But how about a Popsicle or even a few ice chips? I'm afraid I'm going to be sick if I don't eat."

Darla grinned and nodded as she walked toward the door. "Let me see what I can do."

Drew should have been back by now. He had to make his rounds and check in at the lab, but he had traded schedules with Dr. Willis so he could be off for the next day or so. Where was he?

Lish was thankful that Anne had offered to go to Babies R Us. She knew Della was aching for another child, and she didn't want to have to send her to the baby store. But if the baby came this week, Lish needed a car seat to take her home in. Mary Jane had had reflux so bad, she must have spit up on their old car seat a hundred times. The cover was worn out from all of the washing, and Drew insisted they throw the whole contraption away when she graduated from the infant seat into a forward-facing one.

Now Lish closed her eyes for a moment. She was thankful for Della too. Della could handle the kids. She could handle them for a year if she had to. Poor Della. She was the brightest and most capable person Lish knew, but she and Peter had trouble making ends meet.

She checked the "labor and delivery" file Drew had brought from home. In it was the article she wrote for the paper about the importance of creating a birth plan. She had delivered both Andrew and Mary Jane without any anesthesia, and she'd avoided the usual grogginess and headaches some of her friends had complained of postpartum. With each birth, Drew had had one of the nurses immediately snap a photo of the mother-child bonding after he rested the baby on her chest, and these photos were framed and hung in their bedroom as a reminder of the momentous occasion.

Besides her husband, she didn't want any family in the room for several hours. They would both need time to connect with their beloved little one. Then, by the afternoon, the rest of the family could meet the new arrival. First her children, who would be anxious to meet their younger sibling. She wanted Drew to take a photo of their faces at their first sight of the baby; she would put them in a frame she found at Metropolitan Deluxe that read "my family" and hang them in the nursery as well. Now she read the closing of her column,

While I've encouraged you to go with the flow during much of your pregnancy, in this particular case, you can't plan or be specific enough. If you don't have a vision, you will be frustrated and powerless, and your first hours with your baby will be decided by well-meaning medical professionals and family members who may not fully realize what this initial bonding means to you and your child.

Lish put down the article and looked out the window as an extremely sharp contraction began. She heard the baby's heart rate slow on the monitor and there was suddenly a warm pool beneath her. Blood. She pressed the call button for the nurse just as Darla walked in with a Popsicle on a tray.

Darla dropped the tray and ran out in the hall. "She's hemorrhaging!" she called down the hall to the nurse's station.

Lish's eyes clouded over, but she could still hear Darla and the others.

"Fetal distress," Darla said, her voice trembling as two other nurses crowded around and checked the vitals.

"Get Dr. Hunter and Dr. Chang," another said. "This is going to be a crash C-section, and it may have to happen right here."

"We're with you, Dr. Sutton. You're going to be okay." Lish nodded, but she couldn't open her eyes. The sound of her baby's heart in distress was deafening. She heard a nurse paging Drew, and she was aware of a cool swab being rubbed across the lower half of her belly. The last thing she felt was the tube scraping the back of her throat as the anesthesiologist shoved it in.

Chapter Six

Della

Della stared at a wall of car seats in aisle five of Babies R Us in a North Charleston strip mall. Anne had called earlier that morning and said that she had to stand in for a Sunday bell ringer who was sick.

"No problem. I'll go," she'd said to Anne, though in truth she feared she might have an out-and-out breakdown winding her way through the aisles of a baby superstore where all those infants would beam at her from the boxes of merchandise, their Gerber-like faces so perfectly round and sweet.

Della decided not to read about all the bells and whistles of the car seats. She simply bought the most expensive one, which was beige and remarkably bulky, grabbed three different brands of pacifiers, and headed to the checkout without looking one single baby picture (or real-life baby, for that matter) in the eye.

Peter had given his blessing for her to make a morning of it, so she stopped in Starbucks to crank out a chapter of her novel. The manuscript was due to her editor in four short months, and once she started teaching full time, she would rarely have more than thirty minutes in one sitting to work on it. She bought a venti Frappuccino and settled in with her laptop.

It was kind of nice to be off the peninsula on a Sunday. The bells, which Anne described as jubilant, always made Della sad somehow. Sometimes she would even put on Peter's old Walkman with the Springsteen cassette (stuck there for years) to tune them out. Last week she'd spent a good twenty minutes stomping around the house, screaming, "Born in the U-S-A!" until Cozy walked by with her fingers in her ears.

Just then the guy behind the counter called out, "Is there a Della Limehouse here?" She saw him clutching the receiver to his chest. She blushed, partly because now all of Starbucks knew that she didn't own a cell phone, and partly because she'd told the man at the counter that her name was Felicia when she ordered her coffee. (She was trying to get into her character's mind, so she thought she'd try her name out.) She ran over, grabbed the receiver, and pressed her finger to her other ear to block out the jazz music. "Hello?"

"Something's gone wrong with Lish and the baby," Peter said from the other end of the line.

"What do you mean?"

"Drew's beeper went off a few minutes ago. He ran to the car saying something about a crash Caesarian."

Della could hear Andrew and Cozy squealing in the background. "How many weeks is she?" Peter whispered.

"Thirty-two."

Now Della let out a deep breath and her stomach turned. She looked out to her car where the fancy car seat rested against her passenger side window.

"I haven't said anything to the kids," he said. "You better call Anne and get to the hospital."

When Della arrived on the fifth floor of MUSC, she found Anne sitting next to Phil Rainey, the head priest from St. Michael's. They were both still in their vestments, holding hands in a prayer. Drew was in full scrubs and a face mask, pacing in front of the doors of the operating room.

Anne looked up and reached out to grab Della's hand. "They won't let him in."

Della looked at Father Rainey, who used to come to her nana's house and deliver Communion when Papa was having a tough Sunday. He

had given Della her first Communion when she
was ten, and he had married her and Peter on a
a mild October evening nine years ago. His wife
had even sewn Della a tiny, beautiful embroidered
day gown when Cozy was born. That had meant
a lot to Della. It was something Nana would have
done had she been alive. She christened Cozy in
it after much pressure from Anne, Lish, and Peter's folks. Then she tucked the gown away in the
bottom drawer of an old bureau, and she had not
looked at it (or darkened the door of church) since.
She had nothing against this kind, older man. But
she did have a bone or two to pick with God.

Lish and Drew were active at the old affluent
church of her childhood, and Anne, who inher-
ited Nana's unwavering faith, had served for a decade as a bell ringer. It wasn't so much that Della
blamed God for her current struggles. (She knew
she only had herself to blame for her adult life.)
But she did have a lot of questions about her childhood.

In the same way that she couldn't bear to go to
Babies R Us, she couldn't bear St. Michael's. She
could hardly abide the sight of the beautiful, well-
heeled families dressed to the nines and kissing
one another on the cheek during the passing of
the Peace. Those families seemed whole and con-
tent in a way that broke Della's heart each time
she laid eyes on one. She'd had to turn away from

Lish's kitchen window this very morning, even as a couple of these families strolled by on their way to worship as the bells rang out their forlorn toll.

She knew she was both self-centered and pitiful. And she didn't actually want the church families to be ugly and unhealthy, did she? No, no, no. These were the thoughts that ricocheted around the walls of her mind on Sunday mornings as the bells pealed from the top of the steeple in her exceedingly North of Broad life.

"Good to see you, Della," Father Rainey said. "I'm sorry it's under these uncertain circumstances."

Della nodded. "Me too." She took a seat by Anne and tapped her foot so fast and furious that Anne had to reach out, hold her knee, and ask, "Trying to wear a hole through the floor?"

Finally, Lish's young obstetrician walked out of the operating room and lifted his mask above the Phish do-rag he had over his head. There was a swath of dried blood on the back side of his forearm, a spot he must have missed when he scrubbed his arms moments before. Della dragged Anne over toward Drew. The doctor nodded and put his hand firmly on Drew's shoulder. "Congratulations, Dr. Sutton. You have a new daughter and one tenacious survivor for a wife."

Drew let out a deep breath and nodded. He looked to Della and Anne and grinned. "Thanks be to God!" Anne clapped her hands together and bounced on the balls of her long feet. Father Rainey shuffled over and patted Drew on the back. "Yes, indeed, son!"

"The pediatrician will meet with you shortly, Dr. Sutton," the OB said. "The baby is well, but she'll need to be on a breathing machine for the next few days or so until her lungs are fully developed. And we're going to have to observe Lish for several hours. She should be waking up any time now."

Drew stepped back as the baby came out in a warming crib with thin tubes of oxygen stuffed in each tiny nostril. Her pinkish hands were no larger than a benniseed wafer, but they were perfect as a doll baby's, each with their own little rounded fingernail. Anne gasped and Della swallowed her tears and cheered as two nurses rolled the infant down the hall toward the Neonatal Intensive Care Unit. Drew walked alongside his infant daughter, his hand clutching the edge of the plastic bassinet.

Della and Anne stood in the hallway as they rolled Lish over to the observation room. Her cousin looked as though she was sound asleep, but her fingers were swollen and her ankles and toes were streaked with dried blood. The two women took a seat by her gurney at the nurse's invitation and sat for several minutes watching Lish's chest rise and fall.

Della should call Peter to let him know that he was an uncle again, but she couldn't move. Neither she nor Anne could stop studying their closest relative and friend who never failed to possess a kind of valor and grace no matter how gritty or challenging the circumstances. While Della and Lish were born a few months apart and (with the exception of grad school) they had always lived less than a ten-minute walk from one another, Della felt as though they inhabited different universes. One of the hardest things about her current struggles was that they were further evidence of what she had suspected since they were adolescents planning their lives beneath Nana's loquat tree—that Lish's life was on a trajectory out of her reach. One she was either incapable of possessing or simply didn't deserve, for a reason she couldn't or wouldn't ever know.

"What are you thinking about, Del?" Della turned and realized Anne must have been studying her for a while.

Anne reached out and touched her clenched hands.

Della had written some love poems for a therapist friend who was trying to woo a woman in his yoga class, and he'd given her five free sessions where she'd tried to work out some of what was stirring inside of her. "You know the other day my therapist made me tell him about what it was like for me when your daddy died."

Anne shook her head. Della and Lish were in second grade and Anne was only in first when Nana delivered the news during a summer swimming lesson at the YMCA.

"I can't remember a worse day." Anne bit her lip.

Della nodded. "I remember the visitation, standing in front of the casket. When Nana and Papa entered the room, I ran over and asked Nana to hold me. I wanted to be in her arms so bad."

"She was everyone's favorite," Anne said.

"Yeah." Della felt her ears redden and she tapped the floor again. "Anyway, Lish pulled me back and held me tight. 'Let Nana and Papa see their son,' she'd said. 'You stand here with me.'"

Della looked back at Anne, who was studying her intently. She bit the inside of her cheek and added, "Lish was always showing me things like that—even on the day her own father was being laid to rest—things that I'd never thought of. You know?"

Anne gave Della a sympathetic smile. She just didn't seem to have the anger or grief that surrounded Della like the humidity itself, thick and stifling. Anne must have made peace with it a long time ago, Della thought.

* * *

Yes, Lish had her act together, Della thought, gazing at her cousin with a kind of wonder and curiosity. Lish's eyes fluttered for a moment before she settled back into her sleep. Her cousin was bright, conscientious, organized, and cool-headed. She knew when to keep her mouth shut, what to keep personal. While Della was usually complaining about her marriage, Lish rarely uttered a negative word about Drew. Was this discretion or satisfaction? Either way, it created a sense of otherworldliness about their marriage. As if it existed on a plane far beyond Della's.

The truth was, Lish had had her choice of men to marry, and she'd chosen wisely. And now her body had produced three perfect, beautiful children, to whom she was dedicated to loving, teaching, wiping, and feeding day after day.

Della thought back to the sad day of her uncle's funeral. She had wept more than her cousins combined, and Lish had comforted her, giving her a piece of Dentyne from Nana's purse.

Drew came in just as Lish began to stir. He rubbed her hair out of her eyes and softly kissed her forehead.

"You did good, baby," he said. She opened her eyes and rubbed her neck. "How's the baby?"

"In the NICU, breathing strong. She looks like

a Cecilia to me." Della smiled. She was earnestly happy for Lish and relieved that all had gone well. She loved her cousin deeply despite her inability to stop comparing their lives. She would do anything for her, and she knew the reverse was true.

"Hey, Anne, Del." Lish looked their way. "I didn't see y'all there."

Anne stood and walked over to her sister's side. "We're here." She took her hand. "Congratulations."

Peter jumped on the Doctors Sublimes' king-size bed with Andrew, Cozy, and Mary Jane while Della hung the freshly washed and pressed infant day gowns in the nursery. After Della stuffed the last little diaper into the drawer of the changing table, she walked into the master bedroom and leaned against the bedpost. "I've got good news, gang! Mama and the baby are coming home this afternoon."

"Hooray!" Mary Jane said, falling into Peter's brawny arms. He lifted her upside down and spun her around the room, chanting, "Mama's coming home! Mama's coming home!" before he gently tossed her in the center of the bed. Andrew cheered, then took off his pajama top and made the crude sound Peter taught him where you cup your hand in the opposite underarm and pump like a chicken.

"Stop that, man." Peter chuckled. "Your mama won't invite us back if she sees you doing that. Let's save that for when you're with the guys—your dad or me."

Andrew allowed himself two more pumps, his two flawless rows of white, square teeth showing in his full-out laugh.

"Why'd you teach him that, Daddy?" Cozy's hands were on her hips.

He pinched her rosy cheek. "Ah, come on, pumpkin. Loosen up and maybe I'll show you how."

Cozy looked at her mama and rolled her eyes. "Boys," she said.

Peter packed the clothes as Della bathed Mary Jane and Andrew and put them in matching blue gingham sailor outfits—a dress for her and a shorts suit for him. She settled them in front of an episode of *Curious George* while she continued to straighten up the house.

This used to be Della's home, the one she shared with Nana and Papa. She had spent every summer here until the ninth grade when Nana persuaded her father to let her move in for good and attend The Pinckney School for Girls. Her father agreed; nothing could persuade him more than education, and he was weary of getting in the middle of the fights between Della and her stepmother.

As for her mother, she was off living the life of a beatnik. Had been ever since Della was in grade school. She secured small fellowships and grants to teach or write all over the world, but the truth was, she spent much of her time experimenting with drugs and searching for a mate who could fund her habits.

When Della's mother was a senior in high school, she'd spent a year in Paris studying art history before attending college. A group of Columbia University students took her to an inn on the Left Bank that later became known as the Beat Hotel, a haven for young American expatriate painters, writers, and musicians. She met Allen Ginsberg and William Burroughs that year, and she became particularly close to a young beat, Gregory Corso, who helped get her first poem published in *City Lights*. She was now known as one of the few female voices of the time. It sounded implausible, a Charleston girl from South of Broad on the tail end of the beatnik movement. But that's precisely where she ended up thanks to a little bit of talent, a perspective that was particularly gothic, a spirit of adventure, and something that one could argue is even more potent than the aforementioned three: physical beauty. Not unlike Della, Kate Brumley knew how to woo a man. She was in control of her feminine charms, and she never hesitated to use them to her advantage.

Now Della stood at the large doorway that led to the front piazza and garden. She could recall waiting there for hours for her mother to come for a visit, every six months or so. She'd count raindrops, count cars, count mosquitoes and how many she slapped at as they attempted to nip her arms and legs. Usually her mother was several hours late. Occasionally she didn't show at all and would phone in the evening, having missed her train or flight. "I can't make it right now," she'd tell Nana. "Could Della come up to see me in a few weeks?"

Then Nana would bring two cups of hot tea—Della's was mostly milk and sugar—out to the front piazza and place them on the wicker side table. She'd pat a place next to her on the joggling board and hand her granddaughter the china cup with the blue Italian scenes of a bridge and a woman carrying a basket of fruit on her hip.

"Something's come up with your mama," Nana would say. The little girl would sip the milky sweetness and relax into her grandmother's soft side. Nana would gently scratch her arms and shoulders with the ends of her fingernails until Della had little goose bumps on each. They'd stay this way for an hour or so, Nana rubbing her back as Della listened to the cacophony of city sounds—cars, trucks, mourning doves, crickets, and restless fenced-in dogs that seemed to chant, "She's not coming. She's not coming this time."

She understood now that Nana was her true mother. She was there for her, and she offered a stable, genteel way of life. Nana provided everything for Della. Love, presence, even financial support. She knew her dad had sent a check each month, but Nana paid the tuition at The Pinckney School, purchased the fine wardrobe, procured the piano lessons, and hosted the grand debutant ball at Hibernian Hall for all three of her granddaughters.

Della wished she could rest against Nana on the joggling board right now. She had more ahead of her than she could manage—a full-time teaching job and a December deadline for her fifth novel, and she was only eighty pages in. The summer was racing by, and she knew there wouldn't be any time to write when school started. Worst of all, her heart ached for a second child. She'd be thirty-eight next month, and she knew her biological clock was ticking. She and Peter had talked about having two or three, but how? How could they manage and provide?

Suddenly, Mary Jane shrieked and then wailed. Della ran in to see if she was all right.

"Andrew pushed me!" Mary Jane's cheeks were red and streaked with tears.

Della looked to Cozy, who nodded to confirm the accusation.

Then Peter ran in. He heard the cry all the way

from the driveway where he was tying Cozy's bicycle to the top of the old Prelude.

"C'mon, Andrew." Peter led him by the shoulders. "Into your room for a while."

As the Doctors Sublime drove up in their Volvo SUV, Della waved and called to the children. She saw Lish in the back seat retying a bow on the sleeve of Baby Cecilia's day gown. Drew helped Lish out of the car and gently pulled the baby carrier out. Lish turned toward the piazza and took a deep breath as Andrew and Mary Jane ran toward her. Cozy stayed on the piazza and leaned into Della, who rubbed her back up and down until the goose bumps formed.

"Hold me, Mommy!" Mary Jane lifted up her pudgy little arms to Lish.

"No," Drew said. "Mommy can't hold you for a few weeks, remember? She has a boo-boo that will get worse if she lifts anything heavier than the baby."

Lish bent down and pulled Mary Jane to her and then Andrew. "It's good to be home. I missed you both so much."

Della could see tears brimming in Lish's eyes as she took each of her children by the hand and walked toward her. "How can I ever thank you, Del?"

"Don't even." Della flapped her hand and kissed Lish on the cheek. "Rosetta's got lunch ready, and we're going to get on out of your hair. Call me when you need a break, and we'll come pick up the two little monsters." She pulled back and looked Lish in the eye. "Enjoy this sweet homecoming."

Lish nodded and Peter shook Drew's hand before Cozy jumped on his back and they walked toward the car. As Della waited for Peter to check the bicycle, she watched Lish and Drew and their three beautiful children go into their magnificent home, where the table was set and a warm quiche Lorraine and fresh fruit salad were waiting for them on the dining room table.

When they drove up to their home on Radcliffe Street, Della noticed the weeds in the front yard and an unruly vine that had wound its way around the railing of the front steps. A random cat with a severed left ear lounged in the sun at the edge of the rusted screen door. The feline stretched when she saw them pull into the drive and then she slunk down the stairs and beneath the house as they headed toward the door.

Inside it was sweltering hot. Like walking through pudding or the inside of a giant oven. They all ran to Cozy's room, slammed the door, and turned on the window unit.

"Isn't it great to be home?" Peter grinned, reached for Della's waist, and pulled her close.

"Yeah!" Cozy shouted as she fell back on the graying sheets of her bed. They were Della's childhood sheets. The ones she slept on when she was growing up on Legare Street. When Nana died, she'd intercepted a bag of bedding and towels Lish was packing up for Goodwill. "We could use those," she'd said.

Now Della literally bit her tongue as a lump formed in the back of her throat. She wanted to grab her child and run back to Legare Street.

She stepped away from Peter.

"Well," he said. "That shrimp trio is waiting on me out there. I guess I better get back to work."

Cozy tugged on her mother's shorts. "Tell me a Binklemeyer story, Mama." The Binklemeyers were a family Cozy and Della made up a few months ago. They lived in a town called Someplace Small, and Peachy and the kids, Burl and Bernice, walked to the ice cream store and rode their bikes down winding dirt roads that led to the forest where the occasional bobcat and even wild boar had been spotted. Burl had a lisp that made him a little self-conscious, and Bernice, while younger, often acted like a know-it-all (which grated on Burl's nerves). But all in all they got along pretty well and went on all sorts of jaunts that ranged from the amusing to the harrowing, including a romp through the peach fields, a climb up the local water tower, and a swing on a rope their grandfather had tied to the biggest tree on the edge of a nearby river.

Della nodded, and they curled up together and began their ritual. Cozy started with a line ripe with conflict like "The Day Bernice Lost Her Two-Dollar Bill" and Della worked to fill in a story with Cozy guiding her with a giggle or a "No, no, no. I was imagining something like *this…*" The story could go on for nights, and if it was really good they would act it out after it was finished.

"Okay," Della said, pulling her close. "Start us off."

Cozy nuzzled up to Della and nestled in the crook of her neck. She twirled her mother's thin golden hair around her fingers and squinted her eyes. "Burl Finds a Stray Pup in the Woods."

Della chuckled. Cozy had been wanting a real live pet ever since Andrew got a Boykin Spaniel last Christmas. She had sat and rubbed the dog's back whenever she'd had a chance over the last few days, and Della had overheard her asking Andrew if she could take him home for a spend-the-night party.

"I don't think so," she'd interceded. "You'll get a pet one of these days."

"When?"

"When we have a bigger yard."

Cozy had put her hands on her lips and shaken her head. Well, if she couldn't have her pet now, she'd give it to Burl and Bernice and watch them enjoy him in their safe and peachy world.

"Okay," Della said. "Burl was looking for insects for his science project one autumn afternoon when he heard a whimper coming from the bottom of the hollowed-out tree beyond the gates of the peach field."

Cozy inhaled and tried to suppress a grin. She gave a nod as if to say, "Go on."

That night when the house cooled down and Cozy fell asleep, Della sat at the kitchen table writing. After a dinner of frozen pizza, Peter had gone back out to work on his sculpture. They'd already spent the commission money on materials, a new set of tires for the Prelude, and three school uniforms for Cozy. Della could hear the faint scratching sound of a palmetto bug scurrying across the clean dishes that were drying on the rack in the sink, and she wondered how much it would cost to get someone to come and spray.

Her novel was based on a true story about a Latin teacher who was stalked by one of her students, a teenage boy who lived around the corner from her. The woman sympathized with the strange and lonely young boy who was a social outcast, but she would soon learn that he was more dangerous than she had ever suspected.

This manuscript was Della's second attempt to

write a plot-driven novel with commercial appeal in hopes of "earning out" her advance and actually receiving a steady royalty check. She had tried this with the last novel when she wrote about a Charleston socialite who had an affair with her husband's ne'er-do-well brother, but it became more about the ne'er-do-well and his guilt over betraying his brother. His introspection and his childhood flashbacks took over the book, and *Publishers Weekly* had called it "character-driven and contemplative." Words her MFA professors would have applauded but not exactly the ones that stimulate sales. She knew reviews like that might seal her fate as a mid-list author, unable to make a living writing.

Peter came in shirtless with his blue jeans resting low on his hips. Sweat dripped down his neck and across his strapping chest. If she described his body in one of her books, her editor would say, "Yeah, right. Make him more realistic." He had worked construction to put himself through the Savannah School of Art and Design, and he couldn't have a better build.

He poured two glasses of water from the kitchen sink and put one by her side. The pipes were warm and the heat from the water clouded the tops of the glasses.

"Hey," he said. "How's it coming?"

She hit Save and looked up. "Okay."

He cleared his throat and talked through his plan to transport the shrimp he was sculpting for a new seafood restaurant in Asheville. They should be ready by the end of next week. His father, a shrimp boat captain in McClellanville, had an extra-long flatbed truck and was usually happy to lend it with enough advance notice.

"The café's going to put me up at the Grove Park Inn." He softly clinked his glass against hers. "I was thinking maybe we could drop Cozy off at your dad's and make a night of it. Maybe go out to dinner, come back to the room, enjoy the mountain air, and see if the five-star springs on the bed work."

She shifted in her seat. The back of her thighs stuck to the Formica chair. She shrugged her shoulder. "I don't know. We'll see."

He took a look around the kitchen, wiped his forehead, and turned back to her. He watched her for several seconds as she typed.

"What's going on, Del?" He leaned in close and she could see a drop of sweat dripping off of his nose. "You've been pouting most of the summer. And you haven't exactly warmed up to me more than once or twice."

She exhaled and shook her head. What should she tell him? Either the truth or another lie to get him off her back for a moment.

"I don't know," she said. Their windows were

open, and she heard two men shouting in the distance; she couldn't tell if there was anger or elation in their tone.

"I think you do know." He stroked her hand. His fingers were long and his joints were prominent. There were protruding veins on the tops of his tanned hands that worked their way all the way up to his elbow. "You need to talk to me, baby."

She rested her pointed chin in her small hand.

"Is it the job? It's going to be too tough to teach full time and make your deadlines?" He looked around the kitchen. "I don't see why we can't move out to Mount Pleasant to a decent public school district. Or even homeschool. My buddy, Tyler, and his wife are doing that, and their kids are already speaking Spanish fluently. They know all about ancient history, and they take these terrific field trips to archaeological digs and stuff."

"No." She scowled, then swallowed hard. "If we're going to give Cozy a decent shot, she needs an exceptional education. Plus, she's an only child. Only child plus home-school equals socially awkward adult. We've got to do right by her."

"We're doing right by her," he said. "We're here for her. We love her. What's more important than that?"

Della shook her head.

"Okay," he said. "Let's brainstorm. See if we can figure something else out."

"I want another baby." She pursed her lips. "How are we gonna figure *that* out?"

He drummed his fingers on the table. "Della, things are tough right now. We're in a recession. Let's give it a year or two and see where we are."

"I'm running out of time, Peter."

"You're thirty-seven."

"I'll be thirty-eight in August. The risks go up significantly after that. Also, it's not as easy to get pregnant."

"We'll give it a good try." He leaned in to her and nuzzled his damp forehead against hers. He smelled like salt and burnt copper. "Hey, I've got a thought. We can start practicing now."

She pulled away and looked at the computer screen. Then she started to type again as a car with a booming bass zoomed by.

He downed his water and cleared his throat. He watched her until she looked up at him.

"Things have been tough for too long now, and I'm tired of waiting," she said. "I feel like we've been waiting for our careers to take off since before we were married. I've stepped out and taken on work that wasn't ideal. What about you? I think we need to face reality."

Peter pulled on his fingers until his knuckles popped. "Della, I love what I do." He rubbed his bleary eyes and met her gaze. "You used to love what I do too. What do you suggest? That I start selling insurance? That I get my real estate license? That I try to get into med school with an art degree? What?"

"Insurance," she said and her voice gained strength. "Insurance would be dandy, Peter. My friend Michelle's husband sells life insurance, and they live in a roach-free house with air conditioning. They go to the dentist every six months. They take vacations where you buy a new bathing suit and get on an airplane. They drive a car that was bought after 1989!"

She took a sip of her water and slammed it down. "They have three children who they clothe and feed and educate. They have a backyard in a decent neighborhood, and a jungle gym and a dog and a membership to a swimming pool!"

He turned away from her and looked out at the window. "So *that's* what you want now?"

She held her head in her hands and didn't answer. *Yes*, she thought. *That's what I want now.* The nuclear family life. Heck, it could be at the end of a cul-de-sac in a cookie-cutter suburb. She didn't care! Why had she abhorred that life before? What a holier-than-thou artiste she had been before she had a child! How shortsighted. How unrealistic. How lacking in pragmatism. She was sick of it. Her life. Sick to death of it.

When she thought he was asleep, she climbed into bed next to him.

He was in his boxers, face up in the bed. It was too hot for sheets.

She lay quietly down and rolled away on her side.

"I don't understand it, Della." His face was outlined by the street light pouring through the open window and the sheen of perspiration.

"Mmm?" She turned back slightly.

He propped his head on his elbow. "Why it is that you suddenly act as though you've been gypped?"

He waited for her to respond, but she didn't. He sat up, slid on his shorts and flip-flops, and walked steadily out of the room and onto the back porch, where he flicked on the light and started to work again.

She closed her eyes, too tired to call him back, too confused to deny his supposition. She heard the scrape of his crimper against the copper. It formed a steady rhythm above the sounds of the city on a humid summer night—a horn in the distance, muffled voices, the click of a rusty bicycle chain as a stranger pedaled along the crumbling sidewalk.

In minutes, she was asleep.

Chapter Seven

Roy

The week after his St. Michael's interview, Roy settled back into his routine of visiting the sick and jobless, setting up for the weekly Alpha program, studying the lectionary, and writing Sunday's sermon. His mama and Candy Mills were in charge of the upcoming Vacation Bible School, and they kept Rose busy making decorations and learning songs and the accompanying motions. They chose the "Beach Party" theme by Lifeway, and Roy had come home at night to a performance of his mama and daughter singing, dancing, and hanging ten on pretend surfboards as they sang, *"Beach party, surfing the Word... Beach party, surfing the Word... Beach party surfing the W-o-r-d of God."*

He had to chuckle watching Mama in her flip-flop heels and cut-off miniskirt as she squeezed her nose and did the twist all the way to the ground with Little Rose cheering, "Go Granny!"

Roy wouldn't describe his mama as a devout believer, but she sure did get credit for simply rolling up her sleeves and going to work. He had her and his daddy (who'd died of a heart attack less than a year after Jean Lee) to thank for getting him to church in the first place.

Back when Roy was a kid, his folks didn't have the purest of intentions when they decided to switch their membership from Robbins Neck Baptist to Church of the Good Shepherd. Truth was, his daddy had taken a liking to partaking of a cold Budweiser every now and then, after a buddy handed him an iced can at the Darlington Speedway one hot afternoon. And Roy Sr. decided he couldn't reconcile his Saturday refreshment with his Sunday worship at the Baptist church, so his wife suggested Good Shepherd where the Junior League ladies she greatly admired attended. Then off the family went with great hopes of climbing the social ladder while Roy Sr. savored an occasional Bud on a steamy day without remorse.

No, their reason for switching denominations wasn't all that pure, but God works all things for the good of those who love him, who have been called according to his purpose. It turned out there weren't many young folks at the Episcopal church, so Roy and Chick were called on to serve as acolytes nearly every Sunday. There was an older spinster lady, Miss Ruby Nuttall, who spent months preparing them for confirmation when they were in middle school. How often Roy recalled sitting in Miss Ruby's parlor on Wednesday afternoons breaking down the Nicene Creed line by line. Miss Ruby always had a large dish of caramel cubes within reach, and he still remembered relishing them one by one during her theological discourses about the Trinity, the virgin birth, and most thrilling of all, the resurrection, as a kind of warm and ardent yearning began to form in Roy's heart.

The following spring when Bishop Boatwright came and laid hands on his head during the confirmation ceremony, Roy felt the presence of God. There was no denying it. It was like a surging heat that was both forceful and tranquil. It started around the crown of his head and worked its way down to his fingertips and toes until his whole body felt like it had fallen asleep. It was all he could do to stop from laughing out loud when the heat concentrated itself in his gut, and he knew as soon as he felt the fire that he'd been called out of one world and into another.

He kept on being a regular boy during this sanctification process. He played football, delivered papers, listened to Garth Brooks, and got into the typical late-night trouble. But he also joined the

Fellowship of Christian Athletes and became the president of the Clemson chapter by his junior year in college. And Jean Lee, whom he started dating the first day of high school—well, she went right along down this path with her hand in his as if there was no other plan for her life. She had gone to dental hygiene school in Anderson to be near Roy during college, and they married their senior year before he took a job as a youth minister in Winnsboro to get a feel for what it was like to work in a church day in and day out. After a few years, he was recommend for seminary, and they headed to Pittsburgh for a three-year program at Trinity. Jean Lee conceived during his third and final year in seminary, and a few months into the pregnancy she pulled aside the dentist she was working for to show him a funny white spot on her tongue that turned out to be cancerous. The doctors delivered Rosebud as early as they could and quickly began chemo, but Jean Lee was gone before their baby girl was three months old.

Roy didn't understand why some things turned out the way they did. He hated what had happened to his wife and his daddy, too, but he knew God wasn't out to punish him. It was just sin. Plain and simple. Roy traced its origins back to the garden where darkness and death first entered human lives—not by God's choice, but by man's. And

Roy took heart in the fact that sin, whose end result is always death, was only half the story of this life. The narrative didn't simply end there like so many people thought. There was a whole 'nother half and it involved a way out of this predicament. Roy clung to Miss Ruby's belief that a provision had been made, a sacrifice on behalf of all mankind, and that's what buoyed him when his little girl climbed up in his lap and said, "Why did Mama die?"

It was just a week after Roy's trip to Charleston that he received the call.

"Reverend here," Roy announced into the receiver after Skeeter ran in and pointed to the flashing red light on line one.

"Hello, Roy, this is Heyward Rutledge from St. Michael's."

"Hi there, Heyward. Hope you're well."

"Well," Heyward said. "I don't want to beat around the bush, sir." Roy thought he could hear a pen being tapped on something on the other end of the line. He sat back and then Heyward said, "I'll be a whole lot better if you accept the call to be the rector of St. Michael's."

The words hit Roy like a blindside chop block. One might have thought with the dream about flying and the red-headed angel that this was the most obvious of conclusions, but Roy didn't see it coming.

After he caught his breath, he closed his eyes tight and said, "I didn't think it would be me."

"Well, it is," Heyward said. "It is you. The search committee, the vestry, the bishop—we're all in agreement on this."

How? he thought. *How in the world could y'all think this was a good fit?*

"I—" It was one of those rare moments when he didn't know what to say next.

"Well, don't sound so surprised, Roy. The timing is right—the bishop had us listen to a few of your sermons he had on tape, and I tell you, we believe you're just the man we need to light a fire under us."

Roy's ears popped when he swallowed. He heard Candy's husband, Milton Mills, cranking the lawn mower in the front yard of the church, and he could see Skeeter's shadow in the hall outside of the door as she listened in.

"Heyward, I've got to be honest." (He might have prayed right then and there, but he didn't.) "I didn't expect to be chosen, and I'm not sure it's right for me or for you."

There was a long pause and Roy imagined Heyward looking up at the search committee, who it suddenly occurred to him might be gathered around the phone at this moment.

"Well, I don't know what would make you say that," the man on the other line said. "You're what we need. It was unanimous from our end. Why don't you…" There was a pause. "Take a little time and call me back in a few days?"

"All right," Roy said. "I appreciate you giving me some time. I'll call you by the end of the week."

"Okay, Roy," Heyward said. He cleared his throat, and Roy imagined the search committee leaning in to hear more. "We'll be looking forward to your call."

That night Chick and his wife, Nikki, came over with a pound of barbecue, some slaw, and a nice-sized watermelon. Ms. B. had called Roy's home, prematurely, to discuss the installation date and the reception to follow, and Mama was so excited about the idea of him moving to Charleston that she was just about to bust. She had looked up the church online and taken a gander at the three-story rectory on Meeting Street, and she and Rosebud were already picturing themselves there, sipping tea on an upper piazza.

"St. Michael's Church." Chick put a wad of to-bacco behind his bottom lip and shook his head. They were on Roy's front porch watching Chick's twin boys, Buster and Jake, play monkey-in-the middle with Rose. The boys were only a year older, but they were nearly a foot taller than the little girl, and her effort to jump up and grab the football as they tossed it back and forth was all but hopeless.

"Supper's ready!" Mama called from the kitchen window. Jake softly threw the ball at Rose so she could win a round, and then Buster tousled her hair and led her toward the back door with his hand on her little shoulder.

"Yeah," Roy said after the kids slammed the screened door. "Isn't this the strangest turn of events?"

Chick nodded and turned to Roy. "Whatcha goin' do?"

"I want to say no," Roy said. "Every fiber of my being is saying, 'No, those folks are going to eat you alive, Bub.'"

"Yep," Chick said. He spit a little tobacco juice off the front porch just behind the azalea bushes. "I can't argue with you there, brother."

The only person who dreaded Charleston more than Roy was Chick. He had taken that Neanderthal comment to heart back when they were kids, not to mention all the times Aunt Elfrieda told them that their grandpa (her brother) had married beneath himself and that the ill effects of that would go on for generations unless they wised up, gave up an interest in farming and football and speed racing, and started acting and talking like civilized gentlemen. In fact, Heyward's old words and Aunt Elfrieda's were almost like a decree over Chick, and he seemed almost determined to live into them. His efforts to become the consummate small-town Bubba were made with a kind of fervor and bitter surrender that Roy didn't fully understand.

After a knee injury in college that gave Chick no prospects where pro football was concerned, he bought a patch of land off of Welsh Neck Road to farm and promptly let himself go. He gained a good forty pounds, stopped wearing shirts with sleeves, and had a profound disdain for anything that seemed remotely cultivated (and this somehow included church). When their mama offered to pay for voice lessons for Buster, who, according to the music teacher at school, seemed to have perfect pitch, Chick refused. "No. That's not for a boy like him," Roy remembered him saying one afternoon while his mama made a teary plea. "There's only one place outside of school for my kids—that's the speedway or the ball field."

"Boys, come on in and eat," their mama now called. She looked them both over and added: "And Chick, spit that tobacco out right now. You won't be able to partake of that when we visit your brother in Charleston."

Roy reached out and firmly patted her elbow.

"Mama, please stop talking like this thing is a done deal."

She looked away from him, toward the little two-lane highway that ran in front of his house. An eighteen-wheeler was barreling by. It had a large bumper sticker on the back that read, "God is good. All the time!"

"All right," his mama murmured. She turned her back to him, the sparkles from her bright-green eye shadow catching the porch light. "But you and I need to talk."

Their leisurely supper ended with Nikki's homemade banana pudding and a history lesson about Charleston by Rose, whose granny had been pumping her with all sorts of romantic musings about horse-drawn carriages and hoop skirts and a row of houses as colorful as a rainbow. Chick and his brood headed home, and Roy tucked Rose in bed after a little more *Heidi* and the Lord's Prayer. As he turned out the light, she sat up and said, "Daddy?"

"Yeah, sweet pea?"

"Don't you want to move to a pretty city?"

He leaned his head against the door frame and crossed his arms. "You know, I'm not sure, Rose."

Her little head was tilted and he could see her pointing upward with her index finger. "Well, you said that God would show you, and now they've called and said they want you."

He nodded and the verse "You have hidden these things from the wise" blipped across his mind before he could fully tune it out.

"Maybe it's that simple, but somehow I don't think so. I need to feel like I'm supposed to go, sweet pea." He came over and sat next to her in the dark. "It would be a big change for you and me both. The kind of change that would affect our lives for years to come, and if I don't feel an absolute confirmation, I can't go."

She lay back down and he tucked the sheet and comforter around her side so that she looked like a burrito or a caterpillar in its cocoon.

"What's a confirmation?"

"A yes."

She nodded her head and lay back down. "Good night, Daddy."

When he went back downstairs, Donny, Mama's new husband, was watching the news in the den while Mama unloaded the dishwasher.

Roy poured himself a cup of coffee and sat down at the kitchen table. He took off his collar and noticed he'd gotten a smudge of banana pudding on the top edge.

Mama sat down next to him, picked up the collar, and said, "I'll take this home and see if I can get that out with a little OxiClean."

He smiled at her. "Thanks, Mama."

She took a deep breath and reached over to grab his wrist. "You need to do something for me, all right?"

He nodded as the steam from his coffee rose between them.

"You need to be open to this call. I'm not saying this because Charleston is a nice place and the church is downright gorgeous, not to mention the rectory." She squeezed his wrist, and he looked up into her dark brown eyes. "I'm saying this because sometimes we're asked to go where we don't want to go. And it's not to torture us. It's because there's something there that only we can do. There's a purpose and a plan, and if we don't follow, we miss the blessing. And so does everybody else who we were supposed to love on."

He sat back and looked at her. She looked wise beneath the caked-on makeup and the orange tanning parlor glow. In her eyes there was a light, and it wasn't just the reflection of the overhead lamp.

"I underestimate you, Mama."

She smiled and the crow's-feet on the edge of her eyes that she worked so hard to conceal were more lovely than he could ever describe. She patted his hand, then took a sip of her own coffee. "We only get one go-around. Better make it count."

She stood, flipped the switch on the coffeepot, grabbed her gold purse, and said, "Sometimes you don't even need to pray or think on something. Sometimes you just know." She grabbed her keys, gave him a nod, and said, "Let's go, hon," to Donny who turned off the TV, took her hand, and nodded to Roy as they walked out the door.

Early the next morning Roy heard little footsteps and then the sound of Rose plinking on the piano. The summer sun was already blazing through the blinds, leaving a pattern of slats across his bed. He sat up and felt the same heat in his gut as the day the bishop placed hands on his head when he was twelve.

He took several slow breaths as the heat surged through his body, and he knew the Spirit was upon him.

"Show me the way, Lord," he whispered. "Show me, and I will follow."

When the tingling subsided, he went on down the stairs where Rose was playing one of the VBS tunes on the piano.

"Listen, Daddy," she said.

"All right." He sat down at the bench beside her and put his arm around her. Then they slowly belted out the song together. *"Beach party, surfing the Word... Beach party surfing the Word... Beach party surfing the W-o-r-d of God!"*

Chapter Eight

Lish

In the living room sat four bouquets full of pink and yellow roses and hydrangeas and lilies. Anne and Della had left the tags in their plastic pitchforks, and now Lish opened each one and smiled. One was from the downtown neighborhood association, another from her editor at *The Post and Courier*, one from the infectious disease department at MUSC, and another from her book club. On the love seat, there was a pile of gifts to open, presents in slick white wrapping paper and pink satin ribbons with thick ecru tags bearing the names of the local children's boutiques.

She opened a gift from her next-door neighbor, a pale pink day gown with white smocking, and immediately wrote a thank-you note. Her stationary and stamps were set up on the side table along with her address books from the children's school, St. Michael's Church, the Country Club of Charleston, and the South of Broad Neighborhood Association. However, on the front of this envelope she wrote, "By hand" in the bottom left corner.

After she sealed the envelope, she opened the next box, a Charleston Bonnet from a friend in her Pilates class. As she reached for the next gift, her incision began to burn, and she leaned back and stuffed one of her grandmother's small satin throw pillows beneath her head.

The living room was the only room where she had not changed the furniture. Nana had left it to her—the pale yellow and orange Oriental rug, the yellow-and-white-striped Chippendale sofa, and the antique chairs Nana had bought during a trip to London. This was the room where she and Anne sat eating fruit salad and deviled eggs after their father's funeral when she was eight. She could still remember her mother and Nana standing at the doorway greeting the guests. Nana had put baby's breath and daisies in her granddaughters' hair, and Anne kept leaning over into Lish's bun to smell the flowers.

The year her father died, Lish became adept at holding back tears when need be. There were enough of those around Nana's home with Della's mother postponing her annual visit or their grandfather, Papa Brumley, shuffling home from his music store each day where he'd walk silently up to his room, put on a record (more often than not, the art songs of Richard Strauss), and stare blankly into the trees behind the piazza until the wetness formed in the corners of his eyes.

But despite the grief, Lish loved the summers she and Anne spent in Charleston with their grandparents. 18 Legare was a haven, especially compared to the naval bases they were dragged to after their mother married a naval commander the year after their daddy's death. Lish and Anne had moved three times in three years during their adolescence: Millington, Tennessee; Earle, New Jersey; Fort Worth, Texas. Each time, Lish missed the crumbling beauty and the thick, humid air of Charleston. The smell of low tide and sitting on the piazza listening to the rain hiss when it hit the ground, or the sound of the blind man who pounded the street with the top end of his merchandise, calling, "Brooms for sale," until someone came out of a house and bought one. Best of all were Nana's stories, which she told them at night in the hammock of the upstairs piazza. She'd recount tales about their father and Della's mother and the mischief they got into as children. And she'd tell them about their great-great-great-grandfather, an old Charleston merchant for whom the street they lived on was named.

Now Lish could hear the tap of her husband's fingers on the laptop in the upstairs office across from their bedroom. He was e-mailing photos of the baby to their family and friends and uploading a new album onto his Facebook page.

As she rose from the love seat, she was astonished by the ache in her gut, and she shuffled to the kitchen to take another Tylenol with Codeine. Once the pill took the edge off, she slowly stepped up the stairs and made the rounds, retucking the children in for the night. She listened, as always, to Mary Jane's breathing. The toddler suffered from asthma from time to time, and Lish couldn't rest until she bent over and heard her breathe deeply in and out several times. Of course, Andrew's room was a disaster—Tinkertoys, broken crayons, and plastic bowling pins were strewn across his floor. Della and Peter were great with the kids, but they left a mess here and there. She checked the Pull-up he still wore at night, kissed his forehead, and tucked the covers in around his sides. He rubbed his eyes with the back of his hand and rolled over.

On the back piazza, Lish sat for a moment and took in what she was feeling. A kind of overwhelming gratefulness. A relief that she and Baby Cecilia were all right. It could have been bad, but it wasn't. The chances of both a mother and child making it through a placental abruption were slimmer than she'd like to remember from her med school days. She felt blessed—undeservedly so. She sat back and let out a deep sigh. The truth was,

Lish had all she ever wanted: a houseful of healthy children, a loving husband, a caring community, and the comfort of a familiar, beautiful home.

Drew, as if on cue, came out on the porch and rubbed her back. "How ya doing?"

She nodded. "I'm great. Come sit with me for a few minutes before I wake the baby to nurse." He took a seat on the wicker chair across from her and propped his foot up on the table. He leaned his arms back and stretched.

"So I got an interesting call today." He put his arms down and examined her.

"From whom?"

"The CDC."

"Again? Boy, they don't like taking no for an answer, do they?"

He cleared his throat. "The thing is, they've raised the salary on the position by another $100,000, *and* they offered to pay the first year's mortgage on a house of our choice." He shook his head in disbelief. "I asked them if they'd change the title of the position to Director of Influenza Research, and they agreed." He sat up and leaned toward her. "I'd have a team of researchers at my disposal, Lish. I'd be in charge of my own lab, and the budget is practically limitless. We'd be working on improving the swine and bird flu vaccines, and we'd be on the front line of whatever comes next. Heck, we might even get a few trips to Capitol Hill out of it. Imagine that?"

"I don't want to move to Atlanta, Drew." She met his eye and spoke in a gentle, earnest tone. "Not now, with the new baby." When Lish reached for a mosquito that had landed on the back of her neck, a piercing pain shot through her side. She quickly returned to her original position. "Do you really want to uproot the kids and move away from our family? Our home? We talked this through a month ago." The incision throbbed, and she was wishing for another pill.

He bit the inside of his jaw and looked out over the landscaped garden. He rubbed his upper arm with the heel of his opposite hand. "This is my career, Lish. And it could be *the* opportunity of a lifetime." He tilted his head, and she met his eyes. "And not just that—we could be part of something huge. You know?"

She could hear the snorts of the baby in the nursery as she slowly roused. Cecilia let out a little whimper. The milk burned as it came in. It started in Lish's armpit and filled the ducts until her breasts began to drip.

Drew noticed the two circles of wetness on her nightgown. "You're tired. It's been an exhausting week, and the baby needs to eat. Let's talk about it in a few days. I can keep the CDC on ice for a little while."

After Lish fed the baby, changed her diaper, and tucked her into the bassinet, she went back onto the piazza. As she sipped the thermos of water she always kept by her side during the first weeks of nursing, she spotted the young doctors from Drew's fellowship program, Melanie and Robbie, to whom they rented the carriage house. They were coming back from their nightly run around The Battery after the city cooled off. Their bodies were young, taut, and muscular; their legs were long and they glistened beneath the street lights.

They were supposedly just friends, but she had to wonder as Melanie pushed Robbie's bare, wet shoulder and he chuckled. Lish saw residents and other young members of the fellowship program going in and out of their little house from time to time, and early one morning she had watched Melanie push the new ER doctor, Craig Michaels, down the stairs without his shoes on. She had thrown his loafers at him (or aimed them, rather), then slammed the door behind her. The doctor had stumbled out of the wrought-iron gates and into his Jeep, speeding off with no regard to the speed bumps or the Children Playing sign Lish had fought to put up on their street.

Now she remembered the days when she and Drew courted. She was living in the carriage house with Della and Anne before Nana died. She actually had a boyfriend she'd been on and off with since college who was trying to make it in the music world in Nashville, and Drew had a girlfriend in medical school at Vanderbilt. They would carpool together to see them. After the third trip, as they were approaching Nashville, he reached over, put his hand on her knee, and said, "Who are we kidding, Lish? Let's turn this car around and head back to Charleston."

They did just that, driving all night. They ran straight to Folly Beach, threw down a blanket, and watched the sun come up, imagining the messages on their respective answering machines from their significant others. They were married the following year and lived on ramen noodles and Kraft Macaroni & Cheese through residency. As soon as they both started getting a real paycheck (Lish joined a well-established pediatric practice downtown, and Drew accepted a prestigious job with the infectious disease department at the Medical University), she threw out her birth control pills.

Two months later she was pregnant with Andrew. It seemed absurd to leave Andrew every day so she could be with other children, so within six months of his birth, she left her practice and started to write a blog about motherhood. *The Post and Courier* found it and asked her to write a weekly column, which she'd been doing ever since. Wyrick Publishing had offered her a book contract, but she'd never found the time to get to that. Her family was her priority.

When her nana, Cozy Brumley, passed away just before Andrew was born, Lish and Drew were able to buy Anne and Della out of their portions of the house and move into 18 Legare Street, where an architect renovated the back portion with a large family room and vaulted ceilings. He also put in a small swimming pool, and the famous landscape designer, Benny Chestnut, updated the garden while preserving the old beauties: the magnolia, the rose bush, and of course, the loquat tree in the back corner where she and her kids harvested the fruit every June just like she did as kid. In fact, she had created a baby food with a little loquat in it a few years ago, and she sold it at the farmers' market downtown from time to time on Saturday mornings.

She could not imagine leaving Charleston now. After her father died, she spent the rest of her childhood and adolescence fantasizing and then strategizing about how to get back here. She hoped that Drew wasn't serious. He'd turned down the CDC offer twice before, and each time MUSC had lured him back with a hefty raise. He knew how she felt about raising their children here among her family and friends. These were her roots. Drew grew up in a suburb of Cleveland, and he always said he loved Charleston because of the sense of place, the history, and the realness of it. When he figured out a way for them to buy Nana's house, she'd said, "You've made my dream come true," and he held her, rubbed her bulging belly, and said, "That's what I like to hear."

The euphoria she was feeling an hour ago seemed to have dissipated, which was odd. She knew when she nursed, oxytocin was released, and she should be feeling it even stronger than she did before. Maybe it was the talk with Drew or the pain medication or simply the physical trauma of the emergency C-section. She rubbed her bloated belly and couldn't imagine it ever going back to normal. She was sure she'd never wear a bikini again. Good-bye youth.

She noticed a thump in her head. Right on the top as if she was standing beneath a dripping faucet. The baby cried out. Surely she was not hungry again. Lish gave her a few moments to settle down, but she got louder and louder, and Lish feared she would wake up the children.

Now she stood over the bassinet for a moment and watched the child kicking and snorting and wailing. Her face was red. Her gums looked hard and smooth.

Lish took the baby out to the wicker couch on the piazza. She winced as Cecilia latched onto her breast. She held her close so that she wouldn't wriggle and kick the sore spot below in her gut.

Everything was tender. Achingly so. As the milk burned and released, Lish noticed the thump on her head strengthen. She had never felt it before. It was like a kind of Chinese water torture. *Hurry,* she thought as she rubbed the top of her skull. *Hurry up and eat so you can go back to sleep.* Then the unforeseen thought crossed her mind as she held the baby tight, *You could hold her so close that she wouldn't be able to breathe. A few minutes, pulled tight to your breast, and she'd be gone.*

Lish shook the thought off. She tousled her hair, but the pounding was still there.

"Drew," she called over her shoulder. "Drew, please go downstairs and get my pills."

Chapter Nine

Della
August 29, 2008

Just as Della's planning period ended, the phone at her desk rang. She hoped it was Anne, who was on her way home from an interview in Atlanta for that bell ringing program in England, and since Della was the one who convinced her to make a move, she couldn't resist answering it.

"Hello, this is Della Limehouse," she said.

"It's me."

"I'm so glad you're taking matters into your own hands, Anne." Della balled her free hand into a fist. "How did it go?"

"Della," Anne said. "I need you to do something for me right away."

"Sure. What?" Della could hear Anne's old Saab rumbling down the highway.

"Listen to me," Anne said. "*Please* go check on Lish as soon as you can."

"Okay," Della said. "I mean, I don't get out of here until four this afternoon. Why do you sound so freaked out?"

"I don't know," Anne said. "It's just something in Lish's *voice*. Drew is at some conference in California, and she called me a little while ago, but she couldn't even get any words out. I don't have a good feeling. I just want you to go over for a little bit this morning if you can. I've got a five-hour drive before I'll be home."

"So you're telling me that something is going on with Lish that can't wait until four?" Della nervously rubbed her forehead as a large pack of seventh graders piled into her room just before the third-period bell sounded.

"That's my next class," Della said.

"Della, do this for me, okay?"

"Okay." Della exhaled as her students claimed their seats. "I'll see if I can get someone to cover for me here."

By eleven a.m. Della was knocking on Lish's front door. *Where is Rosetta?* she thought. There was no answer, but she could hear the screams of the baby from upstairs. The window was open, and the baby was calling in a chant that seemed both rhythmic and horrible. It rose and fell every few seconds.

When it was clear that no one was going to answer, Della lifted the urn of the potted ficus on the right side of the front door and pulled out the hidden house key. She had to try it a few times before the large brass lock slid back.

"Lish?" she called as she followed the screams of the baby up the stairs.

The baby was writhing beneath a soiled blanket in her bassinet. Her face was red, but her lips were pale. Lish sat in a glider chair on the other side of the nursery looking out of the window as though she hadn't heard a sound. Della looked out and saw that Mary Jane was half-dressed in only a shirt and underwear, sitting on a bench, trying to coax a lizard into a bucket while Andrew straddled one of the lower limbs of the loquat tree. He threw a Matchbox car down to the ground and it made a crashing sound.

Della grabbed the baby and pulled her close. "Lish?" She squeezed her cousin's shoulder as the baby continued its rhythmic wail. "Lish, what's going on?" Lish flinched, grabbed the top of her head with both hands, and shook it back and forth.

"Lish!" Della said. "Lish, look at me."

With her hands still grasping her head, Lish looked slowly up at Della as though she vaguely recognized her, then she turned away and shook her head again.

Della turned to the wailing baby, watched her pale legs kick furiously, and wondered what she needed. What could she do to calm her for a moment? She just needed a moment without the screams so she could get Lish's attention. When Della changed her small diaper, she saw that feces had dried around Cecilia's bottom, and beneath it was an awful rash the color of a cranberry. It looked like the bedsore she saw on Papa the day they discovered the nursing home had been neglecting him. As the baby wailed, Della examined her round, little mouth. Her gums were dry. Her tongue had no saliva on it.

Della gasped. This baby was dehydrated. Her heart started to race.

"Lish, talk to me," she called. She grabbed her cousin's knee. "Cecilia needs to eat. Do you have any formula?"

Lish continued to hold and shake her head. "I can't stand up. It will hurt too badly."

"Can you nurse her?" Della asked. She knew Lish was a purist; Andrew and Mary Jane were both breast-fed solely for the first twelve months.

Della tried to hand the wailing baby to Lish. Her tiny hands were curled into fists and her toes were spread out like little fans. She was so tense and miserable. Hungry. Della wondered when she had eaten last.

Lish pushed the baby away. She shook her head no and then she grabbed the back of her neck. "I can't make it stop," she said. "It's been hitting me over and over."

"What?" Della said. "Make what stop?"

"The pelts," she said. "The pelts on the top of my head."

The baby continued to cry. It was a dry, hoarse cry. Della could no longer bear it. She took the infant in her arms and ran across the street to Nana's old neighbor, Martha Emerson. Martha was bedridden, but she still had all of her help—a round-the-clock nurse and a housekeeper who cooked and cleaned every day.

"Please," Della said to the housekeeper. She suddenly remembered her name from childhood. "Miss Janie. Can you watch those children across the street? There's an emergency, I think. I have to get this baby some food."

"Sure," said the woman (who seemed elderly herself). She walked slowly across the street and toward the garden where Andrew was chasing Mary Jane with the lizard.

Della found Lish's car keys in the foyer, strapped Cecilia into the baby seat, and raced to the Harris Teeter, where she bought formula and a bottle as the baby wailed. Della's home was closer to the grocery store and it seemed time was of the essence, so she made a snap decision and raced to Radcliffe Street, pulled into her driveway, and ran into the house.

Peter was on the piazza, replacing a rotten spindle. "Hold her," Della said as she thrust Baby Cecilia into his arms. She filled the bottle with warm water, put two heaping scoops in, and shook, then she ran out to the porch and handed it to Peter. The infant girl began to suck at the plastic nipple as he took his place in the rocking chair and tilted the end of the bottle higher and higher with each ounce she gulped down.

He looked to Della, whose heart continued to pound. Who was only now aware of her hands trembling as she leaned back against the railing and breathed deeply.

"What's going on?" Peter did not take his eyes away from Cecilia. He must have remembered from Cozy's infant days that the nipple must be filled with milk or she'd take in air.

"Something's wrong." She looked at him. The top of his wide forehead, the protruding veins of his skilled hands, with some muck from the rotten wood of their piazza beneath his fingernails.

"It's Lish. She's not coherent or something." Della bit her bottom lip until it turned white. "She wouldn't respond to me or the baby crying, and the kids were running wild in the backyard." She tried to catch her breath and think clearly. "Drew's out of town. I've got to get back there, Peter."

He nodded. "I can call it a day," he said. "Leave the baby here, and go see about Lish."

She swallowed hard. Her mouth was dry. "Okay," she said. "Do you think you could pick up Cozy at three?"

"No problem." Baby Cecilia grasped his rough forefinger with her little hand. "I'll fish the old stroller out of the shed."

"And can you call my work and tell them there's a family emergency?"

"Sure," he said as he propped the baby on his shoulder and patted her back. She belched and relaxed. Then he walked toward the kitchen where the telephone was as Della raced out of the house and into her car.

Before she put her keys in the ignition, she ran back in the house. "One more thing, Peter!" she called from the foyer.

He was hanging up the phone and he turned around so she could see the baby against his chest.

"What's she doing now?" he asked.

Della looked at her little face. She pressed her hand gently down on her warm back. It was rising and falling slowly. "Snoozing, I think."

"Like riding a bike, baby. I've still got the touch." He grinned tentatively and swayed back and forth.

"If I'm not back in an hour, please give her some more formula. I'll call you if it's going to be longer than that." Della scurried toward the door and then turned back again.

"If she's wet, change her and use a clean dishrag for a diaper. She's got a terrible rash and should be changed right away."

He looked her way, put his finger to his lip to shush her, and nodded.

When Della arrived back at Lish's, the front door was wide open. She called to her cousin as she stepped inside. There was no sign of anyone— not the kids, not the housekeeper, not Lish.

In the kitchen, mold grew on three plates of what must have been lasagna from a few days ago. There was a bowl of curdled milk with a few bloated Cheerios floating on the surface. A couple of flies darted back and forth between the trash can and the moldy plates. The refrigerator door was slightly ajar, and as Della went to close it, she saw the thick droplets of condensation on an uncovered chicken carcass and an unclosed carton of organic milk.

Before she raced upstairs, she took a quick look out of the back door and spotted Lish curled up with her knees to her chest beneath the loquat tree. She rocked back and forth with her head face down.

Della ran out to her. "Lish?" She saw that she was in a camisole and some flannel pajama bottoms. Her fingernails were bitten down to the nubs and her right thumb was bleeding. A mosquito landed on Lish's shoulder and started to nip her; she did not swat it away.

Della sat down, brushed the insects off, and started to gently rub her cousin's back. "I'm here. Talk to me."

Minutes passed and Lish continued to rock. Della noted a prominent vein protruding from the side of her cousin's long, thin neck; she watched the afternoon sun filtering through the loose strands of her rich brown hair. From across the street, Della heard Andrew and Mary Jane. As she craned her neck, she spotted them chasing one another behind the white picket fence of Mrs. Emerson's front yard. George, the gardener, sprayed them with the hose from time to time, and they shrieked with laughter. Janie was on the porch smiling and clapping.

On the opposite side of Lish, Della noticed a hole Lish must have dug with a stick in her pristine garden. It was a few inches wide and went down a good four or five inches. The soft, freshly dug dirt smelled like pluff mud and low tide.

It was humid and miserably hot. Probably still in the mid-nineties. The limbs of the tree seemed to sag from the heavy air, and the rotten fruit that had fallen to the ground was decaying on the grass around them. Della cleared her dry throat. "You've got to tell me what's going on, Lish. I can help. I'll do anything I can to help you."

Lish shook her head. She seemed unable to speak. She looked up once and her eyes were pink and swollen. She started to rub the top of her head with her dirty fingertips.

"There is a pounding on my head. It won't stop. I can't sleep." She turned to look Della dead on. "When I stand up, it's unbearable." She looked back down. "It's terrorizing me."

"A pounding?" Della's bright blue eyes raced back and forth as if she was speed reading.

Lish shook her head and then her eyes seemed to glaze over. She leaned back against the trunk of the tree and closed her eyes. "Leave me alone, Della. I need to sleep."

When Anne pulled into the driveway a few minutes later, Della was holding Lish's hand as she seemed to be in some kind of a waking trance beneath the tree. She put her cousin's hand gently down and ran out to meet Anne.

"Where is she?" Anne peered over Della's shoulder.

"She's in the back, in a kind of waking sleep, I think." Della's face was pale.

"What happened?" Anne asked. "When did you come by?"

"When I got here late this morning, the baby was screaming and the kids were running around the yard. Lish was just sitting in the glider in the nursery. It was like she wasn't really there." She reached out and squeezed Anne's hand. "The baby's mouth was *dry*. There was hardly any saliva. I don't know when she'd been fed last."

Anne's round green eyes bobbed up and down as Della stared into them. She turned her head from Lish to Della over and over.

Della followed her eyes to the backyard. She cleared her throat. "Anne, the baby had a rash that was worse than anything I'd ever seen. It was raw, and she was caked in feces."

Bile rose in Della's throat as she recalled it. She thought she might gag, but she took in a deep breath of the heavy air as Anne paced back and forth wringing her long, freckled hands. She closed her eyes and Della thought she might be praying. Then she looked up, tucking her red hair behind her delicate shoulders. "What should we do now, Del?"

"Okay." Della spread out her fingers, attempting to make sense of this and take charge. "I'll call Drew and you call Rosetta. We'll call her obstetrician, and if need be—" She paused and looked up to the carriage house, where the tall, blonde

MUSC resident was bolting up the stairs in her white medical coat. "Todd Jervey."

Della hoped the young woman didn't see Lish in the backyard. She wanted to protect her somehow. She wanted to pull down a screen over 18 Legare, and she remembered Nana closing the shutters when Papa was weeping in the crow's nest. "He's having one of his spells," she used to say.

"Did she talk to you?" Anne asked as her eyes anxiously followed the medical resident into the carriage house.

Della nodded. "She says something is hitting her head." She exhaled as they watched the young woman in the carriage house throw off her coat and pull a wineglass down from the cabinet.

Anne unclasped her delicate hands and touched Della's bony elbow. "Maybe she just needs a decent night's sleep. She probably hasn't had a consecutive eight hours for six weeks now."

Della nodded and turned back to Anne. "I think there's more going on here than that."

In Lish's Day-Timer in the upstairs office, they found the numbers they needed. Anne went to call Rosetta on her cell, while Della spotted Lish's fancy iPhone and attempted to call Drew. Della and Peter were the last people on the planet who didn't have cell phones. It used to be something they'd admired about one another. At art shows and book signings they'd say, *No one can track us down at a moment's notice.* Or they'd pipe up sarcastically when a friend or colleague gave an exasperated sigh when asking for their number, *How did we ever live before cell phones?* Now she found it rather embarrassing. It took her whole minutes to navigate this foreign device. When he didn't answer his mobile, she paged him. He called back ten minutes later.

"Why'd you page me, honey?" He sounded as if he was out of breath. "You knew my presentation was this afternoon."

"This is Della, Drew."

"Della?"

"Yes. Something's *wrong.*"

She heard him breathe in and out, in and out and then, "What do you mean? Are the kids all right?"

"It's Lish," Della said. "She's curled up in a ball in the backyard in a kind of catatonic state. The kitchen's disgusting. We don't think she's fed the baby for a while. Maybe *a day* even. How long have you been gone?"

He cleared his throat. "Three nights," he said. "I don't understand. Where's Rosetta?"

"I have no idea. Anne's trying to reach her now." She tightened her grip on the phone. "Something is truly amiss here, Drew. I think Lish needs some kind of medical help, maybe even *psychiatric* help. I don't know." Saying those words out loud made Della teary. She felt the perspiration burn beneath her arms, and she willed herself to keep her voice strong. "You need to get home right away."

"She's just tired, Della." She could hear him tapping rhythmically on something. He said a muffled, "Thank you. Yeah, see you there," to someone. Now he was back. "It's exhausting. Taking care of three. Don't go jumping to any drastic conclusions on me now, okay? Let me talk to her."

Della walked the phone out to Lish, whose eyes were now closed.

"She's sleeping, I think," she said to him.

"Don't wake her. Just have her call me as soon as she's up. I've got my final presentation tomorrow morning, then I'll catch the first flight out."

Della's ears popped as she swallowed hard. "You should catch the red-eye tonight. I don't think you understand what I'm saying, but you've got to believe me."

"Look, Della," he said. "I know you're concerned, and I appreciate you being there. Just have Lish call me when she wakes up, okay? I know how she works. It's exhaustion."

"No, it's more than that—" Della heard the click of his phone. "Drew?" He was gone. She was so angry and scared, she was seeing little black spots. How could he not hear the urgency in her voice? She looked down at the sleek, thin device. Where the heck was the Shut Down button? Should she shut down the phone? If she didn't get a cell phone soon, she was going to start feeling downright dis-enfranchised.

Anne stood in the doorway with three pro-nounced lines across her freckled forehead. "Ro-setta said Lish kicked her out day before yesterday just after she let herself into the house like usual."

"Seriously?"

Anne nodded. "She said Lish pointed to the door and told her to get out for no apparent reason. The kids were crying and saying, 'Mama, we want Rosetta to make us pancakes.' She said they fol-lowed her out to the front gate and begged her to come back, but Lish kept saying no and pointing to the street corner where Rosetta catches the bus."

"This is nuts," Della said. "Did she say any-thing else?"

Anne lowered her voice. "She said Lish hasn't been right since she came home with the baby. That she's been sleeping a lot and letting the baby cry for a while before she nurses her. She's been short with the kids. Rosetta says she mentioned it to Drew a couple of weeks ago, and he said he would see about it."

"This is unbelievable." Della leaned against the wall, and one of the oil paintings of the Morris Is-land lighthouse tilted slightly. "Drew is convinced she's just exhausted. He wants her to call when she wakes up." She straightened out the painting and turned back to Anne. "I don't agree with him. I think it's something else."

Anne peered out the window at Lish and back to Della. "What should we do?"

Della looked up at the ceiling and around at the familiar crown molding of the upstairs hall. How many days had the three of them run up the stairs and down the corridor in a game of chase or hide-and-seek. "Settle down!" Nana would call. "Don't disturb Papa." Papa was often on the third-floor crow's nest, listening to an album on his old phonograph. He'd volunteered to fight in World War II, well into his mid-thirties, and when he came home, he was never quite the same. "He got real sad after the war," Nana had told them once when she was tucking them into the king-size bed in the guest room they shared from time to time. "And then when he lost his son, well, that about did it. He hasn't been able to shake it for more than a few days since then."

Now Della squeezed her eyes shut and then opened them again. "I'll get Peter to take Andrew and Mary Jane to our house for the night."

"I'll keep the baby," Anne said.

"Okay," Della said. "There's formula and a bottle at my house. I'll stay here with Lish until she wakes up. We'll call Drew. Then I'll see what kind of state she's in."

Anne nodded and they headed to the nursery where they found a well-stocked diaper bag to which they added blankets, baby soap, powder, a pacifier, and a pair of white pajamas with pink and green polka dots.

Della walked to the doorway and watched Anne zip up the bag. "Sometime you'll have to tell me how that interview went."

Anne sniffed the rank air of the nursery and shook her head. "It's not what's important right now."

"Say something, please." Della grabbed Lish's shoulders. She'd woken up an hour ago, but she'd swatted away the phone every time Della handed it to her.

When Della called Drew back, he exhaled and said, "I've arranged to have my presentation moved up to eight a.m. I've booked a noon flight out. Don't do anything until I get home, okay?"

"Not okay," she said. "I don't think you're hearing me, Drew. Your wife needs you now. This is more than exhaustion, and it's scaring me."

Drew exhaled. "Della, I've seen this before with Lish. If you can just get her to have a good night's sleep, she'll be a new person tomorrow. I need you to hang in there."

Della was beginning to feel a little crazy. Could

sleep be all Lish needed? Had this happened before?

"Call you later," he said before she could respond. *You're a lot of help, Drew. A real rock.* She shook her head in disbelief.

Della called the middle school principal and told her she needed a sub for tomorrow. She didn't offer an explanation, and she didn't pretend to be sick. She was thankful that she was not questioned.

"I'm calling your OB," Della said as Lish sat at the kitchen table and scraped at a cut on her shin with her unfiled fingernails.

The on-call physician, a Dr. Chang, called back. She had a kind voice, and Della explained it all to her.

"She may be worn out, or there could be another medical cause," the doctor said. "Let's see if she'll talk to me."

"This is the on-call obstetrician." Della handed the phone to Lish.

Lish managed to find her voice for a moment. Her hands trembled as she held the receiver to her ear. She answered "no" four times and then handed the phone back to Della.

"If she's not better after a good night's sleep, I'm sure her doctor would like to see her in the morning," Dr. Chang said.

"But—"

"Look, Ms.… I'm sorry. Tell me your name…"

"Limehouse."

"Ms. Limehouse." She cleared her throat. "I'm not sure I can discuss this with you. I'm not her physician, and you're not an immediate family member."

"I'm the only one here." Della tugged on the phone cord. "I need some guidance!"

"If you're that concerned, you should take her to the emergency room," Dr. Chang said. "They can properly assess the situation. All right?"

"Okay." Della nodded, and the doctor said a quick "Good-bye."

Outside a squirrel scurried across the wrought-iron fence, and two mourning doves took flight. They landed on the telephone wire and began their soft five-note coos.

Suddenly Lish scampered up to the nursery, holding her head; Della quickly followed her. She watched her pad around the room until she turned to Della and screamed, "Where's my baby?"

"Let me explain," Della said, but Lish ran past her and grabbed a silver letter opener at the desk just outside of the nursery. She turned to Della, her legs wide and firmly planted, her arm outstretched with the sharp end of the letter opener pointing toward her cousin. "Give her back!" Lish screamed, and she lunged at Della.

Della grabbed her wrist, but she couldn't stop

the letter opener from cutting through the sleeve of her shirt and the surface of her shoulder.

She pushed Lish back, took a look at the wound, put her hands up and said, "Please, Lish. Listen to me." But Lish came right back at her with the letter opener, which Della dodged. When she saw Lish lunge again, she ran back down the stairs and out of the house. She jumped in her car and locked the door.

She grabbed the steering wheel as if to steady herself and watched her knuckles whiten. When Lish didn't come out of the house, Della reached for the cell phone, which she was glad she'd tucked in her skirt pocket. Without hesitating, she called Mrs. Jervey, who still lived in Todd's old family home on South Battery. Mrs. Jervey gave Della Todd's mobile number, and she dialed it right away.

"Hello?" a deep voice said before the third ring.

"Todd, this is Della." She sucked her teeth and continued to firmly grasp the steering wheel. "I need your help."

When Todd arrived, Lish was slumped against the bottom of the staircase with her head between her knees. She rubbed the top of her head as if she had just hit it on the corner of a table. She'd put the letter opener down a few minutes before when Della offered her a sip of water. Della had discreetly grabbed it and put it on top of a chest in the living room.

Lish took a small sip of water and looked up at Todd. Her eyes were puffy and bloodshot, and her pupils were dilated. Yet she looked him in the eye and seemed to recollect who he was.

"Todd?" she said. "Thank you for coming." She pressed her fingertips into her skull. "I can't find my baby, and I have this awful thumping on my head."

Della took a step toward her. "Remember what I told you about the baby?" She talked as calmly and gently as possible. "The baby is with Anne. She went for a little visit, and she'll be back soon. The children went to a sleepover at my house."

Todd helped Lish lie down. He put the glass of water by her side, stood up, and rubbed the back of his sunburned neck. Despite his beard and a couple of extra pounds, he still had his boyish look—a thin frame, fair skin with freckles, and strawberry blond hair.

When Lish closed her eyes, Della looked at Todd. It had been ten years, but his soft hazel eyes were familiar and comforting to her. He tugged at his bearded chin as if to think for a moment and then looked back at her. "I think we should take her to the emergency room."

Della swallowed hard. "I know Drew doesn't

want that. He thinks she's exhausted. He wants me to wait until he gets back tomorrow."

Todd shook his head. "Della, if he saw her, he would want her to be checked out. We need to run an organic etiology—to rule out a medical cause for this. There could be a metabolic or thyroid problem." He looked at Lish and then back to Della. "It's pretty unlikely, but a brain tumor is another possibility." He grasped her thin shoulder. "And the letter opener incident shows that she could be a threat to herself or someone else."

Della had not considered any of those things. She was sure Drew hadn't either.

"Can we call Drew first?" she said. "Maybe if you talk to him…?" She lifted her shoulders and threw her hands up as if in a plea.

"Sure," Todd said. He popped the knuckle of his forefinger. "I'd be happy to."

They paged Drew twice and waited for him to return the call. Della paced the floor and Todd walked around the house, noting Lish's framed articles and a high-profile cover story the local paper ran about the loquat baby food she'd created. Next to it there was a photo of the handsome couple in Venice at San Marco Square, embracing one another amid the pigeons.

An hour passed without a response from Drew. When Lish started to stir, Todd watched her intently from the foyer. Suddenly she sat up on the sofa, looked at Della, and said, "Get out of my house," then began to weep.

"Okay," Della turned to Todd. "Let's take her."

Lish didn't fight them, and she walked willingly into the emergency room. Right away, she was recognized by the attending physician and the head nurse, who whisked her out of the crowded waiting room and into a bed where they pulled a gray curtain around her.

Della and Todd told the attending doctor, a young guy by the name of Rob Suarez, what they knew. He nodded and seemed to give Todd a knowing glance. "We'll draw blood and do a metabolic panel," he said. "We should know in an hour or so if this is something organic. If the blood sugar and electrolytes are normal, I'll call in Dr. Swan, the attending psychiatrist, who may want to talk to you, Mrs. Limehouse."

Della nodded. "Okay. I'll be here."

Todd sat with Della in the waiting room, and they watched an obese woman pacing back and forth with a steaming cup of coffee in one corner and an elderly man holding the hand of a young girl in another. He was whispering to her in Spanish. Her eyes were big and nearly black, and when she looked up she met Della's stare head on. Della smiled at the beautiful girl. Who knew what they were waiting for? The girl looked back down to the pattern of her skirt—circles upon circles of lavender and yellow.

"Have you eaten?" Todd asked.

"No." Della became suddenly aware of her empty stomach.

He nodded toward the sliding door that led to the street.

"Let's pick up a quick sandwich. This always takes much longer than you might expect."

As he led the way next door to an all-night pizza and sub joint, she looked up at him and let out a nervous chuckle. "Well, I never thought we'd meet again under these circumstances."

He gave her a tenuous smile. "Listen," he said. "This is life. You take it as it comes."

He held open the door of the little dive. It smelled like beer, cigarettes, and pepperoni, and Della had a faint memory of eating there in the middle of the night when she was in college.

Todd pointed to the meatball sub on a menu. "This is good. Wanna try?"

After they got their food, they walked back to the hospital and took a seat on a bench in a little garden outside of the emergency room.

Della looked at the meaty sub, the parmesan cheese oozing out of the white bread. She took a sip of her Coca-Cola and looked at him. She wanted to ask him what would happen to her cousin tonight, and what he thought was really going on. But she decided to wait. She knew he wouldn't want to speculate until they ruled out the medical possibilities. She watched him unwrap his sub.

"So the whole eating-healthy thing hasn't made it onto your radar yet?"

He chuckled and took a hearty bite. A little smudge of tomato sauce was in the corner of his mouth, and he wiped it away with a thin napkin.

"Nah," he said. "I don't grind my own flour or anything yet. I've spent so many late nights in the lab or the psych ward that I've learned to survive on anything that's open after midnight, and that's not usually the unprocessed stuff."

Della nodded. The sub was surprisingly delicious.

"Yeah, we can't afford all of that stuff. It's great and all if you're wealthy, but one trip to Whole Foods and my *whole* paycheck is gone."

He nodded. "Oh, don't tell me the famous author doesn't make enough to buy organic?"

Della exhaled. "Famous? What's the definition of famous? Receiving a seventy-two-dollar royalty check, maybe, every four months?"

He popped open a bag of chips and his hands seemed strikingly familiar to her, the freckles across the knuckles, the scar on his thumb where she knew he once caught a fishing hook on a friend's bad cast. He looked up. "I don't know why you say that with a hint of disdain, Del." He took a bite, and she could hear the loud crunch. "You look to me like you've got the life you always wanted." He leaned forward. "I've seen your good-looking husband and your beautiful little girl. Mom sent me that article in *Coastal Magazine* about you all, the one about artistic couples of the low country." He took a sip of his Sprite. "Plus, you're managing to do the thing you always wanted."

Della nodded. She noted a bat swooping between the corner of the hospital and the parking garage. A city bus lurched to a stop and a couple of third-shift workers exited its doors.

Della thought of her crumbling home just down the road. She thought of the finger-length roaches ducking in and out of her utensil drawer and the yard full of scrap metal and the stray cat lounging on the front stoop. She thought of her dinosaur of a computer and the novel she was only a third of a way through. She was too close to it to know, but she suspected it was the weakest of the bunch.

What made her think she could write about a stalker who committed murder? Had she ever stalked someone? Had she ever been a witness to a murder? Or shadowed a detective who arrived just after the scene of a crime? No, no, no. She was an idiot to try and write one of those kinds of books. And what were her intentions? To make money? To remake herself as a plot-driven novelist?

Her mother, if she were alive, would immediately peg the manuscript as her daughter's attempt to sell out. An unsuccessful one. But Kate Brumley, the highly anthologized poet, was an abysmal mother, Della admitted now. She never needed to worry about providing for her daughter because Nana was the present and responsible grown-up in Della's life. What did Katie Brumley know besides how to catch the eye of a strung-out beatnik at a shabby hotel in Paris with her well-proportioned curves and her piercing blue eyes? Or how to string a few words together so that they captured the kind of out-of-body experience one felt during an LSD trip? The older Della got, the more she disdained her mother.

She watched the third-shift employees in their hair nets, gray-green scrubs, and thick-soled shoes as they took their turns moving through the wide revolving doors.

Todd cleared his throat. "You've done very well. You can't deny it."

"Oh, yeah?" She looked at his gentle face, his hazel eyes glistening from the light of the street lamp. His head was tilted with a half grin, expecting her to agree with him. "Right now it feels like a façade." She exhaled. "I've got too much on my plate, you know? And none of it is what I really want."

"What's on your plate?"

"Well, I'm teaching English full time to middle-school kids to make ends meet—grammar, sentence diagramming, recess duty, nasty parents, the whole nine yards. I love the kids, even the entitled ones, but it's tough working a nine-hour day, then coming home, taking care of a child, and writing at night. I have to write a book every twelve months that will sell only a few thousand copies. I sit at book signings where half the people don't even look my way—or worse, ask me for directions to the bathroom." A car honked in the distance. A radio blared suddenly and then faded. "I'm a mid-list writer. It's not exactly something an author aspires to. In fact, it's kind of a curse."

He balled up the empty paper bag from his meal and tossed it in the trash.

"Aside from making sure your cousin is okay, and I think she will be, what *do* you want?"

Yes, that was Todd. The consummate mental and emotional surgeon—aiming the scalpel at your heart when given the slightest opportunity. She remembered their long walks on the beach, how he would probe and probe her about her motherless childhood, about her desires, about how she felt when he took her in his arms. She used to find it wearisome. To answer all of those questions. She missed the spontaneity she'd had in previous relationships, and she was annoyed by his constant need for her to self-reflect.

But that was in her twenties. Tonight, just outside of the emergency room where her cousin (on whom she relied in a way she couldn't quite explain) was being poked and prodded in search of a medical cause for her mental state, Della was overwhelmed with the desire to take stock. She was about to turn thirty-eight, and she was not at all where she thought she would be at this point in her life. She wanted to tell someone how she really felt.

She took a deep breath and let it go. "The truth is, I just want to raise my daughter the best way I know how." She looked up into the night air above them. "And I want more kids. I love raising children. I know that sounds awfully 1950s, but it's the truth. It's the best thing I've ever experienced." She crossed her legs and tapped her foot as he waited for her to continue. "And I want time. Just a little time. Time to write a novel I can be proud of. Time to read. Time to take a walk." She shrugged her narrow shoulders. "And I'd settle for central heating and air and neighbors who don't deal drugs, you know?"

He nodded, peeled the lid off of his disposable cup, and tilted it up. Then he surveyed the street, looked back at her, and said, "You do have too much. You're going to have to think of a way to cut some things out."

She raised her eyebrows. "I'm all ears, Dr. Jervey. Tell me how to simplify my life and make twice as much money, will you?"

As she watched him rub his chin, Lish's cell phone rang. Della pulled it out quickly and looked hard for the Talk button. She punched it as soon as she spotted it.

"Drew?" She pulled the phone to her ear.

"No," said the voice on the other end. "It's Anne, Del. Where are you? How's Lish?"

Chapter Ten

Lish

It hurt to swallow. The thumping was on her head and in her throat now, and she tried to wait as long as possible before she swallowed. She spit in the bedside pan a couple of times to avoid doing it.

The curtain was pulled back and the young attending said, "Dr. Sutton?"

Before she could stop herself, Lish swallowed. It burned, and she pictured the fire-breather she and Drew applauded at a Venice street show during their trip a few years ago. The man would put the flaming torch down his throat and hold it there for whole seconds before pulling it out and holding up its snuffed end with something between a wince and a smile on his face. Several in the audience, including Lish, would toss a coin in an empty hat, and the man would reach for a sword in the open case beside him and in he would plunge it, down beyond his tongue into the soft and tender shaft of his throat. Now Lish nodded and grasped her neck.

"Are you able to talk?"

She nodded again.

She had once been in this attending's same position a decade ago during her third year of medical school. She remembered making her worst rotations first in an effort to cross the particularly sad and miserable places off her career list: ER, Oncology Unit, Psychiatry Ward. She recalled one particular night in the ER, watching a doctor examine a woman who had been brought in naked from the downtown market in the middle of the night. Lish had draped a gown over her body as the rest of the staff rushed out to meet three ambulances in the driveway. (A bus had overturned on I-26 and there were five injured passengers who needed immediate help.) Lish remembered gently laying the gown over the woman who was curled up in the fetal position on the floor. She had recoiled at the woman's awful stench and the grime beneath her finger- and toenails.

"I can't find my puppy," the woman had said. "Have you seen a little black labradoodle around here?"

The attending physician rolled his eyes as he pulled Lish to the side. "Page the on-call psychiatrist," he'd said. "This one belongs on President Street. It's a tough night, and she needs to move on."

Lish wanted to ask, "Before you examine her?" but she knew better than to question an attending.

She had nodded and paged the doctor, who agreed with the attending after his assessment. The woman put up a fight, scratching the psychiatrist across the forehead, and he had to call the judge and have her involuntarily committed. One policeman had to hold her down while another put handcuffs on her. She cursed at them and kicked them, and they both had beads of sweat on their foreheads by the time they walked her to the door. Lish had watched the psychiatrist sign off on the court papers. "Poses an immediate threat to herself and others," he'd written, and she walked with the policeman and the woman, kicking and screaming, over to President Street to the Institute of Psychiatry, where the doctor took her in a holding area and gave her a shot that knocked her out. Lish could still see the woman's pale, thin legs like toothpicks protruding from the gray gown when the doctor picked her up and carried her to a gurney by the elevator.

She knew the attending wanted to see if she needed to take the same walk to President Street. He wanted to quickly rule out any organic cause and move her out and over to the Institute of Psychiatry.

"You recently had a C-section?"

"Yes." She felt the saliva pooling on her tongue, and she stopped herself from spitting. "About six weeks ago."

"Are you still taking your pain medication?" He looked up from his clipboard after he asked the question.

"No. I ran out maybe ten days ago." She didn't know when she ran out, but she couldn't remember the last time she took one.

"Have you been drinking during the last twenty-four hours?"

"No." Had she? She didn't think she'd had a drink since the baby was born.

"Do you have diabetes?"

"No."

"A seizure disorder?"

"No." Once a boy, one of her patients, had a seizure in her office. He'd slapped her jaw hard as she and his mother tried to restrain him. Her cheek was black for a week.

The doctor tapped his pencil. "Family illness that might pertain to how you are feeling?"

Family illness? She tried to picture the members of her family—Drew, the children, Nana, Papa, Mama, Rick, Mama's husband, and then her daddy standing on the piazza on Rutledge Avenue, waving to her as she rode her bike over to East Bay Playground the week before he died.

She swallowed. It burned. "No."

"Recent head injury?"

She held her head. "No, but it hurts."

"Tell me about your head."

She blinked and her eyes seemed dry. She put one hand on the top of her head and the other on her throat. Her breasts were sore and hard, and she knew her milk was drying up. She couldn't recall the last time she'd fed the baby.

"I've had a thumping here for weeks." She pointed to the place where there was a groove. Where the two sides of her skull came together. "It hurts worse when I stand up. And even worse when I walk. It seems in synch with my heartbeat. And it's in my throat too."

He nodded. "Okay. We're going to draw blood first. You know how this goes."

"Yes," Lish said. "A quick organic etiology. You want to see if I'm physically sick or just plain crazy." She still had her hand on her head.

The young doctor cleared his throat and looked down at his chart. He scratched the back of his neck and seemed to search for the proper response as if it was written on the clipboard.

"No response necessary," she said. "Send in the nurse."

An hour later, the psychiatrist came in for her

mental status examination. It was Sharon Swan. She'd been a year ahead of Drew and Lish in medical school. She was several years older than the other students, had gone back to school later in life, after her kids were in grade school. Lish always wondered how she managed it. She had a great deal of respect for Sharon Swan, and she thought it was mutual. At a cocktail party not six months ago, Sharon had complimented Lish on her recent column about detecting ADHD in young children.

The woman reached out her soft, middle-aged hand. "Hello, Dr. Sutton."

Lish nodded. She couldn't bear to swallow any more so she spit into the bedpan. "Hello," she whispered.

"I'm sorry you aren't feeling well." She took out a pen from the pocket in her coat. "I need to ask you a few standard questions, so bear with me."

"Okay," Lish said.

"What's your name?" The doctor watched her spit before answering.

She wiped her mouth with a tissue from the counter. "Lish Sutton."

"Do you know where you are?"

Lish nodded and held her throat. She saw the doctor studying her fingernails. She removed her hands from her neck and noticed the dried blood and dirt on her fingertips. "The emergency room at the Med U."

"Do you know what today is?"

Lish narrowed her eyebrows and shook her head. She thought for a moment. She remembered taking the kids to their first days of school last week, but she had no idea what today's date was.

She shook her head. "I know it's August."

"Do you know the day of the week?"

She took a guess. "Saturday?"

Dr. Swan's face flickered briefly, just enough that Lish guessed she was wrong.

"Have you had any suicidal thoughts?"

Her head hurt.

"I need relief, Sharon."

"Have you had any thoughts about hurting someone else?"

She thought of the baby and the fear of smothering her. She remembered staring at the new set of kitchen knives from Williams-Sonoma that were in a decorative wooden block on the counter. When Drew left town, she threw them away in a neighbor's garbage can. Did she grab a letter opener today?

Dr. Swan stared at her, and she tried to breathe. She shook her head no even as she felt the burn of the tears in her eyes.

Dr. Swan took a deep breath and slowly nodded her head. She didn't look down at her chart.

Her next question was, "Can you spell the word *world?*"

Lish pictured the felt map of the world in Andrew's room. How he liked to take the penguin out of Antarctica and move it over to Madagascar— the world according to Walt Disney. "W-o-r-l-d."

"Can you spell it backwards?"

"D." Lish's head throbbed. The pounding was more pronounced now.

"W."

She grabbed her skull and shook her head no.

Dr. Swan bit her lip. She gently reached for Lish's shoulder as if to steady her. "I'm going to tell you three words, okay?"

Lish nodded.

"Boat, car, and chair," said the doctor. She took a deep breath. "What three words did I tell you, Dr. Sutton?"

Lish spit again. "Boat-car-chair." She looked up at Dr. Swan. "Are you going to send me to the Institute, Sharon?"

Dr. Swan met her eyes, reached out, and gently squeezed Lish's shoulder. "Let's finish the examination, okay?"

She looked away and then back to Lish. "What were those three words I told you?"

"Boat…" Lish grabbed her head. She swallowed. It burned. She grabbed her neck and dug the tips of her fingers into it.

She looked up at Dr. Swan. "I'll go, Sharon. Send me to President Street. I'm not going to put up a fight."

Dr. Swan looked at her. Then she gently patted her back. "Lish, I think it would be the wisest thing to do," she said. "We'll find out what's going on and we'll help you." She tucked a strand of hair behind her ear and looked Lish dead in the eyes. "You're going to be all right. You hear me? And I'll do anything I can to help you."

Dr. Swan consulted with the nurse, who quickly brought Lish a pill containing one milligram of Ativan. She took it, and it hurt all the way down.

Dr. Swan explained her decision to Della. Then the doctor and a security guard walked Lish over to the Institute of Psychiatry, where a nurse with soft, kind eyes met them at the front desk.

Lish was thankful for Dr. Swan and the nurse and the Ativan, which was making her feel light, very light, and remarkably sleepy. She stretched out on the bed in the room where the nurse had led her. The nurse pulled the covers over her. The sounds of the hall faded away. She thought she heard someone in the next room calling out, but it immediately became muffled and even the muffled sound was gone within moments. She was surrounded by darkness, and she closed her eyes. She felt as if she were floating.

Chapter Eleven

Della
Friday, August 29

Della scrubbed the dried lasagna off the plates she'd been soaking all day. She was in the kitchen of 18 Legare Street, where she'd been cleaning clothes and sheets, mopping the floors and scrubbing the surfaces of the bathroom and kitchen. Drew should be home from the airport by now. He'd called her at two in the morning before Dr. Swan sent Lish over to President Street, and when she told him that Lish was in the emergency room, he exhaled deeply and said, "Okay."

He was practically silent when she called him this morning and reported that Lish had been voluntarily admitted to the Institute of Psychiatry. He let out a groan and she said, "Dr. Swan says she's going to be okay. She just needs a few days there… a little time to get straight, you know?"

"Hmm," he said faintly.

Now she heard someone fiddling with the lock, and when she went toward the foyer, Drew flung open the door and stood before her, seeming taller than usual in his straight-leg jeans and crisp white oxford. His salt-and-pepper curls seemed to gleam, and his fresh-shaven face had a squeaky-clean glow to it.

"Della, thank you for your help." He gestured subtly toward her car with his elbow as he stepped inside. "It's time you leave."

She wrinkled her brow. "Have you been to see Lish? Tell me what's going on."

He picked at an invisible fleck on his shirt sleeve, then looked down to meet her gaze. "You really care about Lish?"

"What?" she said. "Of course I do."

"Mmmn." He crossed his arms, and she noticed the small black tufts of hair below his knuckles.

He took a cursory survey of the house before staring back at her. "You care about her and yet you drop her off"—he pinched his brow—"a successful physician and mother of the decade, for crying out loud"—he inhaled—"at the emergency room for a *psychological evaluation?*"

He shook his head and now refused to meet her eye. He looked above her at a portrait of Andrew hanging at the bottom of the stairwell. She watched as he gently kicked the door closed before counting off her offenses on his hands. "You threatened her reputation; you allowed her to be prodded and drugged and forced to sleep in a closet of a room next door to a teenage girl who swallowed a medicine cabinet full of pills for the second time in a month." He cupped his chin and narrowed his eyes. "Yep, you really care about her."

Della's stomach lurched. "But Todd advised—"

Drew raked his hair with his right hand and looked at her dead-on now. "I asked *you* to wait until I got home. It was twenty-four hours, and you couldn't do it, could you? You and your old ex in *my* home deciding what is best for *my* wife?"

Della bit her lip. "Drew, come on!" She took a step toward him and met his gaze. "She was not right. The kids were in potential danger. And I thought she might be too. She needed help, and we didn't know what kind."

He quickly leaned down, inches away from her face. "Don't be so dramatic, Della! This is not one of your fictional plot trajectories, all right?" He pointed his index finger toward her. "This is my wife's life. Her reputation. She has never endangered our children. Not for a second, and you *know* that."

"The baby hadn't eaten. She was dehydrated." Della got her footing and spread her hands out before him as if she was carrying a large and fragile bowl. "I don't think you understand." She clenched her thin fists. "Your wife couldn't move. She couldn't get up. She was practically catatonic, and the one time she did move, it was with a sharp object in her hand coming toward me."

She took a deep breath and lowered her voice. "You know I love Lish. All I want is to protect and help her."

He nodded toward the door. "Get out," he said. "Lish doesn't want to see you now or for a while, all right?" His nostrils flared and for the first time Della noticed a small mole beneath his chin. "I can take care of her. Rosetta will be back. Melanie, the doctor who lives in the carriage house, can help. She'll have all the support she needs. Now go."

Della threw down the dishrag, strode through the foyer, and slammed the front door. She felt as though she'd been kicked in the stomach. What an out-of-touch cad. He had no idea. Poor Lish.

As she walked to her car, she saw a shadowy figure in the passenger seat of the Suttons' Volvo. It was Lish, still strapped in, gazing in the opposite direction. Della wanted to run over, knock on the window, and tell Lish she loved her, but she could feel Drew's eyes on her as he stood on the piazza waiting for her to exit.

Now she walked toward the gate, shaking her head.

* * *

When Della arrived home, it was dusk. The night was cooler than usual and all of the rickety windows were open. She saw the thin strips of paint peeling off of the sills and wondered if they had lead in them.

As she walked through the foyer, she saw that Peter and the children had painted a mural on the hallway walls. One image was of Burl and Bernice and their newfound mutt, Beauregard. The other was of a bed and three little monkeys jumping on it. In the background there was a mother monkey wagging her finger at them and a Dr. Monkey, much smaller, in the distance, scratching his head as he talked on his cell phone.

In the kitchen Della saw an open, empty Domino's pizza box and the browning skins of some apple slices on paper plates. A half-drunk pitcher of lemonade was on the table, attracting a lone fly.

She found them all in the backyard in between the tool shed and two half-built, headless crustaceans that stood four feet tall. Peter had laid out a blanket, and they were listening to the crickets. No one was in anything matching and Mary Jane's dress was on backward. But they were clean. They had been fed, and they were listening to the crickets.

"Mama!" Cozy shouted when she turned and spotted her. She ran and jumped into her arms, and then Mary Jane and Andrew danced around her, chanting, "Cousin Del, Cousin Del!"

Then Andrew rested his head against her hip and said, "Where's Mama?"

"And Baby Cecilia?" Mary Jane asked, her cheeks flushed from the excitement.

Della rubbed their heads and found her gentlest voice. "Mama's at your home and Baby Cecilia is with Aunt Anne, but I imagine your daddy will be picking you and her up real soon."

Peter rolled on his side, cocked his head on his hand, and looked at Della.

"Cozy, why don't you take Andrew and Mary Jane into the kitchen and let them pick out a Popsicle for dessert?"

"Okay!" she said and they quickly followed her.

Della sat down next to Peter on the blanket, half wanting to collapse into his arms and tell him what her last twenty-four hours had been like, half wanting to keep it to herself, the frightening parts with Lish and her conversation with Todd Jervey over meatball subs in the middle of the night.

He sat up, tapped her sandal with his bare toe. "How's Lish?"

"Not good." Della suddenly felt the weariness from the night spent at the hospital. For the first time, her eyes were beginning to blur. "She's had some kind of real mental break. A postpartum thing, I think."

She teared up. "Drew just chewed me out for taking her to the emergency room." She rubbed her eyes with the tip of her index fingers as the kids came running down the rotting back steps.

"He wants me to stay out of it. Says I overreacted." Her lower back ached, and she leaned over to stretch it out. When she sat up, Cozy jumped into her lap, and it was as if the very weight of the little girl's body breathed a new kind of life into Della. Holding her daughter was a kind of resuscitation. Something that jump-started her heart and got her blood pumping. *I am someone's mama*, she told herself. *Someone is depending on me. I've got to keep it together.*

Cozy reached up and played with Della's earring, a silver drop with turquoise that dangled just below her ear. "Tell us a Burl and Bernice story, Mama."

"Yeah!" said Andrew, "but make it one about Burl, okay?" He crossed his arm, a miniature version of his disgruntled father with black, curly hair and long, dark eyelashes. "Bernice is a brat."

Cozy rolled her eyes, and Mary Jane watched her older cousin and tried hard to do the same thing but seemed to get dizzy in the process. Della reached out her hand to steady the little girl.

"All right, Andrew," Cozy said, and she wrapped her arms around her mother's neck as if to claim her for her very own. "I guess it can be a Burl story even though it's Bernice's turn."

"Someone give me a line," Della said.

"I've got one," said Peter, rolling down on his back.

"Okay, Daddy." Cozy turned to him, grinning with expectation.

"Burl's Mama Seems Sad, and He Wants to Cheer Her Up."

"Mmm," Cozy tucked a strand of hair behind her mother's ear. "That sounds pretty good."

"Yeah," Mary Jane added. "Tell us why Burl's mama is sad."

After Drew picked the children up, Della tucked Cozy into bed. She had a stack of quizzes on her desk to grade before her first class tomorrow morning, and she had to be at school at 7:30 to take roll. If she got behind now, the whole quarter would spin out of control.

Peter was in the yard, welding a head on one of the crustaceans. She knew he didn't have a commission, so why was he wasting his time and materials? She hoped he'd given more thought to the idea of a new career, but she doubted it.

As she put the pillow over her head, she wondered how she could check on Lish without Drew's disapproving glare in the background. She'd give it a few days and then start with an e-mail to test the waters. As she closed her eyes and tried to feel a thumping in her own head, she wondered what was going on in her cousin's brain. How did it all start, and how could they get it to stop? As the sound of the blowtorch halted, she removed the pillow from her head and suddenly recalled the rest of her conversation with Todd.

"So you never married?" she said after she unloaded on him in a way she hadn't with anyone in a long time.

He shook his head, looked up at the indigo sky and then back at her until their eyes locked.

"I've only been in love once." He bit his lower lip, looked down at his feet and then back to her. "And you pretty well ripped my heart out."

Della tried hard to swallow. They had been engaged for six months. Todd was on his way to residency at the University of Colorado where they had an established program that specialized in his real interest, the revival of electroshock therapy to treat severe depression and bipolar disorder. She was going to go with him to Boulder—until she had her epiphany that she should follow in her mother's footsteps and write. Once she received her acceptance letter from NYU's M.F.A. program, she knew she had to go for it. And that very next summer she met Peter.

"Oh, come on." She brushed him off like she used to do when he got too intense or emotional.

"You're a nice, attractive, successful guy. I'm sure you've had to beat off the women with a stick."

His eyes glistened in the thick air. He nodded and wiped his brow. "If you're wondering if I'm over you..." He leaned in and gently patted her knee. "I can't say the answer is yes."

Now she wondered, as she did from time to time, if she made the best decision, not to marry Todd Jervey. Did she follow the right career path? Did she marry the right man? All she needed to do was open the door by her bed and see Cozy sleeping soundly, her eyelids fluttering, to know she could never call it a mistake. And yet it was hard. Not at all what she imagined.

Todd would take her back now. She knew that from the look in his eyes, and she wondered, for the good of them all, if she should go.

Chapter Twelve

Lish

Drew pulled two chairs beneath the loquat tree so they could have some shade. Lish took a seat, and they watched the children jump over the rotating sprinklers while they talked.

Drew shook his head and reached his arm around her. "How are you feeling?"

She cleared her dry throat and swallowed slowly. It didn't burn or throb like it did in the emergency room, but she braced herself just in case. Each time she swallowed, she curled her toes and squeezed her hands into fists. The thumping in her head was significantly dulled. She was barely cognizant of it. It was as if an occasional raindrop hit the top of her head.

"Your cousin and your sister really let you down." He squeezed her shoulder. "Drama queens.

None of this would have happened if I'd been here."

Lish's breasts ached. The milk was gone, and an hour ago she had scooped the powdery formula into a bottle that Drew shook hard before feeding to Cecilia. The Ativan that the on-duty psychiatrist at the Institute prescribed made her feel groggy and slightly nauseous. She would taper off of it as soon as she could.

Now Lish felt Drew observing her. He saw her toes curl and her hands ball into fists every few seconds. He wanted her to respond, but all she could manage was a steady nod.

He rubbed her back with the palm of his hand. "You know what we're going to do?"

She turned to him and worked to meet his steady gaze. "Mmm?" she said just above a whisper.

"We're going to have a normal week. Get back in our routine. You know?"

She nodded, and he continued to rub her back in tight circles. She pictured the circles, his hand going around and around between her shoulder blades, and it made her dizzy.

He leaned in and talked in the voice he used to convince her of something. It was a skillful blend of consideration and vim. "We've had a lot on us, honey—the baby coming so early, entertaining the kids all summer, the conference, and the job offer"—he touched his cheek to hers and whispered—"it's gotten us all out of whack. I think each one of us could benefit, and you especially, from getting back in our workaday, school-year routine."

He removed his hand from her back and turned his chair to face her. "Today, we'll take a walk with the kids like we used to do on Sunday afternoons, and tonight I'll pick up a couple of steaks from Earthfare and put them on the grill." He tapped her knee with his fingertips.

"When's the last time I've done that?" He leaned back and shook his head. "Man, it must have been months." He looked out over the garden and back to her. "Then Monday, I'll help you get the kids ready and we'll drive them to school, all right? I'll go to work, Rosetta will stay here and help you with the baby. Okay?"

She nodded slowly.

"The hospital made an appointment with the doc Sharon suggested, right?"

She nodded again.

"When is it?"

"Tuesday afternoon." She winced, and he mistook it for a smile.

"Great." He grinned and patted her knees. "Two days. I bet you'll be feeling a lot better by then."

Lish braced herself for her swallow. She nodded her head and tried for an earnest smile.

"Okay?" He furrowed his brow until she looked back at him. She noticed a pocket of skin at the top of his nose. It was almost a perfect square.

He leaned even closer. "It's going to be okay, honey. Things are going so well on so many fronts."

She looked up at the trees and noticed the hazy afternoon light filtering through the branches as he continued. "We've got three beautiful, healthy children who have the greatest mother I've ever known." He paused and touched his index finger to his lips, then removed it to continue. "Work couldn't be better. Word from the NIH at the conference is that the R01 grant is going to come through any day now, and the CDC keeps sweetening the pot on their offer." He shook his head vigorously, and she noticed a small stream of sweat rolling down his cheek. "I'd be a fool not to consider it."

CDC. She started to sing the ABC song in her head using CDC over and over.

He licked his lips until they glistened and looked out over the garden. "Maybe I'll be able to convince the center to set up a satellite office for my team here in Charleston." He looked back to her. "But Atlanta wouldn't be so bad, right? For a few years anyway? For a quantum career leap?" When she didn't respond, he looked back out to the garden, setting his eye on the rosebushes that outlined the carriage house. "But maybe we can do our research here. Have our cake and eat it too."

He grinned and took a deep breath. "We're going to get you right in no time, Lish." He tilted his head to the side and gazed at her. She tried to meet his eyes, but it took an effort for her to focus. "We have so much ahead of us, and I want you to enjoy it. Every last second of it."

She instinctively reached up and tore down a leaf like she used to do when she was a kid. The loquat leaf was about the size of a magnolia's, with a slightly lighter green tint, but it was the underside that was unique. It was a pale green and felt just like the outside of a ripe peach, fuzzy and remarkably soft. She stroked her forefinger across the bottom and remembered her daddy sitting with her beneath the tree when she was young. He'd reach up high, tear off a leaf from a long branch, and rub it against his cheek for a moment before handing it to her.

"Wanna feel something good?" he'd say.

And she'd rub it between her finger and thumb and then against her own cheek. It felt just like the outside of the small, gray velvet crèche figurines he had given her the year she was chosen to be Mary's Donkey in the St. Michael's Christmas pageant. She must have been four or five. She had a place in the center of the stage beside Mary and Joseph, and she was able to watch Baby Jesus, who was actually the new baby girl of her next-door neighbors on Rutledge Avenue. She still had the little figures tucked away in one of the Christmas boxes in the attic. It was always one of the first decorations she displayed each season. She usually set them on the breakfast table in the kitchen so Andrew and Mary Jane could play with them. They had reenacted the story with them so many times that the fuzz had rubbed off of the rounded edges of Mary's shoulder and the donkey's pointed ears.

"How does that sound?" Drew pulled her back with his confident voice. She watched him blink several times. "A normal week?"

She nodded and mustered a "Good," though her voice sounded, even to her, as though it was coming from the bottom of a well. She could barely hear it.

Now Mary Jane came racing over and leapt, soaking wet, into her lap. "Hold me, Mama." The little girl collapsed into Lish's sore chest.

Just as Andrew moseyed over, rubbing his long, damp eyelashes, the baby let out a cry from inside the house. Drew consulted his watch. " 'Bout that time."

Lish knew she should rise and put together the bottle, but she felt weary. It seemed to take a great effort to move any muscle in her body.

Mary Jane reached up and stroked the back of her hair. "When are you going to play with me, Mommy? We haven't played Candy Land in a long time." Lish closed her eyes. The stroking felt good. The tug on her scalp made her feel awake, but she couldn't seem to think of how to respond to her daughter.

Drew leaned in and took Mary Jane's plump little hand. "Let's go find the water guns in the shed. It can be me and you against your brother."

"Yeah!" Andrew formed a fist and pumped his small tanned arm. "Bring it on!"

Drew peeled Mary Jane away from Lish, though the little girl still reached out for her mother. "Better go feed that hungry baby," he said as Lish curled her toes and swallowed.

Now she slowly stood and walked toward the kitchen, where Rosetta was mopping the floor.

The older woman stepped back when Lish entered. Lish turned to look at her. Rosetta had been avoiding her all day, and she wished she knew why, but she didn't have the nerve or energy to ask.

Rosetta nodded toward a fresh bottle on the counter. "Just made it."

"Thank you," Lish said as the baby continued to wail. She grabbed the warm bottle and made what felt like a tremendous effort to walk up the stairs to the nursery.

Baby Cecilia kicked and wailed even louder

when she caught sight of the bottle. Lish lifted her awkwardly and sat down on the glider and put the bottle in her mouth, forgetting to put on a bib. The baby grabbed the bottle and sucked, and Lish watched the little bubbles form at the bottom end as her infant gulped it down in a matter of minutes.

Lish's swallowing started to burn just slightly for a moment as she held the baby over her shoulder to burp. The thumping on her head was still very distant, but she kept batting her eyelids, expecting it to worsen. The baby belched, then she twisted and turned and fussed again. Lish could see by her bulging diaper that she needed a change.

She placed her on the changing table and opened the drawer underneath where the diapers and wipes were stored. She stared at the wipes for a long time, dazed. The baby was on her back with her dirty diaper open. She cried, kicked, and eventually spit up some of the formula in chunky streams that rolled down her chin and into the folds of skin around her neck.

Lish wasn't sure about what to do next. She curled her toes as she swallowed. *What comes first*, she thought to herself, *pulling the dirty diaper off or opening the clean one and putting it beneath the dirty one?* She feared she would upset the baby more if she did it out of order. She was not sure how long she stood there, her back tightening, staring at her kicking, spitting child.

There were footsteps on the stairs and then Rosetta was there, striding through the doorway. The woman stepped in front of Lish and finished the job. As Lish turned around to head back to the glider, she saw Drew standing in the doorway, his shirt damp from the water gun fight. He studied her the way she'd seen him study a patient with an unidentified flu or a virus growing in a Petri dish. She sat down; she glided. Her mouth was filling with saliva. It was time to swallow, and she braced herself.

Drew guided Lish through the next couple of days. Though she moved in slow motion, she felt better, especially when the sun hit her face, blinding her momentarily, or when she stood in the shower watching the steam rise up and form beads of moisture along the thick windowpanes in Nana's old bathroom.

The baby smiled at her every time she walked into her room, though this bothered Lish. She didn't deserve a smile from Cecilia. Her heart ached when she saw those rosy lips tilt upward to reveal the pink gums behind them. She tried to smile back and meet her daughter's eyes, but she was ashamed of the kind of mother she had been to her so far.

As for Andrew and Mary Jane, it seemed to Lish that they had never asked so many questions:

"What's for supper?"

"Where's my Triggerhappy Transformer?"

"What are sequins made from, and how do they get to be different colors?"

"How do you get cooties?"

"Can we go to the Piggly Wiggly and buy the Popsicles like Uncle Peter has in his freezer?"

"What are you staring at, Mama?"

"Did you hear me?"

"How come you say, 'Uh-huh,' and you don't know what I said, Mama?"

Rosetta didn't usually take care of the children, but she had been willing to help with the baby. She fed Cecilia every two and a half to three hours and changed her several times a day. She bathed her in the nursery sink in the mornings, and then she laid her on her stomach on the floor of the den and put a shiny silver rattle in front of her.

"Don't want her head to get flat," she told Lish.

Lish knew this was a good idea. She remembered writing a column titled "The Value of Tummy Time" shortly after Mary Jane was twelve weeks old. The column warned against positional plagiocephaly—a condition where the skull flattens if a baby is left on his or her back too long—and it outlined the benefits of tummy time, including trunk stability, limb coordination, and head control, all of which would aid the baby in turning over and crawling as he or she grew.

However, Lish could hardly stand to watch Cecilia on her belly. The child grunted and struggled to lift her head in a way that made Lish cringe in both sorrow and sympathy.

On Tuesday, she stood in the doorway and watched her daughter's pink arms collapse. Her little chin hit the floor, and she did an out-and-out face plant where she breathed into her blanket and made a muffled cry that tore at Lish's gut for whole minutes until Rosetta grabbed Cecilia, rocked her, and stuck the pacifier in her mouth.

Lish described this scene to Dr. Cussler, the psychiatrist, during her first meeting with him. She had driven her car over the new and majestic Cooper River Bridge to Mount Pleasant, where she found his office in a little home in the Old Village.

He had asked her about her medical history and her family history, and now he seemed to be giving her time to talk. He was young, barely thirty by her estimation, and sort of nerdy with a small frame, a pasty white complexion, and a red paisley tie that clashed with a green striped shirt. She noted the wide gold band on his left ring finger and wondered if he had any children. *What kind of mother was his wife?*

He scratched his eyebrow and swooped a swath of his thin mousy brown hair out of his face. She knew he'd read her discharge papers, and she wondered if he thought she was trying to minimize and rationalize her thoughts and actions.

He screwed his long nose up, and for some reason he reminded her of the easily irritated rabbit from the Winnie the Pooh books. "Before we develop our goals and come up with a treatment plan, I want us to do a rating scale."

She swallowed. Her throat didn't burn right now in his office. His office reminded her of a dentist's office. It smelled like new carpet and something more. Whatever it was, she noticed that her nose tingled the way it did when the dentist put the mask over it and turned on the laughing gas. She felt relaxed. She felt like his big green leather chair could swallow her up; she wouldn't mind if it did.

He wiped his shiny, narrow nose and brought his pen back to his yellow legal pad. "All right, Dr. Sutton, on a scale of one to four"—he looked up at her briefly—"with four being the highest"—he looked back down—"I want you to rate your overall outlook on life right now."

She settled even further into the soft padding of the chair. Her legs made a squeaking sound as she leaned back and closed her eyes. "Four."

He scribbled on his pad as though she was telling him something that was essential to the survival of all mankind.

She sensed him looking up, and she opened her eyes but couldn't seem to sit up straight. "Rate

your interest in doing your usual daily responsi-
bilities."

She pushed herself up a little. "I'm interested,
but I don't have the energy, and I think that's because of the Ativan." She slouched back down.
"I'd say a drug-induced two."

"So how would you rate your energy level?"
Didn't she just say that? "The same."

He nodded and wrote some more. Then he in-
tertwined his fingers and narrowed his eyes. She
gnawed on the inside of her cheek as if she expected to lose feeling there soon. He said in a
hushed tone, "Rate your feelings of helplessness."

She took a deep breath. Honestly, she felt very
helpless, but she thought it was the medicine. She
bit down so hard on her cheek that she reached up
to rub the outside of it.

"We need to do this after I taper off of the anti-
anxiety pills."

He nodded. "We will, but let's continue with it
today. Right now, rate your feelings of helplessness."

She sucked her teeth and felt the pain pounding
in her cheek. "Two and a half."

"Okay. Rate your feelings of hopelessness."

She rolled her head as if she was warming up
in her aerobics class. "Two and a half." *Should she
say two point five?* She breathed in the newness
of the room. What was making her nose tingle?

Maybe it was a new coat of paint or the leather of the chair. There was a window behind her and the sun filtered through the half-opened blinds, creating a horizontal pattern of slats of light across the arm of her chair and her lap. She felt relaxed here.

Dr. Cussler cleared his throat. "Have you felt, during this time, that you are a failure somehow?"

She gradually nodded *yes*. The room was very quiet. All she could hear was the hum of the air through the vents.

"Rate your feelings right now about that."

"Three." She closed her eyes. The AC cut off, and his voice seemed louder and clearer.

"Lish," he said. "Have you considered harming yourself?"

She kept her eyes closed. She sat very still. She swallowed and it barely burned. She searched her brain. *Had she?*

She could hear him sniff. He was trying to hold back a sneeze. He rubbed the tip of his nose and said, "On a scale of one to four, rate your thoughts about harming yourself."

He sneezed. "Excuse me."

"Two," she said.

Her lap felt warm, but she was not hot. She thought she could feel her heartbeat in her ears. She opened her mouth, and her ears popped just like they did when she was on an airplane.

Dr. Cussler seemed both miles away and right across the room from her.

She thought she heard him swallow. "One more question." He paused. "Have you had any thoughts about hurting anyone else?"

She felt her eyes moving back and forth beneath her eyelids. She searched her mind. She wanted to be honest. She wouldn't get better unless she was honest. She thought of the knives on the kitchen counter and how nervous they made her the day Drew had left for his conference. How she had thought, *The baby is vulnerable*. How she had watched her infant sleeping in the bouncy seat on the kitchen table. How she had picked up the whole block of knives and walked them over to the neighbor's trash can and threw them in. Did she actually think she would use a knife to harm Cecilia? Or was it just their proximity to the baby that made her uneasy? Should she connect those dots in her mind?

She wanted to weep, but she held it in.

"Rate your thoughts of harming someone else," the voice called from across the room.

She squinted her eyelids. She twisted in the chair. She sat upright and met his stare.

"One."

She felt stronger, somehow, as she started to cross the grand Arthur Ravenel Jr. Bridge that spanned the Cooper River connecting Mount Pleasant to Charleston. As she passed by each of the mighty, slanted cables that held up the longest bridge of its kind in the Western Hemisphere, she noticed the bright afternoon sun filtering through the clouds above her, and when she reached the crest of the bridge she felt as though she was ascending into the rays of light. As though each of the cars, including hers, was on its way to someplace so brilliant and so high it could take your breath away.

Dr. Cussler wanted to see her once a week for the next six weeks. After the rating questions, they came up with a treatment plan. She could taper from three down to two Ativan a day starting this Sunday. He believed this would help with her sluggishness, and he hoped to have her off of them in six weeks. He would keep her on her current 25 milligrams of Zoloft for one more week, then he would raise it to 50 milligrams for four weeks. If all went well, he would raise it to 75 milligrams. By six weeks she would be off the Ativan and on 100 milligrams of Zoloft. He expected her to be back to normal, or close to it, by Thanksgiving.

Chapter Thirteen

Roy
September 6, 2008

On moving day, Ms. B. met Roy and Rose at the front of the rectory with the keys to his new home and a warm loaf of banana bread. It was all he could do to keep Rose from dancing as Ms. B. led them from room to room in the enormous three-story rectory that sat on the corner of Meeting Street and St. Michael's Alley.

"It's okay," Ms. B. said after he told Rose to settle down. "I'd be twirling too if I were her." Ms. B. took Rose's hand and swung it back and forth. "Tell your daddy it's time to celebrate."

Rose smiled at the impeccably dressed older lady in her pale yellow pantsuit and double-strand pearls with a gold hummingbird brooch on the top of her left shoulder. The bird's wings were spread wide, and Roy imagined the creature taking flight, buzzing around his new home in search of a flower.

Before long the moving van arrived, with Mama, Donny, and Chick less than twenty minutes behind it. When Mama stepped one foot onto the piazza, her jaw dropped so low you could see the three fillings on her bottom molars. Then she started asking Ms. B. a gazillion questions.

"How old is this place?"

"It was built in 1785."

"How high are the ceilings?"

"Ten feet."

"On each floor?"

"Yes, I believe so." Ms. B. looked to Roy and smiled as his mama stepped closer, pinched her elbow. "Tell me what else I should know about it, darlin'."

Ms. B. pointed to the piazza entry that led to Meeting Street. "This neoclassical screen door is of particular note." She pointed toward the back where the white clapboard became brick but not like any brick his mama had ever seen. "And so is the line of original brick outbuildings. They are connected to the house now via the butler's pantry, but they used to be a separate building which included the kitchen, laundry, stables, and slave quarters."

"Look, Granny! Horses!" Rose took her grandmother's hand and they ran out onto Meet-

'Can ... oy chuckled as Mama pinched off
... k hair doohickey she had clipped to
led ... niskirt. She quickly twisted her long
ho ... r and clipped it on the top of her head.
e- ... waved along with Rose as the carriage
d ... inted out the rectory.
e ... live here!" Rose hollered, and the group of
... s smiled and nodded. Mama smoothed out
... rinkles in her jean skirt and nodded. "That's
... , folks!"

Ms. B. turned to Roy. "Such enthusiasm!"

He rotated his bum shoulder forward and looked
own at her. "You can say that again."

Pretty soon the men got to work unloading
boxes and hanging pictures, and Mama sat with
Ms. B. in the kitchen looking at swatches of paint
for the formal living room.

"I'm fond of this lavender here," Mama said.
"How 'bout you, Ms. B.?"

Ms. B. raised her eyebrows. "Well, since this is
the gathering spot for many a meeting and even
a tea or party, it might be best to go with something neutral."

"Mama?" Roy called over his shoulder as he
held up his picture of the Clemson End Zone over
the fireplace in the den right off of the kitchen.
"We've got eight rooms upstairs. You can pick one
just for yourself and paint it any color you like."

"Oh, my!" Mama pointed to the swatches. "
I keep that lavender one, Ms. B.?"

"Why yes, of course." Ms. B. carefully pu
the swatch out and handed it over to Mama w
leaned in and said, "I saw this black-and-whi
striped bedspread the other day at Marshall's, a
I'm going to buy that thing and fix me up a ni
guest room for me and Donny."

"That sounds lovely," said Ms. B.

Then Roy could hear Mama whispering.
"'Course, the truth is, Rose and I are hoping Roy
will meet someone down here and get back going
on that big family he always wanted." He turned
and watched her squeeze Ms. B.'s hand. "Will you
be on the lookout for someone to introduce him
to, Ms. B.?"

Ms. B. looked back and saw Roy shaking his
head in disbelief. "If it pleases Father Summerall,
I will keep my eyes open."

"Oh, thank you." Mama clicked her silver nails
together. "You're as lovely as Roy said."

By nightfall, he and Rose had placed some plastic lawn furniture on the upstairs piazza, and they
feasted with Chick and Mama and Donny on one
of the umpteen casseroles Ms. B. had stacked in
the freezer. As the sun set over the picturesque
rooftops, a flock of pelicans flew right by them
at eye level on their way to roost.

"Good gracious, those birds are big, Daddy!" Rose said.

"They are, sugar," he said with a nod. He was seeing everything through her eyes and was not surprised when she climbed into his lap and said, "Don't you feel like this is a dream?"

He pulled her close as Mama looked on grinning. "Maybe so, Rosebud."

When Roy arrived at work the next day, he found a stack of resignation letters on his desk from the staff of St. Michael's, including the assistant rector, the youth minister, the children's education director, the bookkeeper, the organist and choirmaster, the office manager, the sexton, the housekeeper, and the receptionist. (Back at Good Shepherd, it had just been Roy and Skeeter and a whole lot of volunteer parishioners, and he had spent many a day scrubbing toilets and sweeping floors.). He had heard this was the protocol when a new rector took over a church, but he had no intention of getting rid of anyone unless, after getting to know them well, he realized they directly opposed his vision for the place.

He called them all together in his office, took a seat on his desk, and tugged at the collar encircling his wide neck. Then he held up the stack of resignation letters and smiled at this group of well-dressed, bright-eyed strangers, his staff. "I'm not accepting any of these right now." He looked to each of them. "Let's get to know one another. My hope is that we can be a team." He glanced out at the nine a.m. hustle and bustle of Broad Street before pulling out the well-worn Bible Miss Ruby gave him after his confirmation.

"Let's start with a little Scripture and prayer. We can do this every morning if you'd like. And we can pray for each other. You know, let each other know what's going on in our work lives and home lives so we can look after each other."

"Wow," the youth minister said. He was a clean-cut young fellow with the exception of his tattered sandals and the tiny silver dot on the side of his nostril. *Is that an earring?* Roy wondered. The youth minister nodded his head with confidence. "I like what you're saying, Father Roy." He reached out his hand. "By the way, I'm Keith Norris."

"Me too," a woman piped up, her eyes brimming with tears.

Roy leaned toward her. "You're Keith Norris?"

"No." She shook her head and chuckled as she brushed away a tear. "I'm Trish Dickerson, the office manager, and I like what you said about praying for each other."

Roy put down his Bible gently on his desk. "Well, we can start right now, Trish." He saw a box of Kleenex on a bookshelf and held it out to her. "If there's something you want to share."

She nodded and reached for the box. "I'm just so relieved you're keeping us on." She looked out of the window. "My husband is in real estate, and he hasn't had a sale in almost a year." She looked around the room at the staff, and Roy wondered how well they knew one another. "And my mama broke her hip and needs to move in with us." Trish's shoulders began to shudder as she silently held back her weeping. "And I tell you the truth, she's not the easiest person to live with."

Roy walked over and patted Trish's shoulder. Then he motioned for them all to come together and pray for her on the spot.

When they were finished, she blew her nose and nodded her head. "Thank you," she said as she looked around the room. "Thank you so much."

Then Roy opened his Bible right in the center and read aloud the first full psalm he could find. It was Psalm 121:

I lift up my eyes to the hills—
where does my help come from?
My help comes from the Lord,
the maker of heaven and earth.
He will not let your foot slip—
he who watches over you will not slumber;
Indeed, he who watches over Israel
will neither slumber nor sleep.
The Lord watches over you—

the Lord is your shade at your right hand;
the sun will not harm you by day,
nor the moon by night.
The Lord will keep you from all harm—
he will watch over your life;
The Lord will watch over your coming and
going
both now and forevermore.

Roy could feel a kind of peace taking root in his own heart as he read the words. God was watching over all of them, even him. And when he looked up at this staff he hadn't known yesterday, he saw them as he thought they really were—people longing for mercy and love, and he knew that ministering to them and having them minister to one another was one of the things he was brought here to do.

By the end of the week, he'd met with the vestry, though Heyward Rutledge, the senior warden, was a surprising no-show. Roy tried all the numbers for him listed in the church directory, but the junior warden, Commander Carleton with the eye patch, recommended they proceed without him. Roy made his pitch to start up the Alpha Course in mid-October (which he all but insisted the leadership and the staff should take), and the vestry approved the small budget for this endeavor and seemed willing, if half-heartedly, to participate.

Roy also met with Ms. B. twice that week (at her strong suggestion) to plan his installation, which sounded like a whole lot more hoopla that he was hoping for, with an engraved invitation to all the clergy in the diocese, a trumpeter, a bagpiper, a quarter peal of the church bells, and a reception for three hundred in the Parish Hall.

"Is all this necessary?" he said to Ms. B., who stood in his door asking for the proper names and addresses of the folks from Ellijay he wanted to invite. "I mean, I'm a little uncomfortable with all of the expense, and I don't want too much of a to-do."

Ms. B. clucked. "It's quite necessary, Father Summerall. You're the fifteenth rector who has taken the helm of this church in over two hundred and fifty years, and it's cause for a celebration."

On Friday, Roy walked down to Waterfront Park to write his sermon. He was a little fretful since it was his first one to this congregation, and the Gospel from the lectionary was a spiky one: Matthew 18:15–20, where Christ tells his followers how to treat a brother who sins against them. He could bypass the spikes for this time and head straight to the last verse, where Christ promises believers that if two or more are gathered together in his name, he will be there in the midst of them.

That was an uplifting one, and he really wanted to start on a high note. The verse meant Christ would be there at that moment even as Roy preached. But as he started to write the sermon, he kept going back to Matthew 18:18. It was a verse that both haunted and perplexed him as Christ said, "I tell you the truth, whatever you bind on earth will be bound in heaven, and whatever you loose on earth will be loosed in heaven."

As far as Roy could tell, it meant that the stuff we do in the here and now has an eternal ripple. That was pretty frightening if you stopped to think about it. And yet, as he stared at the words, this came to his mind. *What we do here counts. And we often get sidetracked, even with the best of intentions, and before long we are building our lives on a foundation that might not be what we were made for.* He realized as he wrote that this was a perfect invitation to Alpha. He would put forth these questions:

Why am I here? Where did I come from? Where am I going? For anyone who thinks there might be more to life than meets the eye right now, for anyone who has questions about life or God, no matter how simple or even hostile, you need to come have dinner with us in the Parish Hall every week for ten weeks starting on Tuesday, October 19. And bring that friend or neighbor who has these questions too.

* * *

The next day was Saturday and he was getting a little antsy about how his first Sunday would unfold. It was just him and Rose in the big, rambling house now. They spent the morning riding bikes around the peninsula, and in the afternoon he put on his old Clemson jersey and she put on the orange cheerleading uniform he bought during his last trip to a game, and they spent the afternoon watching the Tigers pummel The Citadel with a final score of 45-17. Around four, he heard someone ringing up the one-ton tenor bell in the steeple tower, and he remembered that there was a wedding in the church that a priest from Columbia was officiating.

Rose ran out to the piazza and called him. "Daddy, come quick!" When he ambled out, his knees aching too much for a thirty-five-year-old man, he saw her pointing toward the street where the tall, redheaded woman was walking toward the steps that led to the bell tower.

Roy looked at the striking woman he'd spotted the day he came for his interview and then down at Rose who was watching him. "Do you think that's an angel?" the little girl said. "Like Mr. Jackson told us about?"

"Maybe," he said. "But my guess is she's a bell ringer. A really tall one."

Rose cocked her head. "Can we see the bells? You haven't shown me yet."

He looked down at her. She was so eager that she was bouncing on the balls of her feet.

"I tell you what." He gently rubbed her little back. "There's a TV in the narthex where you can watch the bell ringers ringing. We'll head over there and take a quick look at the end of the wedding."

"Yippee!" Rose said. She pulled her plastic chair up to the edge of the second-floor piazza. "Now I'm just gonna sit here and watch."

"Okay," he said. He went and got her some lemonade and sat beside her as the groomsmen and bridesmaids lined up outside the sanctuary, and then came the lovely young bride on the arm of her father.

"That might be you one day," Roy said.

She smiled and took a deep breath. "Yeah."

As the bells sounded at the end of the ceremony, they ran to the narthex and Roy flipped on the television. The eight ringers were standing in a circle facing one another as they took turns pulling on the long ropes of the pulleys that rung the enormous bells two floors above them. It was the most jubilant sound Roy could imagine, and just as he was about to tell Rose the long story of the bells, the priest from Columbia grabbed his arm and introduced himself.

The priest, a fellow by the name of Mike Dunlap, bent Roy's ear for nearly twenty minutes about national church politics as the last guests filed out and the bells stopped ringing. Just as the priest's wife tugged on his arm, Rose hollered, "Daddy!" She was pointing at the television. "Look!"

Roy peered at the screen and saw the tall, redheaded woman in the empty tower. She was on the resting bench, in her white vestments, weeping.

"How do you get up there?" Rose asked.

"There's the stairs on the other side."

Before he could stop her, Rose bolted toward the steps. He followed her up two flights and around the narrow, winding stairwell to the bell tower, where she pushed open the door to the room before he could grab her little arm.

"What's the matter?" Rose asked as she stood in front of the woman. The afternoon sunlight flooded the room and he could see Rose's shadow, long and narrow against the unfinished hardwood floors, her little pleated cheerleading skirt swaying from side to side like a bell itself.

The woman sat up straight and wiped her bright green eyes with her wrists. She was speechless and she shook her head, her long, wavy hair moving back and forth across her shoulders.

Rose turned quickly to Roy. "I think she is one,"

she whispered. "I don't even think she speaks this language."

Roy stood behind his child and put both hands on her shoulder as if to steady her.

"We're sorry to barge in on you, ma'am." He reached out his wide hand. "I'm Roy and this is Rose, and we were just—"

"We were watching the TV downstairs." Rose looked the woman head-on as if she was a school-yard friend who had just fallen off of a swing.

The woman furrowed her lovely red eyebrows. "They don't turn that on for weddings."

He took back his hand once he realized she was not reaching out to shake it. He squeezed his daughter's little shoulders. "No. I just turned it on to show Rose. I'm the new rector, and we're still sort of getting to know the place. I'm sorry if we did something we shouldn't have." He wondered if she even believed him. He didn't look like a priest at the moment in his old football jersey (which was getting a little tight) and his well-worn blue jeans.

"Yeah, and we saw you crying on the TV." Rose nodded. "I thought you might be an angel because, well, you're so tall." She leaned slightly toward the woman. "Are you?"

"No." The woman smiled through her tears. "I'm just a bell ringer. One who's having a hard day." She reached out her long, delicate hand. "I'm Anne Brumley."

Instantly he recognized her from childhood. She had grown up with two other girls down the street from his Aunt Elfrieda, and he had seen them walking along the High Battery and down at the East Bay Playground. They were all way too pretty for him or Chick to get the nerve up to ask for a dance.

"My daddy can help you." Rose grabbed Anne's hand and squeezed it. "He's real good at that."

He rubbed the back of his wide neck and smiled.

"Okay," she said more to Rose than to him. She looked up to meet his eye and smiled. "I could use a little guidance."

When they entered the piazza of the rectory, he motioned toward the white wicker chairs Ms. B. had someone deliver yesterday, and she took a seat. She had taken off her vestments, and she was in a lovely dusty-green sundress with the smallest white flowers embroidered around the edge of her skirt.

"I'm going to go get you some iced tea," Rose said. "My granny made it, and it always makes me feel better."

"All right," Anne said. "That sounds wonderful."

She sat back in her chair and twisted her hair into a knot. "She's precious."

"Thanks." Roy shook his head. He had not noticed a woman in a long time and he could feel his face redden. It wasn't anything puritanical, his unawareness of physical beauty. It was just God's way of binding up his heart since losing Jean Lee, and Roy wondered when God would unwrap it and proclaim it healed.

"Here you go." Rose brought out the tea with a paper towel and an orange coaster with a tiger paw. She turned to Roy. "I'm going to go unpack my Barbies upstairs."

"Okay, Rosebud." He watched Anne take a big sip of tea as Rose's feet padded up the stairs to the second floor. She recrossed her legs and put her hands on her narrow, freckled knee.

Doggone, this woman was pretty. If she needed ongoing counsel or prayer, he was going to have to turn her over to the assistant rector.

He smiled at her, and before he could ask she spoke. "I guess maybe I'm having a crisis of faith." She put the tea down and then picked it up for another sip. "That *is* good," she said.

"Tell me what you mean by crisis?" He prayed, *Lord show me how to help this woman.*

She straightened out her sundress and spoke to the ground. "I thought God spoke to me. A few years ago about something specific." She shook her head and looked up at him. "Anyway, I've been waiting and waiting and nothing has happened."

He nodded.

Anne chuckled. "My cousin and sister don't believe me, I think. Anyway, they encouraged me to move on, and I think that's what I'm going to do." She tilted her head and looked at him. "Only, what if I'm wrong? What if I miss what I was supposed to be waiting for?"

Funny how God worked. He spoke to some people very clearly and then it took a long time to materialize. Then he didn't speak to Roy at all about Charleston and embarking on this new ministry and—*bam!* He was blindsided by it. Tackled before he had a chance to run.

"You know, there are some stories in the Bible about promises that take a long time for our human eyes to see. There's Abraham and Sarah, for one."

"Yeah, I thought about that one," she said. "And Sarah took matters into her own hands and ended up with some trouble."

"Absolutely." He could hear Rose singing upstairs. She always had this little music routine she did with her Barbies. "And there's the forty years in the desert and then Zechariah at the temple…"

She bit her lip until it turned white. "Those people were really important, though."

"We're all important, Anne."

She met his eyes, and he didn't look away.

He rotated his bum shoulder and, out of habit, leaned forward. "Look, waiting is hard. Maybe even harder than the surprises."

"But what if I was wrong? What if I didn't hear it right?"

"Well," he said. "I don't think it would be too bad to ask for a little encouragement, do you?"

She took another sip of tea and a strand of wavy hair fell out of her twist. It covered her eye for a moment before she tucked it behind her ear. "Okay."

Then he bowed his head and prayed for her to receive some sort of tangible encouragement.

"Thank you so much." She stood and shook his hand. "And thank Rose for me too."

"I will," he said. "I hope to see you around the church."

Then she walked out of the piazza door onto the street, and he couldn't help but watch her as she walked down Meeting Street, the sun on her back, her pale green dress billowing out.

When a little plastic Barbie shoe fluttered down to his feet, he looked up to the second-floor piazza where Rose was watching too.

"Well, she wasn't an angel, Daddy," she said as the woman rounded the corner where Meeting met Broad, "but she was really nice." Rose licked her little red lips. "And pretty."

He looked up at her and shook his head. She was a little Granny in the making.

She raised her dark eyebrows. "I'm just saying…"

"Get on down here," he said. "Let's have supper."

When she came down, she grabbed his hand. "Daddy, I don't think I can eat another casserole."

"I agree," he said. "What do you say we hop on our bikes and find a pizza joint?"

"Hooray!" She made her hands into fists and cheered. "Only cheese on my half—"

"I know, I know," he said.

Chapter Fourteen

Della

The bell rang and the seventh graders exited Della's classroom, stepping over a pencil sharpened down to its nub and a couple of used tissues someone had discarded relatively near the trash can. *Nice aim*, Della thought. It was only September, but several of the girls had runny noses and coughs and even fevers. Della went through at least one box of tissues a day as student after student stood at the front of the room by her desk (in the middle of a lecture), blowing their noses, examining the contents of the tissue, then blowing again.

Twelve-year-old girls were good at killing time, and they were still relatively fascinated with their own bodily functions. They giggled when they hiccupped; they studied a mosquito bite on their leg for whole minutes, squeezing it and scratching it until a trip to the nurse's office for a Band-Aid was inevitable; and they winced when their throats hurt and asked to be excused just at the climax of her lecture so they could examine their tonsils in the bathroom mirror from every possible angle until Della had to send a fellow student in to call them back to class.

"No, you may not go to the nurse because the cuticle of your pinky finger is peeling a little," Della told one. She wanted to sound irritated like some of the other teachers who hemmed and hawed and rolled their eyes in an exaggerated manner, but she couldn't. She honestly loved her students, and after years of teaching on and off in the public and private schools around the low-country, she remained in awe of how distinct, and sensitive, and full of life each one was, from their gait to their yawn to their sense of humor to whatever quick glance or whispered word from a peer caused their lips to suddenly quiver and their eyes to fill with tears.

She had sixty of them this year, and when she first stared at their names on her roster and looked out at the seemingly homogenous group during the first day of school, she thought, *How will I ever learn their names?* But within the week, each of them said or did something that stuck out in her mind as if to say, "Don't you know? There is no one quite like me, Mrs. Limehouse."

And Della understood how true this was, and

before the end of the second Monday of the school year, she knew their names automatically and could spot them from behind several yards down the hall as they squealed and giggled and shuffled along in the same plaid uniforms with the same haircuts and the same hundred-dollar backpacks and tennis shoes.

Right now they were reading *A Raisin in the Sun* as a class. It was a great American play about an African-American family eking out a life in the south side of Chicago during the 1950s. It was inspired by Langston Hughes' famous poem "Harlem," where he considered through a series of metaphors what happened to dreams that were forever put off.

The majority of Della's students were quite privileged, and they chuckled as they read their assigned parts. There was a somewhat dated African-American slang that Della had to interpret, and this tripped the students up during the first act. But eventually they were captivated by the story and settled into it without letting a foreign word or idiom break their stride.

Today they were reading the first scene in Act II, where Walter, the protagonist, home from an afternoon spent at the local bar, stood on the kitchen table and pretended he was an African warrior. The girls were in hysterics by the time he made up an African war cry and shouted, "Ocomogysiay," with his sister Beneatha egging him on.

Della had read this play a dozen times at least, but this year it penetrated her heart in a whole new way. Peter hadn't had a commission in months now, and two-thirds of her paycheck went to pay their mortgage. He'd had a toothache that he couldn't afford to go to the dentist to check out. (Neither one of them had been to a dentist in a decade.) And they'd had a rat infestation that they'd had to deal with themselves by setting up traps with peanut butter on a sticky, white square.

Della religiously checked the traps each morning ever since she'd found three baby rats curled up like backward c's on the pad beneath the kitchen sink just as Cozy came in to ask for breakfast. She'd slammed the door and ordered Cozy back to her bedroom to put on her shoes while she ran into the backyard and tossed them in the big green trash can. Now every time Della passed the outside garbage container, she pictured those miniature rodents—their small, rigid feet, their shut eyes, their pink ears pinned back on the sides of their little heads.

Last week after Peter looked at the stack of month-old water and electric and credit card bills on the kitchen table, he picked up the phone and called Old South, the carriage company he worked for during college, and he immediately took the same job he had fifteen years ago—giving carriage tours (for minimum wage and the hope of a few decent tips) up and down the peninsula dressed in a polyester Confederate uniform costume in the blistering heat.

In the play, when Walter's disillusioned wife, Ruth, said to her mother-in-law, "Yes, life can be a barrel of disappointments, sometimes," Della nodded her head and knew that it would likely be years before her students understood what Ruth meant.

These girls were blessed, immeasurably so. At the least, their lives were extremely comfortable. They had loving parents, refrigerators full of fresh produce and organic meat, luxury SUVs with leather seats, nannies and housekeepers to keep their mothers sane, vacations that required airline tickets and even passports from time to time, and simplest yet best of all—soft, clean beds in their very own rooms where they could lay their heads at night and dream of something nice like a picnic at the beach or a Wii under the Christmas tree or a purebred puppy wagging his tail at the sight of them.

Their lives were the very ones Walter fantasized about. The ones that were so far out of reach, it was making him crazy. Of course, they couldn't see this. How could they? They might never see it if they stayed on the trajectory their parents had in mind for them: attractive, straight-toothed, and educated young woman lands spot at very decent if not above-average college, meets attractive, straight-toothed young man from similar background, begets another generation of a privileged life, and so on.

Della looked out of her window and spotted the first-grade class walking to the lunchroom, and there in the middle of the pack was Cozy holding another little girl's hand. The girl leaned toward her and made a remark that caused Cozy to laugh and pull away for a moment without releasing the hand. She turned back and smiled at her friend, and they began to swing their arms together until their teacher stopped the group and instructed them to line up single file before they went in to eat.

Now Della knew she must call Todd Jervey. She'd made her decision, and it was time to move forward. In the teacher's lounge, she dialed the number of his pager, and a few minutes later he called back during her planning period. "Della?"

"Yeah." She cleared her throat.

"What's going on?"

"Well…" Her voice sounded unusually high-pitched and unfamiliar to her. "I was wondering if you'd like to meet me for lunch sometime this week."

He paused. She thought she could hear him breathing. He chuckled nervously. "Sure, I can get away for a little while tomorrow or maybe Wednesday, if that works for you."

"Tomorrow," she said. "Blend at noon?"

"Yeah." He paused a second time. "I look forward to it."

She met him outside of the restaurant the next day. He was in his white coat with his name and title inscribed in royal blue thread across the upper left side. He'd shaved off his beard, and he looked younger and a lot like the fiancé she left one July morning after buying a one-way flight to LaGuardia airport.

He held open the door for her and they took a seat at a small table on the back of the piazza. Her favorite black sleeveless dress with the thick, red patent-leather belt had a rip under the arm, so she'd settled for a short brown-and-blue floral skirt missing a button and a brown silk top that still passed for professional despite its significantly scooped neck.

"So." He fiddled with the brass edge of the menu. She crossed her legs and flashed a smile. If she needed dental work, it was well concealed. Thank goodness Nana sprung for braces when she was a teenager and stayed after her about brushing and flossing until the day she left for college. "How's Lish holding up?"

"I don't know for sure." For some reason she couldn't recall what he had just asked. She took a gulp of her iced tea. While it was nearly October, the heat index was still 100 degrees. She regretted wearing the Spanx Lish handed down to her last year, though it did suck it all in. She didn't yet have the midsection rolls that a lot of her friends had acquired, but she had this overall gravity thing going on that was really depressing. Her breasts seemed to droop in a way they never had before, like heavy raindrops dripping down from the roof gutter, and her rear end sort of sagged down, overlaying the back of her upper thighs. Aging was sad, Della had thought as she stood on top of her bed that morning, studying herself in front of their bureau mirror while Peter poured Cozy a bowl of the Food Lion-brand Cheerios.

Now Todd repositioned the salt-and-pepper shakers as he waited for her response. "Della?" he said. "How's Lish?"

Della snapped back. "Oh, sorry." She blushed and let out a guffaw. "Um, she's sent me a few vague e-mails about focusing on her family and getting better." She brushed away a fly that had just landed on the edge of the table. "I guess that doesn't involve me. Or so her husband is convincing her, I'm sure." She blushed and flipped her hair. "Drew was *furious* about us sending her to the hospital that night."

Todd shook his head in disbelief. "I don't see what other choice we had."

"I don't either," Della said. "I think Drew sees what Drew wants to see, you know?"

Todd nodded knowingly, then lifted the white cloth napkin and patted the beads of perspiration on his fair, freckled forehead.

Della repositioned herself in her chair and corrected her posture. "So how's the new job?" She lifted her chin and read the title beneath his name. "Chair of the Department of Psychiatry. That sounds like a pretty big deal." She watched him remove his tortoiseshell glasses and clean them with the tip of his tie. "Is it an administrative drag or do you get to do the research you love?"

He chuckled as the waiter delivered their salads. He'd ordered the Atlantic salmon on mixed greens, and she'd ordered the pan-seared tuna served over tangled lettuce, topped with roasted asparagus and kalamata olives.

"Well, the deal I struck is that I continue with the research." He took a bite. "I've got a great administrative assistant who seems, so far anyway, like she can help me keep the paper-pushing to a minimum."

Della's eyes narrowed. She noted nothing else around but him. Not the clink of the other diners

as they cut and stabbed their food or the hum of
the cars whizzing by. She leaned in. "Tell me about
the research." She knew he'd received some kind
of award for a study he conducted during his fellowship at Johns Hopkins a few years back and
that Lish and Drew had called him the shock doc
because of his interest in electroshock therapy.
"Are you working with electricity?"

He wiped his mouth, looked up, and raised
his eyebrows. She knew it had suddenly dawned
on him that she'd been keeping up with him. He
smiled. "Sort of. But we think we're on to a less
invasive method." He placed his napkin back in
his lap and began to talk with his hands. "There's
a local neurologist I'm working with who came up
with the idea for what's called transcranial magnetic stimulation."

She tried to stop the wrinkles from forming on
her forehead. *What did he just say? Focus.* "You
mean using magnets instead?"

"Exactly." He took a sip of his iced coffee. "ECT
causes seizures which sort of set the reset button
on the brain, but the seizures can be harmful to
the patients and there are all sorts of negative side
effects." He counted them off with his damp fingers. "Significant memory loss, a reaction to the
anesthesia, stuff like that."

"Hmm," she said. "And there's a stigma, right?
I mean, who doesn't visualize *One Flew Over the*

Cuckoo's Nest when you say electroshock treatment?"

He chuckled and took a hearty bite of his greens. "Right."

"So this one is gentler?" She gazed at him until he glanced up, wiped his mouth, and locked eyes with her.

"Much more so." He paused to take her in. She tried to subtly correct her posture and push her shoulders back. He looked her up and down through his round lenses with a kind of warm familiarity. She suspected he wondered at this moment *why* she'd asked him to lunch.

"How?"

He grinned at her and lifted his hand to his head. He enjoyed talking about his work. "We use strong electromagnets to bypass the skull with a magnetic field." He tilted his head and stared into her blue eyes. Then his cheeks turned pink, and he looked down at his plate.

This was easy and familiar. She had hoped it would be, and it was. She nodded for him to continue.

"Then we put a weak electrical current on the brain. It works by reenergizing the brain's left prefrontal cortex, where nerve cells in patients with serious depression become sluggish and don't fire off like they should."

"Mmm," she said. "Noninvasive is the key."

He nodded. "We're preparing a trial that we'll run in a few weeks in hopes that we can prove that depressed patients receiving four weeks of daily, thirty-minute TMS sessions will improve."

"Wow. That's fascinating." And it was, if she stopped to think about it. There were a lot of things Della wished she could reset. She watched Todd's Adam's apple bob up and down as he sipped his iced coffee.

She thought he was onto her; he seemed nervous. She patted his knee and let her hand linger for a moment before he looked up.

"Can we do this again, Todd?" She grinned.

He returned her gaze. "Really?"

She nodded. "Yeah. It's so good to see you."

Yep, she was working it. She admitted it, and he likely did too. Todd was insightful, no denying that, but as she suspected, he seemed willing to go along.

This was what was best, she thought as she walked briskly down Doughty and crossed over Rutledge Avenue. She'd have a class full of students in less than five minutes, but thankfully, they would spend the period reading the play.

As she watched a well-heeled mother walking her daughter through the gates after some kind of trip or doctor's appointment, she nodded her head. Yes, she was going to get the life that she wanted for Cozy, and Peter would be free to pursue his art. They would all be taken care of. Like her students and their easy existences. Like Lish and her family.

Why should she feel ashamed? In fact, perhaps this was the way most women think. They just never actually talked about it. Maybe that very woman, signing her daughter in at the front desk, was at one time this calculated and brazen. Maybe it was only Della who was finally cluing in to how this whole thing worked.

She remembered some of the girls from her high school days who were determined to find a well-off man in college. The ones who sat in the senior hut the day before graduation and proclaimed their goal: "To get hitched to a great guy, of course."

She had scoffed at them. Even her favorite friend, Hilah Roberts, who had a shockingly tight-fisted father compared to the others, all but stated that she was out to marry a wealthy man. She found him at law school, and now she was living high on the hog in Atlanta with four kids and a live-in nanny from China who had been teaching her children Mandarin from birth. Hilah loved her husband, yes, but she made sure he fit the bill. It was a decision she'd made long before she ever laid eyes on him.

It was so obvious, Della thought as cars flew by her down Rutledge Avenue. Had she been an idiot not to see it? The irony was not lost on her. She considered herself an intellectual, and yet she'd missed this most rudimentary of objectives for a woman who was not independently wealthy. It was like when she learned about what sex actually was at the age of ten. She'd been racking her brain trying to figure out what it meant to "do it" after she heard some boys talking about it outside the bathroom at one of the East Bay Playground dances. *Well, I'll be doggone*, she'd said to herself when she consulted a book titled *Human Sexuality* in the public library. She'd sat down on the floor between the shelves and studied the black-and-white illustration. *Of course, that fits inside there. Duh! How could I not have seen that coming?*

Getting together with Todd was not a stretch. She had been engaged to him before, right? She had every right to hit the reset button on her life, didn't she? Todd would love Cozy and provide for them both. And she could have more children whom he would adore. Doctors, especially research ones, weren't rolling in it, of course, but they made enough of a living to go to the dentist, to educate children in a safe, clean, cool environment, and to give their wives the opportunity to raise those children and to even consider pursuing some of their own dreams beyond the bliss of domesticity.

It made Della dizzy to think of money as happiness, to think of money as freedom, to think of money as life, as Walter so shamelessly proclaimed to his mama in *A Raisin in the Sun*. Yes, Della was calculating. And her old self might argue that she was shallow. But she would tell that young girl to sit down and bite her idealistic tongue. She was a mother. Her child needed some security. Mothers were the fiercest, most ferocious beasts in the animal kingdom, were they not? It was time to trade in her lofty (and unfeasible, she now knew) principles for the good of the whole.

Now, as she punched in the code of the wrought-iron gates of The Pinckney School, she heard the *click-clack* of a horse-drawn carriage bustling down a street in the distance and wondered if it was Peter, sweating like a pig in polyester with a gaggle of middle-aged women from the Midwest gawking at him and laughing at his well-timed jokes.

On campus, the seventh-grade girls were chasing one another during the last couple of minutes of recess. And the first graders were out and about, too, running cross country around campus as part of their PE period.

Cozy waved to Della as she bolted toward the gate. Just when Della thought she would whiz on by to keep her time low, the little girl stopped and held open her arms, and Della embraced her as the PE teacher smiled from the other side of the campus lawn.

During last period, Della's third-section class got all the way through Act II, Scene 2 of *Raisin*. When the money from Walter's father's life insurance came in, and his mama allowed him to be in charge of it, he immediately entrusted it to his business partners in hopes that they would open up a liquor store and make their fortunes together.

That evening, he came home jubilant and painted a picture to his young son, Travis, of the beautiful future they would soon share. This picture included a lovely home with a gardener, his wife Ruth in pearls, and best of all, Travis as a teenager filling out applications to the top colleges in the country.

The scene took place on the common room couch, which doubled as Travis's bed in the small ghetto apartment. At the end of the scene, Walter tells his wide-eyed son that he can grow up to be anything he wants to be. At this Travis leaps into his father's arms and Walter, with a voice that is both elated and hysterical, lifts his son up high and promises him the world as the lights black out.

And this afternoon Della was the one who reached for the last tissue from the box on her desk as she tried to keep her shoulders from shuddering for the two minutes before the dismissal bell rang.

Then one of her students, Meredith on the second row in the far left corner, asked, "Mrs. Limehouse? Are you okay?"

Chapter Fifteen

Lish
October 5, 2008

The last few weeks had been easier than Lish expected them to be. She'd seen Dr. Cussler three more times, and her energy level had markedly increased as she gradually tapered from three down to one Ativan pill a day. Despite a faint nausea from time to time, she'd experienced no ill side effects from the Zoloft, and Dr. Cussler had continued to steadily increase the dose.

Now she took the children to and from school without Drew's help, and she cared for the baby on her own at night, though it still took her longer than usual to find the strength to pull herself out of bed when she heard Cecilia's cries.

More than a month of Saturdays had come and gone, and she wondered how Anne and Della were doing. She'd received voice messages and e-mails from them both, and she often wondered how Anne was fairing at her training program in England, but she hadn't had the energy to send more than a one-word reply to either of them. "Fry one fish at a time," Drew told her when she asked him if she should call them back. "And right now you've got to focus on your immediate family."

Lish hoped she would have the strength to invite Della and her family to a Thanksgiving dinner at her home. This was one of the goals she'd secretly set for herself now that it was mid-October, and she was feeling so much better. By then she could show her cousin that she'd made a full recovery, and maybe the two of them could go to England to visit Anne before her upcoming move.

Drew had accepted the position at the Centers for Disease Control, and his start date was the first of December. Lish would finish up the school year with the children and her treatment with Dr. Cussler, and the plan was for her to have the house rented and the children moved by the first of May. That way, she could enroll Andrew and Mary Jane in a school for the last few weeks of the academic year, and they would hopefully make a few friends who they could get together with over the summer.

Of course Lish was sad to be leaving her home, but she knew she should support Drew who couldn't be more excited about the opportunity. He was even able to bring the majority of his MUSC research team with him, including Rob, Melanie, and the two other fellows who had helped create the rotavirus vaccine. The fellows were all thrilled about the chance to work on the new flu vaccine team that Drew would oversee. All of the research showed that a pandemic was likely in the next five years, and Drew might very well play a role in saving a large number of lives through his work.

On Friday, though it was a week before planned, Lish decided to cut the Ativan and move down to a half milligram per day. She had agreed to resume writing her newspaper column and needed as much energy as possible to complete the first article she'd written in months. She knew what she wanted to write about—the health benefits of formula if you are unable to nurse. She was going to critique the brands and cover the bottle sterilization process as well as the general feeding schedule for newborns. Also, she was planning a birthday party for Andrew at Jump-Castle-Kingdom, and she wanted to be able to print and mail out the invitations within the week.

On Saturday, her second day on the half milligram of Ativan, she felt an energy like she hadn't felt since before the baby was born. She even sent Rosetta home early and ordered Drew's favorite dinner from Cru Catering—beef Wellington, roasted asparagus, and a cinnamon crème brûlée. Then she drove to the Wine Shop with all three children and purchased an eighty-dollar bottle of a Cotes du Rhone, his favorite.

Drew raised his eyebrows when he saw the dining room table set with linen place mats and silver and crystal.

"What's all this?" He put his hands on his hips, causing his pale blue scrubs to pucker.

Mary Jane came scampering up in her Cinderella nightgown. "Mama made you a romantic dinner, Daddy."

He lifted her up and rocked her back and forth as he looked at Lish, who had managed to take a shower, put on makeup, and iron a floral sundress with spaghetti straps that she'd worn before she was pregnant.

"So she did," he said. "And doesn't she look nice?"

Mary Jane pulled back, looked at her mama and back to her daddy. She nodded yes and said, "Very."

The next week started off strong for Lish as she sent in her article, mailed the birthday invitations, and managed to make a haircut appointment, but by Friday she felt a little jumpy and her throat began to burn like before.

She continued to have more energy, but something else was happening too. Every time she went to make a bottle for Cecilia, she saw microorganisms growing inside the bottom of the bottle, inching their way up toward the nipple. On Wednesday, the day Rosetta had the afternoon off, Lish refused to expose the baby to the awful germs, and Cecilia went hungry for hours until Drew came home, heard the child wailing, and said, "What the heck is going on with the baby, Lish?"

"There are microorganisms in the bottle," she said.

"You couldn't see them with the naked eye, even if there were," he said. He rolled his eyes before stomping into the kitchen and holding up a bottle up to the light. "See," he said. "Nothing's there."

Andrew raced in from the back garden with his fingers in his ears and quickly grabbed a juice box out of the refrigerator. He turned to his father. "The baby's been crying *all* afternoon. I can't stand the sound, Daddy, so I'm going back outside, okay?"

After Drew made a bottle and fed the baby, who went to sleep almost instantly after sucking twelve ounces down, he came out on the piazza where Lish was rocking in a chair.

He leaned against the railing. "Don't go back down this road, Lish." She watched him set his jaw and look out over their garden. She wondered if he was noticing the last pink blooms on the crepe myrtles along the far edge of the wrought-iron fence. He waved to a neighbor who was walking his dog, then turned back to her.

"You've been doing really well, honey. You've got to get a grip, okay?"

She nodded as if she was in slow motion and swallowed. It burned like strep throat or the time she had her tonsils out. "I'm okay. I think I'm just tired."

He sent her to bed at six o'clock and ordered a pizza for the kids.

Friday, on the way to taking the children to school, Lish's car hit a bump in the road on Meeting Street and she was seized by the fear that she had run over someone. She pictured the basket weaver who sat at the corner of Meeting and John Street, tying the pine needles and sweetgrass into knots that she shaped into exquisite bowls and baskets. Lish was sure she had run over the woman. She could hardly breathe by the time the teacher's aide opened the car door for Andrew and Mary Jane and cheerfully escorted them into the building.

Immediately, Lish drove back to the spot and circled it four times, searching for the body of a thin and elderly black woman. She pulled over, got out, and walked back and forth around the block, examining the sidewalk, looking for traces of blood. She found nothing and circled again and again in her car. Where was the body? Had the woman been carted off to the emergency room?

Andrew and Mary Jane were the last in line to be picked up that day. Lish had spent the entire morning driving around and around the corner of Meeting and John Streets. She had been only three blocks from school, but she was over a half hour late picking up her children. Her eyelids were blinking incessantly, and her throat was dry and sore.

One of the teachers, a young girl right out of the early education program at the College of Charleston, walked with Lish and the children to the car. "Are you all right, Dr. Sutton?"

Lish's throat was too dry to answer. She nodded.

"Mommy," Mary Jane said. She was holding up a large piece of construction paper and talking, but Lish couldn't make out her words.

The aide paused for a moment before gently closing the door. Lish looked at the paper and Mary Jane's proud smile. She couldn't find the words to comment, so she turned back around. With a jerking motion, she put the car in drive and rolled slowly out of the school parking lot.

Rosetta told Lish she wanted to work through the weekend. "Get yourself some rest, Miss Lish," she said, and she walked her up the stairs to her bedroom. Lish almost called Dr. Cussler once or twice on Saturday morning when her throat felt particularly hot and she didn't want to swallow, but she felt better after she drank some cool water and took a long, hot shower before crawling back into bed.

Despite their good intentions, the Suttons hadn't made it to church since Baby Cecilia's birth. They were scheduled to have her christened in November, and Drew said it would be pretty bad if he showed up just for the baptism and then left town.

So on Sunday, Rosetta laid out a beige suit for Lish and a pair of black, sling-back pumps. Drew rubbed her back in the early morning and said, "Let's go to church, all right?" Rosetta brought in a tray with a poached egg on toast and bacon, and Lish sat up, took a bite, and then set it aside. It hurt to swallow. She would call Dr. Cussler on Monday. She didn't want to go back on the Ativan, but she couldn't stand this either.

As she stood in front of the full-length mirror in her closet, attempting to zip up her skirt, Drew came up behind her in his charcoal gray suit and bow tie, rubbed her arms, and said, "You look great, Lish."

Rosetta dressed the children in matching green corduroy outfits and put Cecilia in a pale green dress with little pink sheep smocked across the neckline. She made a warm bottle and put it in the diaper bag along with Cecilia's pacifier and the little blanket with satin edges she seemed to be favoring.

They walked the four blocks to church, a handsome family in their pressed garments and their clean faces and their powdered and perfumed bodies. Drew pushed the stroller as Lish walked between Andrew and Mary Jane. The little girl reached up to hold her hand, and Lish took the hand lightly and began to swing it slightly. But as the historic church bells pealed from the stately steeple of St. Michael's Church, Lish became completely focused on avoiding the sidewalk cracks or the round black circles of dried gum that were splattered across the well-worn sidewalk.

In church Lish couldn't get comfortable. The enclosed wooden pew was hard, and it made her spine ache as she leaned back into it. The children were in their own worship service and the baby was in the nursery. Drew was seated to her right, looking away from her toward the altar and the pulpit whose large, ornate wooden roof seemed precariously perched on two columns. For a moment, Lish feared it would topple over and crush the new rector's head when he took his place in its center and looked out over the congregation as the organist played the last stanza of "A Mighty Fortress is Our God."

It felt like a strong hand was on Lish's throat, pressing mightily down on her vocal cords. She couldn't sing. She made a fist and rubbed her knuckles against the velvet cushion when the spit pooled in her throat and she had to swallow. She wanted to stop this. She'd been doing so much better. How in the world could this have come down on her again? If the hand pressed any tighter, she might choke.

After the young rector, who seemed familiar somehow, read the Bible and began his sermon, she grasped her throat as if to yank the hand off of it, and Drew glanced over and patted her knee. She abruptly bent forward, hiding herself in the high walls of the pews. She didn't want to embarrass him, but she had to get this hand off of her throat.

Drew faked a cough and leaned in. "You okay?" he whispered as the priest moved into the first point of his sermon.

She nodded. She didn't want to disappoint him. She was not going to backtrack now. She sat up and tried to concentrate on the priest's words. He was talking about Abraham's faith. How Isaac asked him where the animal was that they were going to sacrifice as he carried the sticks on his back for the altar they were to build at the top of the mountain.

Before she heard Abraham's response, the thumping started again on her head. She hadn't felt it in months and it was like a small hammer, pounding with force in the very center of the top of her head.

She could hardly breathe; she couldn't swallow. *No!* she thought to herself. She squirmed in her seat. Drew noted her in his peripheral vision. She moved back and forth, then she grasped the top of her head. The pounding worsened. Her throat burned. *No! No! No!* she whispered. Someone in the pew in front of her turned to look back.

The fire in her throat was throbbing in her head now. Drew turned to her. He reached out to squeeze her knee, to steady her, but she pushed his hand away. Then she stood and shrieked like she had been shot, and she felt like she had. "No! No!" she screamed and all eyes were on her, including the priest perched high above her in the top-heavy pulpit.

Drew stood up and put his arm around her, but she pushed him off and continued to scream. An internist in a pew several rows back came forward and the priest made his way down the pulpit stairs and across the aisle to her.

Drew squeezed her shoulders with force. "Lish. Come on. Lish, stop."

She shook her head. She spit. She couldn't swallow any more. She couldn't stand it. As two more physicians from the congregation moved toward them, Drew restrained her from the back, picked her up, and carried her screaming down the aisle and out of the building onto the busy corner of Meeting and Broad Street where she collapsed in a heap at the foot of one of the grand white columns as the shadows of the figures attempting to help rose above her.

Someone was asking Drew questions. Someone was praying with their hands open toward her. She heard Drew tell someone to get the children, and then she spit and shut her eyes until she was lifted and carried toward a car that drove her home with Drew pinning her arms to her sides the whole way.

In her bedroom, he poured an Ativan out of her medicine bottle. She put it on her tongue and he watched her until she swallowed. Then he pulled back the covers and stuffed her under them. Rosetta kept an eye on Lish as Drew paged Dr. Cussler, and she agreed to spend the night and look after the kids once a friend from church brought them home. Lish heard all of this from the bed where her head, heavy as an anvil, rested against a thick goose-down pillow. She knew it wouldn't be long before the medicine would calm her as she entered its thick, heavy haze. She lifted her hand to touch her head. She rubbed the spot where the pounding was becoming duller, and she wondered why she was being tortured so.

Hold on, she said to herself. It will be gone by the second pill.

That night, after Drew forced the second Ativan down her, she stumbled out to the piazza where she crouched beside the rocking chair and took in the fresh air. She could hear Drew check on the children who were all asleep, with Rosetta in the guest bed in Cecilia's nursery. Then she watched him walk quietly outside and over to the carriage house, where he discreetly rapped on the door.

"Hello there, doctor." Melanie stepped to the side and closed the door after he slipped in.

The young woman forgot to close the blinds, and Lish could see Drew taking a sip from Melanie's glass of wine and then a bite of her pasta. The young woman rubbed his back in wide strokes, then massaged his neck. Drew let his head drop so she could get to that spot in the center where he usually had a knot.

"Ahh," Lish imagined him saying. "That's the place." Then Drew glanced over his shoulder, noticed the opened blinds, and turned back to shut them tight.

Chapter Sixteen

Roy
Sunday, October 5, 2008

"Daddy?" Rose tried to twirl the spaghetti casserole with her fork into her wide spoon as they sat at the long antique table in the rectory dining room. The table had belonged to the original owner of the home, a local judge, who had left it as a housewarming gift for the first rector when St. Michael's purchased it toward the end of the eighteenth century.

"You hear me, Daddy?" the little girl said. Roy reached out and patted her hand. "I'm sorry, Rosebud." His mind was on the woman who had collapsed in church that morning. He had found her address in the directory and walked over to see about her, but the husband met him at the front door and said she was sleeping.

Roy had seen a lot of things during his few short

years as a priest, but he'd never heard the kind of suffering expressed in that woman's shriek. It was as if she were choking or burning from the inside out, and he had felt helpless, which both angered and terrified him.

He rotated his shoulder and smiled at his child. "I'm all ears. Go ahead."

"Did a lady start screaming in church today?" Rose had a worried look on her face. She glanced at the twisted noodles on her fork and put them down. "I think you better cut up the pasta for me. That's what Granny does."

"Okay." He reached over with a knife and fork. "And to answer your question, yes, a lady did scream in church today. In fact, that's what I was just thinking about."

"I saw her." Rose stared at him with wide eyes. "When the teacher was walking us over from children's chapel. I saw a man carrying her and then I heard some folks talking about it at the coffee hour." She looked down at her cut pasta and took a bite. "Why do you think she did that?"

"I don't know," Roy said. "I tried to go over to her house and see her when you were on your play date, but she was resting."

"Mmm." Rose took a sip of milk and wiped the little mustache off of her face. "I wonder what's wrong with her."

"Me too," he said.

* * *

Roy's installation was scheduled for that Thursday, October 9th. The Parish Hall was remarkably hectic that week with Ms. B. and her team polishing silver, ironing linens, cooking and baking, and arranging the flowers.

More than four hundred people had responded positively to the invitation, and she decided to double her order of wine and coffee-ice-cream punch and crab cakes and shrimp-salad finger sandwiches from Miss Hamby's.

There was a pang in Roy's heart as he stood at the window of his office looking down on Broad Street at the worker bees who hurried in and out of the ornate wrought-iron gates of his church, carrying tables and china and blocks of oasis and baskets of greenery clipped from their gardens.

He felt the Lord led him to St. Michael's, though the part about actually being here still unnerved him. And there was something else. He sensed a heaviness as he looked out at the faces of the people who walked up and down Broad Street—the worker bees and the businessmen, attorneys, real estate agents, and tour guides.

He didn't know much about the financial world. He made sure to keep his life real simple where money was concerned. He only owned one credit card, which he paid off every month, and he'd bought his used truck outright and paid off his student loans right after he graduated, thanks to his little inheritance from his father. As for his homes, they had been owned through the church ever since he took his first job, and he didn't know what it was like to have a mortgage or be upside down in one. But he understood enough to know that the economy was nosediving, and the people around him, in their designer clothes and luxury cars, must be suffering.

He thought back to the woman in church last Sunday. Her terrifying shriek had instantly brought to mind the dream he'd had of the city South of Broad with the dark, rectangular windows and the people still as stones. Back in Ellijay, folks wore their troubles on their coat sleeves. You could see it in their gait, in their well-worn clothes, in their sagging jowls. And they rarely hesitated in opening up and telling all, in hopes someone would lend them a hand. Everybody knew everyone else's business anyhow, so it was silly to pretend like all was well when it wasn't. But in downtown Charleston, people's mental and emotional states were difficult to discern. Fear and suffering could easily be masked with a fine hairdo, a tailored suit, and a stiff, white-toothed smile, and he worried that he might not be able to put his finger on the very needs of the flock the Lord had called him to shepherd.

Of course, what they needed was the love of

Christ. And the joyful expectation of an eternity with him. That was always the answer for everyone, no matter what their circumstances. But how to find the door that leads to someone's heart? The search always started with identifying someone's longings and needs, and at the moment, this remained a mystery to him.

His first sermon with the Alpha promotion was met with very little response. Only two people outside of the vestry and staff had signed up for the program that started next week, and Roy was feeling discouraged about it.

He often envisioned the tall and beautiful woman in the bell tower. Anne Brumley. He had thought about her more than once since she sat on his piazza sipping tea. With a little research, he'd found out that the bell ringers practiced every Thursday evening at five, and somehow he always found himself walking toward the corner of Meeting and Broad around that time, but he hadn't seen her yet. She was one of the few people he'd met thus far who didn't hide her faith or what was truly on her heart. This gave him hope, somehow. He prayed he might cross paths with her again.

He called the home of the Doctors Sutton each day that week, but he always got the answering machine. On the afternoon of his installation, while his mama took Rose to pick up the dress

Ms. B. had picked out for her at a children's boutique on King Street, Roy walked on over to Legare Street again and knocked on the door.

A woman who introduced herself as the housekeeper answered, but he could see the woman from church, Dr. Lish Sutton, sitting in a chair in a drawing room just beyond the foyer, and he could hear a baby crying somewhere else in the house.

"I was hoping to check in on Dr. Sutton. To see how she's feeling."

The woman looked at his clerical collar and then over to Dr. Sutton. "She's not all the way awake right now."

The baby's cry grew into a wail that echoed through the two-story foyer. The housekeeper looked up to the stairs and back to him. Then she called over her shoulder. "Miss Lish, the preacher's here to see you. I'm going to let him in and go feed the baby."

The woman sitting in the chair looked toward the foyer. She was squinting her eyes as though she were trying to see him from a long distance away.

The housekeeper shook her head in what seemed to be exasperation. "Come on in, Father," she said. "I don't see how it could hurt." She walked to the kitchen, grabbed a bottle, and made her way up the stairs as the baby wailed on.

Roy ambled carefully into the sitting room and

kept a good distance from the woman. He didn't want to startle her.

"Dr. Sutton, I'm Roy Summerall, the new rector at St. Michael's." He reached out his hand, but she didn't move to shake it, so he put it gently down at his side. He tried to meet her eyes. "I just came by to see about you."

The woman continued to stare at him through an invisible haze. He figured she was on some kind of medication. There must be something mental going on, and he didn't want to press her or upset her.

"May I pray with you?" he asked.

She looked down and nodded her head slowly.

"Thank you," he said. He didn't want to lay hands on her like he usually did with someone who was ill, so he stood right where he was, lifted out his hands, and uttered, "Come, Holy Spirit. Be present in this home. Take care of Dr. Sutton and her family. Heal any ailment that exists. Flood her heart with your love."

As he uttered the words, he watched her almost go limp for a moment, and he was afraid she might fall forward out of her chair. He stepped closer so he could catch her if need be. But in a few moments, she sat back up and squinted at him again.

Before long, the housekeeper came downstairs with a red-cheeked baby girl who gave him a wide, gummy smile. His heart did a flip. Oh, he wanted another baby. Was there anything like having one? When the child reached for him, the housekeeper said, "You can hold her." He took her in his arms as the woman went over to Dr. Sutton with a glass of water and a pill.

When the baby started to fuss, the housekeeper said, "See if she'll burp." And she put a cloth on his shoulder and he patted the child's back as he walked back and forth in the foyer admiring all of the family photos.

Suddenly he saw a picture of three little girls, arm in arm on a bench at The Battery and he recognized the redhead at once. It was Anne Brumley who had spent her summers in this home. Then he scanned the other pictures on the wall and found a recent image of Anne, her long wavy hair draped across her shoulders with a big smile and her arm around Dr. Sutton and another woman.

Then he heard, in the distance, the tenor bell being rung up in preparation for the two forty-five-minute peals that would both precede and follow his installation.

He prayed a blessing over the child, then walked into the kitchen where the housekeeper was pulling a roast out of the oven. "I've got a service soon. Mind if I give her back to you?"

"Yes, sir." She opened her arms.

He looked toward the living room and back

again. "I hope you all will call on me if I can help in any way."

The housekeeper nodded. "I'll let Mr. Drew know you came by."

"Thank you," he said. He kissed the baby on the forehead and said good-bye to Dr. Sutton, who seemed to have fallen asleep upright in the chair, though her eyes weren't completely closed.

The installation was glorious. The bishop, dressed in his long, heavy robe and high hat and shepherd's crook, gave a stirring homily about the mystery of grace, and the church presented Roy with a variety of symbolic gifts for his ministry, including an antique key, a silver chalice, a miniature bell attached to a pulley, and a King James Bible that had been handed down by each of the preceding rectors dating back to 1751.

Roy's mama was all dressed up for the ceremony in a purple lacy cocktail dress from the Myrtle Beach Outlet Mall, and Rose looked like an angel herself in a pale pink dress with puffy sleeves and a wide sash, which Ms. B. informed him was made of something called raw silk. And Ms. B. had pulled Rose's hair back in a bun, into which she had tucked some pink rosebuds. Roy felt a lump in his throat when he saw those roses in her shiny black hair.

Even Chick wore a coat and tie for the occasion.

He and Nikki and the kids had made the trip, and his boys looked terribly uncomfortable in the clip-on ties and polyester oxford shirts their granny had bought them at the Marshall's in Darlington.

Skeeter and Candy Mills were there, too, their faces and hair all fixed up, sporting the jewelry they only wore at Christmas and Easter time. They both gave him a warm embrace. And Candy presented Ms. B. with some bright orange cupcakes from the Piggly Wiggly with candy corn on top. The elderly lady graciously accepted the contribution and immediately moved them from their plastic container to an ornate silver tray. She put them front and center on the sweets table alongside the petits fours and lemon squares and slices of hummingbird cake.

Roy stood in a receiving line for over an hour with Rose by his side and Mama nearby in case the little girl grew weary of shaking hands. She didn't. She wanted to know everyone's name, and he was surprised how she looked each person in the eye, smiled a genuine smile, and answered their rote questions about her age and grade.

The bishop was the last in line, and he embraced Roy hard and said, "This is good, son. Very good."

"I sure hope so," Roy said.

The bishop grabbed the young priest's bum right shoulder and looked him in the eye. He pounded the staff once on the linoleum floor and nodded hard. Then he turned around and headed for the beef tenderloin at the end of the table.

Roy could hear the bells as the ringers continued to change ring from the steeple for a good hour after the installation, and when they finally came down to the parish hall to partake of the festivities, he looked around for the beautiful redhead, but she was nowhere to be seen.

After the last guest left, his mama took Rose home to bed and then Roy helped Samuel, the sexton, break down the tables. When the last chair was stacked, he shook Samuel's hand, then walked into the kitchen where Ms. B. and her team were putting all the leftovers in plastic containers and pulled her aside.

"Ms. B., do you know Anne Brumley?"

The lady raised her trim eyebrows and smiled. "Yes, I do." She clamped down the top of a container full of cheese straws. "She's a lovely lady. A bit tall, but that wouldn't bother someone as secure in their skin as you."

He felt his cheeks redden. "I didn't mean…"

The blush gave him away. Ms. B. cocked her head and stacked the container on top of a box of finger sandwiches. "Well, that might be good because Anne Brumley is in England."

"What?"

"She did an exchange program through a bell

ringer association, and she's over there for some time, I believe."

"Oh," he said. He tried not to look too disappointed. He washed his hands and started loading two silver trays full of lemon squares into plastic containers.

After he helped Ms. B. and the worker bees clean the dishes (in spite of their passionate pleas that he not clean up after his own party), he ambled home and found Mama and Rose asleep on her Barbie bed and Donny sawing logs on the sofa in the den with ESPN replaying the NASCAR Talladega race. (Tony Stewart had won after Regan Smith was penalized for his pass.)

When Roy climbed into bed, he looked out of his window at the steeple and the bell tower. It was a clear night and a nearly full moon was hanging beyond the steeple, and he imagined it illuminating the choppy water of the harbor just two blocks away.

It had been a beautiful occasion. So much work on his behalf. He felt both thankful and unworthy. Yet despite Ms. B.'s tireless efforts and the bishop's stalwart support and the presence of his close-knit family filling up his big house with the sound of their snoozes and snores, he felt alone in this world. Alone like he did in those dark days after he had laid Jean Lee's body into the earth. Alone like John the Baptist must have felt after Herod had imprisoned him. Roy remembered when John sent word to Christ, saying, "Are you really the One? Or should we expect another?" It was tough to trust in God's plan for your life when the black void of loneliness engulfed you. When you longed for someone to reach out and hold you, to rest her head against your wide chest and relax in a moment of solace and contentment. Roy braced himself for the awful self-pity that usually followed moments like this. In an effort to stave it off, he put his head in his hands and prayed, "Comfort me. Comfort me, Lord Jesus."

A few days later, he found a note in his box and recognized Ms. B.'s writing. It simply read:

Miss Anne Brumley
c/o The Central Council of Church Bell Ringers
35 A High Street
Andover, Hampshire County
SP10 1LJ United Kingdom
abrumley@gmail.com

For a few days he kept the little piece of paper tucked in his Bible. He wondered what to do. Should he write? Or e-mail? Should he contact her at all? He prayed, but he did not receive any sort of confirmation, so he didn't do a thing.

* * *

Alpha started the following week and it was just the staff and the vestry minus Heyward, who had been missing in action for everything except a brief appearance at the installation. Even one of the people who had signed up after his first sermon dropped away, citing a work conflict. The first session was titled "Who is God?" and Nicky Gumbel went to work answering this question on the video screen as Roy and Ms. B. served up fresh-baked flounder with grits and sliced tomatoes to the participants.

Ms. B. seemed discouraged as well that night. When they were washing dishes, she said, "Roy, I think you ought to include a description of Alpha in your next sermon and see if we can get more people for next week. I can think of a good hundred people that need to be here."

He took the Pyrex dish she handed him and began to dry it. "I sense that too."

"Of course you do." She dipped a pair of salad tongs into the soapy water and he watched three bubbles fly up into the air and thought of Rose.

His right shoulder ached and he rubbed it for a moment. "You know, I worry sometimes, Ms. B. That I don't understand these folks too well. I'm country come to town. We both know that. But I think I'm supposed to be here—"

"I know you are." She handed him the tongs.

"Well, how do you think I can reach these folks? I mean, what makes them tick?"

She turned for a moment and faced him head-on. "Why don't you ask them?"

Roy blinked hard and wondered how to go about that. The thought occurred to him—the Advent prayers. He had once attended a church in seminary where the priest prayed for every member and their specific needs during Advent. Why couldn't he do that? He would pass out the cards over the next few Sundays and ask folks to put their specific requests down.

"Wow." He smiled at Ms. B. who had already piled three trays beside him by the time he came to. "You sure are a wise woman."

"Lady." She winked at him and her twinkly gray eyes smiled.

"Yes, ma'am," he said. "Don't ever stop correcting me."

The following week when Roy picked Rose up from school, she dissolved into tears in the back seat of his truck before the teacher had even closed the door.

"What's wrong, baby?" She had been adjusting to her new life so beautifully. She'd made friends at school and church and had so many invitations to parties and play dates that he could hardly keep up.

He pulled over just beyond the pickup line. Then he got out and moved to the backseat beside her, where he took her in his arms. "What in the world is wrong, Rosebud?" He rubbed her bony little back. "Tell me, now."

He noticed a bright yellow piece of paper that she had crumbled in her hand. She opened it up for him to see. It read:

> *Margaret is turning seven*
> *Hooray! Hoorah! Yippee!*
> *And she'd like you to come*
> *To a Mother-Daughter tea!*
> *Wear your fancy dress*
> *And bring your Mom along.*
> *We'll provide the white gloves*
> *And tea cakes and song.*
> *October 22, 2008*
> *4 pm*
> *124 Tradd Street*
> *RSVP to Margaret's Mom at 224-6741*

When he finished reading the invitation, he looked over to Rose, who was staring at him with a kind of righteous fury in her eyes.

"Oh, honey," he said. "It'll be okay. We could ask Granny to come down for this, or I bet Ms. B. would be downright delighted to take you."

She bit her lip and her round chin puckered as the tears came again.

"I don't want Granny or Ms. B!"

He pulled a strand of dark hair out of her eyes. "I could take you then. Wouldn't that be neat?"

"No!" She looked out through the back window as one smiling, well-dressed mother after another picked up a child from the carpool line.

Then she turned back to him. "I want a mother!"

Roy fell back against the seat.

She pounded him on his arm. Hard. "I wish you would find one. And so does Granny."

He leaned his head back against the headrest. He could feel her staring him down.

"I've been praying about this, sweetie."

"I'm tired of you praying, Daddy." She sat up until he looked at her. "I want you to do something about it!"

He furrowed his thick dark eyebrows and pulled her close to him.

"Please, Daddy!" She relaxed into his arms and whispered. "Please try. I didn't know Mama, except through what you've told me. But I know she'd want me to have a mother."

He pulled back and kissed the top of her head. "You're right," he whispered. "She would."

"So you'll try?" She wouldn't let him out of her gaze.

He took a deep breath and swallowed. He nodded, and she unfolded the crumpled paper.

"If you'll really try, then let's ask Ms. B. to take me to this." She handed him the invite. "'Cause I know it doesn't happen that fast."

That night, Roy got out his paper and pen and wrote Anne Brumley a good old-fashioned letter.

Dear Miss Brumley,
I hope this finds you well. Rose and I kept hoping we would cross paths with you again, but I recently learned that you are in England for an extended period of time. How long?

I hope you are enjoying your exchange program. It must be exciting to study with the experts in the field. I often imagine what it might be like to work for Nicky Gumbel or Billy Graham or C.S. Lewis (if he were still alive). Those are my heroes.

Anyway, I hope you don't mind me writing to you. The truth is, I've been thinking about you ever since we met. This may be unmannerly and forward, but I want you to know I'm a widower. I have been for almost six years now, and my daughter and I both feel as though we are missing a vital member of our family. Kind of like a three-legged stool without the second leg. I haven't been

on a date since my wife died, but I think it might be time.

If you're at all interested in getting to know me in that regard, write back and we can begin a dialogue. If you're not, please don't feel bad. And don't feel strange about coming back to St. Michael's after your exchange program.

I'm trusting God in this, and I know he'll bring the right person at the right time for me and for you if you so desire.

Sincerely,

Roy Summerall

That Sunday, he gave a heartfelt sermon based on the passage from Matthew 6:25–33 about how the Lord clothes the lilies of the field and feeds the birds of the air, so be certain in these uncertain times that he will take care of you. How much more valuable are you than the birds and lilies? Much more. He had the ushers hand out little pieces of paper with "Prayer Requests" written on top, and he asked everyone to put down one request from their heart. (They could sign their name, but they didn't have to.) And he would pray for each member of the congregation. Then he concluded with a second invitation to Alpha the following Tuesday.

Two days later, forty-three new people showed

up at the church for the program! Ms. B. quickly
pulled casseroles out of the freezer and sent some
members of her hospitality committee down to
the Harris Teeter to get some salad makings and
bread, and she served a delicious hodgepodge supper that included lasagna, chicken Divan, egg-and-
sausage casserole, and a garden salad.

"It was a loaves-and-fishes miracle!" she said
to Roy after he walked the last surprise partici-
pant to their car. "The freezer just kept producing
Pyrex dishes with frozen meals. I had no idea we
had so many in there!"

Two weeks later he received a letter with unfamiliar handwriting and a stamp of Queen Elizabeth on the front.

He tucked it in his Bible, and after he got Rose
down that night, he unsealed it.

Dear Mr. Summerall,
Thank you for your letter. It was a true surprise, and I must admit—a delightful one.
Yes, I am learning a great deal here. I am
committed to a six-month exchange program where I'll ring many of the oldest bells
around the country with changing ringers
who are masters and even composers of this
rare ministry and art form. Last week I rang
a two-ton tenor bell in a church in Bath! It

nearly lifted me off the floor on the first hand
stroke. Like the change ringers in Charleston, it is a warm, friendly, and eclectic group,
and I am quite at home here. (I spent several
months in London when I was in college, and
I very much enjoy the people and the cul-
ture, from the charming accents to the time
set aside for tea and scones every afternoon!)

As for your request, I must answer, yes; I
would be interested in getting to know you
better. I am single, and I have never been
married. If we're going to be perfectly honest, I might as well say it has been a long-
standing, fervent prayer of mine to meet
someone. It may not be what God has in store
for my life, but I am willing to take another
step down this road if you are. I'll look forward to hearing from you.
Sincerely,
Anne Brumley (Please call me by my first
name from now on. Also, in the interest of
time, I am happy to receive e-mails as well.
I'm at abrumley@gmail.com)

Doggone if his heart didn't skip a beat when
he read and reread the letter! After the third time,
he immediately thanked God and sat down at his
computer where he spent the next hour typing
Anne Brumley an e-mail, telling her whatever

popped in his mind about him, his family, and his ministry. It was ten paragraphs by the time he pressed Send. He hoped she would write back soon.

Chapter Seventeen

Della
November 25, 2008

"Where's Mr. Pickles, Mama?" Cozy asked. She was eagerly packing her overnight bag with her favorite pajamas and her toothbrush and her stuffed lobster that reminded her of one of her daddy's sculptures.

Cozy was becoming a good reader, and she couldn't wait to show her grandfather. She was only going for three nights, but she'd packed four of *The Magic Tree House* books she checked out at the library and one of the *Frog and Toad* books that she had read ten times over the last twenty-four hours.

It was the Tuesday before Thanksgiving and tomorrow Della would drive Cozy halfway to the upstate, where she'd meet her Pop Pop and her step-grandmother, who simply liked to be called

Sue, and they'd head on back to Pop Pop's house at the foot of the Blue Ridge Mountains where they'd build a fire and roast marshmallows right in the living room.

Della came in with Mr. Pickles, the well-worn blanket Cozy had slept with since she was an infant. Over the last couple of years, Della had patched up two of the blanket's rips with Nana's old sewing machine. One of the patches looked like Pac Man or the main character of Shel Silverstein's story *The Missing Piece*. The other one looked like a pickle—a rectangle with two rounded edges at the top left side of the blanket.

"Do you think you're getting a little old for Mr. Pickles?" Della tossed the blanket to Cozy, who embraced it, found the pickle-shaped spot, and rubbed it against her cheek.

"Never!"

Della had reservations about sending Cozy to her dad's for the holiday. She'd had some tough run-ins with her stepmother growing up, but Sue seemed to have mellowed over the years, and Della's daddy, a gentle (if not timid) soul, was absolutely crazy about Cozy. This would be the second year Cozy had begged to let her go. Last year Della agreed, because she had been desperate to have a little time to meet her book deadline. And it all went well. This year, she planned to meet Todd Jervey at The Woodlands, a five-star inn tucked away in the forest outside of Summerville where they would consummate what had started with a lunch date at Blend a few months ago. Peter would be working double shifts at the carriage company. This was a busy tourism week in Charleston, and Della had told him she'd received a scholarship to a writer's retreat where she could finish the final chapters of her novel, which was due December 1st.

"Okay," he'd said last week when she spelled out the plan. "After work on Thanksgiving, I guess I'll drive over to see my parents in McClellanville." He shook his head and looked at Cozy. "Man, what a lonely holiday."

His words had bothered Cozy so much that on Sunday she set the table with her parents' wedding china and begged Della to cook a turkey breast. Thankfully, Della found one on special at the Piggly Wiggly, and she baked it and made some rice and gravy, and they ate when Peter came home around eight that evening.

"See, Daddy," Cozy had said. "We're just having our dinner early. That's all."

Lish's Thanksgiving invitation to Della's family had been retracted a couple of weeks ago. After a parent at school told Della what had happened in church, Della went by 18 Legare the very next afternoon to see about her cousin. Just as she was pulling up, Drew intercepted her in the driveway and nearly kept her out.

"Della," he said. "I know you mean well, but Lish needs some time to herself right now. She's making strides every day, and the more rest she has, the better."

"I haven't seen her in almost two months." Della crossed her thin arms and looked him fiercely in the eye. "She's my family, Drew. Can't I lay eyes on her?"

Just then Mary Jane and Andrew had come barreling out of the house. They'd run up to Della and squeezed her tight. She had lifted both of them up in her arms and spun them around.

"Where's Cozy?" Andrew said. He peered behind her toward her old car.

"She's on a play date with one of her classmates." She brushed a thick dark curl out of Andrew's eye. "I have to pick her up in a little while. I just came by to check in on your mama." She bent down and rested her hands on her knees so that she was eye to eye with her nephew. "How's she doing?"

Andrew shrugged. "She's fine." Drew came up behind him and grabbed his shoulder.

Mary Jane tugged at Della's hand. "Did you know we're moving, Cousin Del?"

"No," she said, looking back to Drew.

Mary Jane grinned, happy to be the one to divulge the big news. "Yes, we're moving to Atlanta, Georgia…right, Daddy?"

Della squinted her eyes. She knew Lish didn't want to move. She tried not to sound devastated. "When?"

Just then she heard the screech of the big oak door. Lish walked out slowly with a half smile on her face. "Hi, Della," she said before clutching the rail and moving slowly down the steps, one pale bare foot at a time.

Della went to her cousin and embraced her. Her hair smelled like something sweet and clean, like a ripe apple, and her face was made up even though she was still in her nightgown. "I'm glad to see you."

Della pulled back and searched her cousin's eyes. They seemed more dull than usual, or maybe it was serene. She couldn't quite place the look.

"Come in," Lish said. "Have some tea."

The house was immaculate except for a small corner of the room where Andrew was building something narrow and tall with a zillion little Lego pieces. The air smelled of roasting chicken and Febreze and that old musty house stench.

Lish wore a subdued smile as she watched the children play with the Legos. Mary Jane was trying to feed one of the small black blocks to her Madame Alexander doll, the one dressed up like

Little Red Riding Hood, while Andrew added another layer to his tower.

Within minutes Rosetta brought Della a cup of hot tea on a tray with a bowl full of sugar and a pitcher of cream. Drew sat down on the ottoman opposite them and showed Della the article in *The Atlanta Journal-Constitution* about his MUSC research team moving to the CDC.

Della studied Lish, who maintained her dull smile and nodded her head. She turned to Della for a moment. "Isn't it exciting?" she said.

Della took a sip of tea. It was hot, and she winced. "Yes." She put the teacup back in its delicate saucer. "And very unexpected."

Lish raised her eyebrows as the baby began to cry somewhere upstairs. "We'll be back in a few years. Right, Drew?"

He laced his hands together and nodded. "Yep. We just couldn't pass this opportunity up."

Della watched Rosetta carry a bottle upstairs. She repositioned herself on the couch and addressed Lish. "When will you go?"

"I have to be there December first," Drew said. He reached for the article and put it on the bookshelf. "Lish and the kids will come in the spring."

Della looked at Lish, who now seemed weary as she studied her fingers with her eyes half open. She tilted her head slowly to the side as if what Drew said was something she needed to ponder in order to accomplish. She swallowed hard and looked at him. "That's right."

They sat there and made small talk for twenty minutes or so before Della stood and said, "Well, I've got to pick Cozy up. Will you walk me to my car, Lish?"

Drew cleared his throat, and Lish slowly stood and followed Della to the car.

When they made it down the stairs and out into the driveway, Della turned to her, squeezed her hand, and said, "Are you really okay?"

Lish nodded. Her eyes seemed clouded. Like an invisible film was over them. She looked beyond Della at something in the street. "It's taken longer than I thought, but I'm getting there."

Then she turned back to Della with the faintest glint in her eye. "These pills make me feel sluggish. That's the tough part." She nodded as if she was listening to a reassuring voice in her mind. "But I'll get to taper off of them soon."

Della hugged Lish and put her lips to her ear. "You get in touch with me if you need anything, okay?" She squeezed her even tighter. "I'm here for you like always."

Lish pulled back carefully, but she held onto Della's arms as if she needed them for balance. Then she looked down at her bare feet. "I don't think I can manage Thanksgiving this year." She looked back up to Della. "Would it be too awful if I took back the invitation?"

Della chuckled. "No, of course not. Don't give it a second thought." She patted her cousin's arm and waited for her to say more. They stood this way for several minutes, with Lish steadying herself by holding on tight to Della's arms. When Drew walked out on the piazza and started to pace, Della leaned in again and kissed Lish's cheek. "We'll talk more soon."

Then she let go of her arms, climbed in her old car, and drove out of the driveway wondering how she could see Lish again, in private. She would wait until Drew moved in a few weeks. Then she'd be able to get the full scoop and assess her cousin's condition.

When she turned onto Meeting Street and spotted a bell ringer in vestments heading into St. Michael's for practice, she was overcome by a sense of grief. She missed Anne (though Della was the very one who had pushed her to go), and now Lish was leaving in a few short months. There would be no more Saturday get-togethers with their tightknit threesome, no more walks along the beach, no more Nana's house or the loquat tree to remember their shared childhood. Her cousins were her best friends. They kept her on track. They were like sisters and mothers all rolled into one, and now they both seemed very far way. It was a sad and awful realization (their absence in her daily life), and it would take a long time for her to get over this painful change.

That was three weeks ago, and Della had e-mailed and called Lish every few days with no response. (She was counting down the days until Drew took off so she could have a real conversation with her.) Truth was, she had enough on her plate right now. She was ready to seal this deal with Todd and get her life on a new path.

She worried about Peter, but she knew this was best for him. He loathed driving the carriages, and she saw on his bureau the other day a schedule for an electrical engineering course he had signed up for at Trident Technical College. And his father, a big, lovable salty dog from McClellanville, had invited him to work with him on the shrimp boat next summer.

"I'm open," Della had heard Peter say. "We've got to find a way to bring in more income, Dad."

An incident last week reaffirmed Della's decision to solidify her new relationship with Todd. It had to do with a school field trip they had to tell Cozy they couldn't afford. The Pinckney School's science teacher was coordinating an optional (but strongly encouraged) "Sea Turtle Camp" at Kiawah Island during the first weekend in December. It involved spending two nights at the swanky beach-front inn, a tour of the sea turtle hospital, and a private viewing of a release of a fully rehabilitated sea turtle into the ocean.

Nearly all of Cozy's classmates had signed up. It cost $550 and there was no way they could swing it. Della dreaded having to tell her daughter. She had tried to find a way to make it work, but Peter said, "We can't, Della. We can hardly make the mortgage payment this month. Let me talk to her."

Della stood in the doorway of Cozy's room as Peter walked over to where the little girl was on her belly on her bed reading *Merry Christmas, Amelia Bedelia*.

"Sweetheart." Peter took a seat on her bed.

She looked up at him and smiled. "Hi, Daddy."

"Mama and I need to talk to you about something."

She sat up, put the "I can read now!" bookmark the school librarian had given her in the center of the book and placed it on her pillow.

"Okay." She rubbed her eyes.

"It's about the turtle camp."

"Oh, yeah," she said. Her eyes widened. "Miss Jackson is organizing it. Most of my class has already signed up."

He stroked his broad chin, then reached out to hold her hand. "The thing is, Cozy, we're not going to be able to send you this year."

The little girl looked to Della, who had said,

"We'll see," when she brought home the brochure in her homework folder a month ago.

She looked down at her book and rubbed her fingers over the plastic shield the library slides on all of their hardcovers. Then she nodded. "Okay."

Peter swallowed, tilted his head, and examined her. He peered out of her window into the dark street and squinted his eyes.

"Hey, but I've got an idea." He looked to Della and winked as Cozy lifted her head.

"What?" the little girl said.

"You remember Daddy's old johnboat?"

"The one in the shed?" She started to bounce gently on the bed.

"Yeah." He patted her knee. "That's the one."

She nodded and wrinkled her brow. "It's got a hole in it."

"Yeah, but I think I can patch it up with a little fancy metal work." He put his forehead next to hers. "What do you say I take the day off next Saturday, and you and me and your mama take a boat ride over to Capers Island? We'll do a little fishing and look for porpoises. Heck, maybe we'll see a sea turtle on our way."

She lifted her little eyebrows, smiled, and looked at Della.

"Yeah!" she said. She turned to him. "Can we pack a picnic?"

"Sure we can." He grinned and turned to his

wife. He swept his hand across his forehead as if to say *Whew* as Cozy stood up and started jumping on the bed.

"Can we bring some fried chicken, Daddy?"

"Yep." He stood on the little bed and bounced with her. "And some chips and soda!"

"Grape soda?" She grabbed his hands, and they jumped together in time.

"Any flavor you want," he said.

She squeezed his waist. "That sounds great, Daddy!"

Della smiled. How easy it was to persuade her little girl at age six. But it might not be so good for her the Monday after the turtle camp when all the girls talked about their experiences and watched the slide show in the lower school courtyard. And it certainly wouldn't be this easy as Cozy grew up and continued to go to play dates in magnificent homes where housekeepers, cooks, and full-time nannies brought in as much in a week as either she or Peter. It wouldn't be near as easy then.

As Della and Cozy drove to the halfway spot just south of Columbia on Interstate 26, Cozy drew on her sketch pad with her colored pencils while Della worried about the "check engine" light that lit up on her dashboard as soon as they hit the highway. Before she had a chance to fret too much, Cozy said, "How about a Binklemeyer story?" Della nodded as the engine icon faded in and out. They told a long and winding Burl and Bernice Binklemeyer story that started with the line "Burl and Bernice Visit Their Crazy Uncle on His Farm in Illinois."

It began with a flight to Chicago that Bernice nearly missed because she refused to board the connecting flight after she discovered that her lucky marble had disappeared from the little zipper pocket on the inside of her carry-on bag.

She'd had it when they ate lunch at Chick-Fil-A in the airport food court, and she didn't want to leave Charlotte International until she found it. Cozy's eyes widened from the backseat when Della described how Burl had to grab Bernice by the back of her sweatshirt and drag her onto the airplane, kicking and screaming.

Then Cozy squealed with joy when the flight attendant helped Bernice double-check her carry-on bag only to discover that there was a small hole in the little zipper pocket and the marble was actually sitting on top of Bernice's carefully folded purple-and-pink-striped underwear.

"That was a close one!" Cozy said as they puttered down the highway. The engine of the old Honda rumbled when it exceeded sixty miles an hour, and Della had had to tell the story at such a loud volume that her throat now ached.

She looked in the rearview mirror at her daughter and smiled. She thought of her own father driving her down the very same highway to meet Nana. How she could hardly sit still on the trip and how when she saw her Nana's white Cadillac parked at the edge of the filling station, her heart would beat wildly inside the little cage of her chest, and she knew that for the next several days she would be held and sung to and walked around the High Battery as the soft, thick harbor air lifted her thin golden hair off of her cheeks.

Della's childhood had been a sad and frustrating one, with the exception of her time with Nana in Charleston. From an early age, she'd had a vision of what a family was supposed to be, and she knew that hers wasn't it. Every time her mama had come to see her, she thought she could persuade her to stay. Secretly, she had hoped her mama would be sorry and her daddy would be, too, and that they might somehow come together and form the kind of family Della read about in her favorite childhood books—the Browns from the Paddington series, the Ingalls from *Little House on the Prairie*, the Quimbys from the Ramona books, and the Johansens from *Number the Stars*.

Now as she pulled off the exit, she watched Cozy scanning the parking lot of the McDonald's until she spotted her Pop Pop and Sue sitting in their burgundy Toyota Prius. Pop Pop started to wave and Sue let out a tight grin as Della's old Honda came rumbling to a stop.

"Let me out! Let me out!" Cozy called, and as soon as Della opened the door, Cozy bounded into her Pop Pop's arms. "I can read now!" she said. "I brought four books, and I can read them all to you while we roast marshmallows."

He held her tight and rocked her back and forth. "That sounds great, pumpkin."

Sue gave Della the once-over, then looked at the old car. "That thing is a wonder, isn't it? Who'd have thought it would still be running after twenty years?"

"Hi, Sue," Della said. She squinted her eyes and noted her stepmother's ever-widening midsection paunch. "You look great."

Sue cocked her head and crossed her arms. Just before she sent a sharp comment back, Cozy leapt into her arms and she softened a little. She returned Cozy's embrace, then let her gently down before straightening out her pressed oxford blouse.

Della's daddy kissed her on her forehead. "How are you doing, sweetie?"

He didn't ask her about her writing. It was a subject they steered clear of around Sue, who was still angry about Della's first book, a coming-of-age novel featuring a grumpy stepmother as one of the primary antagonists. Even Della had to admit (only to herself, of course) that the character did bear a striking resemblance.

"I'm all right." She tousled Cozy's hair. "I'm going to miss this little girl, though. We're never apart for three whole nights, are we?"

Cozy flapped her away. "Oh, Mama, we were last year, remember?"

Della smiled. She tapped her finger on her chin as if to look back in time. "I guess you're right." She leaned over and kissed her daughter on the forehead. "We were, and I survived, somehow."

Cozy giggled and hugged her mama.

"Well, we'll see you Saturday?" her father said. "Same place, same time?" He took Cozy by the hand, and she dragged him toward the car.

"Yeah," Della said. She handed Sue the suitcase and Mr. Pickles and the stuffed lobster.

"Be a good girl," she called to Cozy, who was already being buckled into the back seat of her Pop Pop's car.

"Have you heard of The Magic Tree House series?" she heard her daughter ask.

When Della got home, she packed her own overnight bag, including a black silk dress she'd had since college and a faux silk nightie she bought at Target last week. Tonight she would clean the house and wash the linens, and then in the morning she'd head to the library where she'd pound out the last chapter of her book before meeting Todd at The Woodlands in the afternoon.

She was at the point where she had no idea if her book was any good or not. Her chapters were getting longer as she had to tie up so many loose ends, and she didn't even get to some of the places she'd hoped to go after the murder—the courtroom, the prison, the congressional floor where they would introduce new legislation regarding stalking and law enforcement-to-victim notification before a stalker was released from prison. The story had a lot of potential, but she just couldn't flesh it all out and make her deadline. It looked like it would end with the inevitable murder in the last chapter—a pretty morose conclusion, even by her standards.

When Peter came home in his Confederate uniform, his walkie talkie still clipped on the outside of his right pocket, he asked, "Coz get off all right?"

"Yeah," she said. He examined her suitcase in the hall. "And where are you off to?"

Didn't she tell him this? She took a deep breath. "A writing retreat, remember? I'm going to finish the book there."

He nodded. "We can afford that?"

"It's free." Her voice was flat, even spiteful. She didn't like how she talked to him, but it was hard for her to stop herself. "I applied and was accepted, remember?" She raised her eyebrow, turned back to the bathroom, and poured the Food Lion version of Comet into the rusting toilet bowl.

He took off his cap and tossed it on the kitchen table. "I'm beat." He pulled a wad of cash out of his pocket and deposited it beside his cap. "Take what you need for your trip."

Then he grabbed a beer and headed out to the back steps, where he surveyed the backyard and shed. He'd been patching up the johnboat for days now. He walked over to it, lifted the tarp off of the rust hole, and lit his blowtorch.

As she scrubbed the grime off of the old toilet bowl, she thought back to her conversation with Todd a few weeks ago.

"Are you sure about this?" he'd said. They were at Kudu Coffee House, looking at the room choices of The Woodlands online. They had only managed to see each other for small chunks of time since they'd reconnected. Both of their schedules were crowded. They'd managed a lunch break here and a walk around the Med U. there, but that was it. This would be the first time they would be alone together for several hours at a time, not to mention a whole night.

He had turned to her. She knew he wasn't asking about the accommodations. He was asking about their going away together. It was a big step. One you couldn't take back.

She had felt as if she was on autopilot. The decision had been made months ago, and there was no need to rethink it again. Her child was in need, her biological clock was ticking, and she and Peter were barely scraping by. She gently tapped his foot with her own, studied the rim of his glasses before looking him in the eye. "Very," she had said. He had leaned forward and discreetly squeezed her knee one quick time.

As she finished her last chapter, she didn't have the sense of relief she usually had at the close of a novel. The book didn't feel right in so many ways, but she had no time (not to mention any idea) of how to change it. She headed out of the library parking lot, into the Honda, and out to The Woodlands. Todd, who was on his way back from a group home in rural Georgia where he was conducting one of his research studies, would meet her there.

As she drove down I-26 and then through Summerville, she thought of the last time she'd made a trip out to The Woodlands. It was the weekend that Todd proposed to her more than a decade ago. They'd had dinner at the award-winning restaurant in the inn and then on a walk through the back gardens, he'd gotten down on his knee and opened a small, black velvet box containing a large sapphire flanked by two diamonds set in platinum.

She had felt like an actress in a play that day. She had gasped, cupped her hand around her mouth, and presented her left hand just like she had seen so many other women do in movies and television shows and even in a few cheesy beach reads she'd succumbed to during her teenage summers.

"Yes," she'd said, and as he slid the ring on her finger, a bee stung her ankle. "Ouch!" She jumped back and reached toward her sandal. She'd mistaken the sting for a bad omen. Looking back now, she chuckled at her immaturity. It was just a bee sting. Why did she have to analyze everything so much?

Of course, she would never say that she regretted marrying Peter. Too much good had come out of their union. And they had given it their all; it just wasn't enough. They had tried to make it, and the world seemed stacked against them. It was that simple.

Now as she drove slowly down the winding roads and then the dirt path that cut through the pine trees toward the inn, she spotted Todd's car— the sporty BMW convertible at the edge of The Woodlands' circular driveway. There was a space right next to him, and she pulled into it and cut off the engine.

She glanced up at the grand house and was sur-

prised to see him, his back turned to her. He was
perched on the railing of the upstairs porch of the
suite they had picked out together. He was looking
out over the back garden as he pinched the crystal
stem of a full glass of red wine.

Now she examined him, his tall, thin frame
repositioning itself on the railing, his strawberry
blondish/gray hair and his freckled neck with the
crisscross of wrinkles from age and sun exposure
now forming across it. He adjusted his posture as
if his mother has just scolded him and breathed
slowly in and out. Then he brought the glass of
wine to his lips.

Della's palms were sweaty and her heart was
beating fast. She watched a young couple come
out of the front door hand in hand and noticed a
churning in the pit of her stomach. The couple slid
into their sleek car and drove off.

Now Della examined her dank palms and
rubbed them on the side of her blue jean skirt. Was
she nervous? Guilty? Fearful? *Yes*, she thought. *All
of the above*. It was like the moment before she
and her cousins dared one another to jump off of
the highest limb of the loquat tree in Nana's backyard. Something in her said, *Don't think, just do
it*, and she knew this was what she should do now.
*Don't think, just put one foot in front of the other
and walk up to that suite, and in no time you'll*

*land on the soft ground of Nana's garden with-
out a scratch.*

She reached into her backseat and pulled out her
suitcase. Below it, she noticed a crumpled piece of
paper from Cozy's sketch pad. She reached for it,
opened it up, and took in what her daughter had
drawn on the way to meet her grandfather.

It was a picture of Cozy and Peter and Della
in the patched-up johnboat, holding hands, with
a sea turtle and several small fish swimming in
the water beneath the boat. There were clouds, a
couple of pelicans, and a bright yellow heart directly above the boat with rays of light surrounding it as if the heart was the sun. On the back of
the picture she had written, "Famly bote tip by
Cozy Limehouse."

Della looked at the words and then back at the
picture. In it, she had a brick-red smile shaped like
a crescent moon that took up most of her face. And
so did Peter. This was how Cozy saw her parents,
or how she wanted to see them anyway. And there
was Cozy herself, right in between her mom and
dad with a pink round O for a mouth and a bubble
above her that read, "Look! A trtle!"

Della didn't know how long she stared at the
wide smiles on her face and Peter's, her heart racing, her palms sweating.

Suddenly she felt a gentle squeeze on her shoulder and then a light peck at her neck. She turned

around and looked up at Todd. She folded the picture over.

"You okay?" He smiled gently down on her.

"No." She shook her head. She tucked the paper in the outside pocket of her suitcase and looked up to him. "I can't do this, Todd."

He studied her face for whole seconds. Then he squinted his eyes and let out a muffled groan, and she knew that he fully comprehended what she was saying. "Not again, Della."

"I'm sorry," she said. "I've had this thing all wrong." She leaned back against the car and crossed her arms. "This isn't what I want, and it's not what's best for my family. Or for you, for that matter."

He took a step back and bit his lip. Whole minutes passed as he kicked at the gravel between their cars. When he looked up, he said, "I don't like it." He inhaled and exhaled deeply. "But I can't fully understand what it's like to be in your shoes."

She blew a loose strand of hair out of her eyes, rubbed her sweaty palms together. "It wasn't right the first time, and it's not right this time." She took a deep breath. "It will happen for you, Todd. I know it will." He crossed his arms and shrugged his shoulders. "Maybe."

Then she slipped back into the Honda, smirking at the squeaky sound it made when she sat down.

She quickly put the car in reverse and puttered out of the gravelly driveway, leaving dust and her old beau and the five-star inn behind.

It didn't take long for her to find a parking place on the outskirts of the downtown market just off Hassell Street. She jumped out of the car and raced over the cobblestones with just her keys in her hand until she reached the center of the market, where she immediately spotted Peter sitting in an empty carriage in front of the basket weavers, waiting for his turn to load up.

He didn't notice Della coming up behind his carriage as he lifted the cap off of his head and wiped his sweaty brow with his forearm. He looked around and nodded at the passers-by. Then he leaned forward to straighten the reins.

"Welcome aboard," he said without turning around as he reached out his hand.

She put her hand in his and let him pull her up onto the carriage, where she took her seat beside him as he slowly turned around.

"Hey." He scratched his chin. "What are you doing here?"

She seized his strong, wide, calloused hands and looked into his dark eyes as the carriage in front of him loaded up and pulled out into North Market Street.

"I haven't been gypped." She felt the lump in her throat rising. "I haven't been gypped at all,

Peter." She tried to hold back the tears. "But *you* have."

He watched the wetness form in her eyes.

She swallowed. "I've gypped you countless times, and you know it." She wiped her cheek with the heel of her hand. "I don't deserve you, but I honestly want to make this work. And I can start by treating you the way you deserve to be treated." She leaned back and took a deep breath. "I hope you'll let me make it up to you, Peter."

A half grin formed across his face. Then his eyes softened, and he pulled her close with all of his might. She squeezed his broad chest and rested her head in the nook of his neck. He smelled like Peter—a combination of metal, perspiration, and sunscreen. It was the smell of her husband. The man she loved. The man she had married and promised to honor.

She pulled back and looked into his eyes. "Thank you."

He reached up and rubbed her cheek with his warm hand. "It's been tough on you, Della. I know it's been tough. But we're going to get through this rough spot. We're going to make it, and we're going to add to our brood and do the best we can for them. I promise."

He pulled her to him. "Stick with me, okay? Trust me."

She cherished the feel of him in her arms. She nodded into his chest. "I will."

He lifted up her face and kissed her until some older gentleman ambling by tapped the side of the carriage and said, "Take that gal for her own private tour."

"Great idea, sir," Peter said. He lifted the reins of his horse and pulled out, heading into North Market and turning left on Church Street.

Della stood up beside him, and he put his arm tightly around her hips. Then he took a right onto Cumberland and a left onto Meeting Street and guided the horse by The Wells Gallery, where they had met for the first time, and then up Queen Street and down King to the High Battery where he had leaned in to kiss her the very next night after watching the reflection of the moonlight on the harbor. They took a left on East Bay Street and another left on Broad and drove right by St. Michael's Episcopal Church at the center of the city, where they'd exchanged their vows on a temperate October afternoon more than nine years ago as the old bells pealed and the sun blazed a reddish pink before setting behind the steeples and slanted chimneys and slate rooftops of the Holy City they loved.

Chapter Eighteen

Lish
December 12, 2008

Lish and Drew had had a friend in residency who took his life just two months after he was married. He had been folding laundry and left a note to his wife on top of the dryer that simply read, "Don't go in the basement." When she came home from work, the dryer was still warm and their towels were neatly folded on the kitchen table. She had taken one look at the note and then cautiously made her way down the basement, where she found him hanging from a rafter with a noose around his neck.

Lish couldn't say she'd thought anything through. But on the Friday after Drew moved to Atlanta, she dropped the children off at school, parked her car at the foot of the new Cooper River Bridge, and walked steadily toward the top. It was mid-morning and there were usually dozens of people jogging across the bridge's pedestrian path this time of day. But it was a gray and foggy day with a light rain spitting on Lish's face, and she didn't see any pedestrians ahead. She was not in any kind of sport attire. Just jeans, an MUSC sweatshirt, and some dark green rain boots. There was no note. No phone call. Just the unbearable thumping in her head that had returned now that she'd lowered her Ativan dose again.

Suddenly a lone cyclist came her way. He was in a helmet and a spandex body suit with his biking shoes clipped to his pedals. She noted the flash of him out of her peripheral vision and the hiss of his wheels on the wet walkway beside her.

Her eyes were on the crest of the bridge, which stood at an impressive 575 feet high, and she was steadily making her way toward it. One foot in front of the other and soon she'd have gone half a mile toward the top as the trucks and station wagons and school buses whizzed by on the other side of the pedestrian walkway, creating a brisk wind and a steady rumble that could be felt beneath her feet as she stepped forward.

When she arrived at the crest, she didn't hesitate. She simply turned and reached toward the top of the tall metal railing where she gripped the wet edge and pulled herself up. The railing was slick and it was hard for her to keep her footing, but after a couple of tries she managed to reach the top. She leaned over the railing in a pike position and just as she swung her right leg over the side, something clutched her left ankle and yanked her firmly down to the ground, where her whole left side hit the wet concrete with a painfully hard thwack.

She came to in the back of an ambulance barreling down the bridge toward the city. She was sitting up on a gurney with her hands behind her back. She ached when she tried to move them and realized that she was handcuffed. On her left a police officer watched her every move, and on her right a paramedic reached out to steady the bandage across the side of her head. As she turned toward him, her skull ached. It pounded all over instead of just at the top. She tasted the metal tang of blood in her mouth and wondered in all earnestness, *What am I doing here?*

She couldn't account for this day. She didn't remember waking up, dressing the children, dropping them off at school. She had no idea that she had walked to the top of the bridge and climbed halfway over the rail before a security guard who was driving to Wal-Mart to work the day shift jerked his car into Park, jumped over the walkway, and pulled her down.

When they arrived at MUSC, the paramedics wheeled her into the emergency room where a young resident stitched up the left side of her head. She opened her eyes for a moment, but all she could see was the latex glove on the doctor's hand as he sewed the skin above her left temple back together.

She didn't know how long she lay in the dark room with the curtain drawn. She heard the static and muffled voices from the walkie talkies of the police officers and paramedics, and she heard a wail from time to time from a baby in the waiting room.

All she could do was breathe in and out. It was the only thing she was capable of, and she felt it might be that way indefinitely.

When the curtain was drawn back she made out the silhouette of Dr. Sharon Swan, who walked slowly toward her bedside.

Lish found her voice before the questions began. It was gravelly, but she managed to form the words. "Yes, I know where I am, Sharon." She swallowed and a pain shot through the left side of her body. "But I don't know why I'm here."

Lish tugged at the handcuffs. A pain shot up her left shoulder. She looked up at the hazy image of her old classmate and whispered, "Do you?"

Dr. Swan gave her a sympathetic nod and then turned to say something to the police officer who immediately unlocked the handcuffs.

Lish massaged her aching wrists. She couldn't yet see the red ring the handcuffs had formed around them, but she could feel it. "Why am I here?" she said.

Dr. Swan gently took Lish's hands and leaned in. "Lish, you tried to jump off the Cooper River Bridge this morning."

Her heart pounded; she could feel it in her throat and her ears. She vaguely recalled walking up the bridge in the rain, but that was all. Now her teeth chattered, and as they did the left side of her jaw pounded with pain.

She tried to find her voice again. "Don't tell Drew. Please don't tell Drew." She swallowed. "I need Dr. Cussler. And I need my sister, Anne, or my cousin Della."

Dr. Swan spoke clearly into Lish's right ear. "I have to admit you to the Institute, Lish. If you comply right off, I don't have to call the judge." She paused and exhaled deeply. "If you don't, I've got to get a court order."

Dr. Swan held a clipboard in front of Lish's face. "Will you sign the admittance papers?"

Lish's hands were swollen. She was not sure she could control them, but she managed to reach up, grasp the pen chained to the board, and sign wherever Dr. Swan pointed.

Then the doctor and the police officer helped

her off of the gurney and into a wheelchair, where they walked her over to President Street.

A young nurse met them at the glass doors. She took the handles of the wheelchair and slowly rolled Lish onto the elevator and up to the psych ward. Once they were in a hospital room, she helped her onto the bed and out of her clothes. Then she draped Lish in a paper gown with no strings or buttons that she could use against herself.

Next she handed her a pill—an antipsychotic, Lish was sure. Before she asked which one, the nurse introduced her to an attendant who would sit and watch her until his shift was over.

"Can I have the phone?" Lish said after swallowing her pill.

The attendant reached for it. "I'd be happy to dial for you," he said.

Lish took a deep breath and nodded. Then she called out Della's number at school.

Chapter Nineteen

Della

At the hospital, Della called her husband and filled him in on what had happened. "Lish wants you and me to drive up to Atlanta and tell Drew in person."

"Okay." Peter exhaled. "Let me tell Joe I need the rest of the day off."

Next Della called Anne in England and had to leave her a message about what was going on. Then she drove over to 18 Legare to see if Rosetta could stay the night with the kids. When she arrived, she found the older woman brooding on the porch swing of the front piazza with Baby Cecilia asleep in the bouncy seat next to her.

"This is my last day, Miss Della." Rosetta stood slowly before placing her hands firmly on her hips. "I told them both in October that I've got a new job come the first of the year." She sucked her teeth. "But I'm not sure neither of them heard me."

Rosetta leaned toward Della. "Now I was going to work one more week, but today I've missed my bus *and* my doctor's appointment, and I'm not happy." She gently pointed her finger toward the bus stop. "It took me three months to get in to see that orthopedist, and I'll have to wait three *more* months thanks to Miss Lish." The woman reached down and picked up her brown velvet hat that was resting on the top of the rocking chair. Then she placed it squarely on her head and whispered in Della's ear, "Something's not right with her. And I can't bear this burden any longer."

"I'm so sorry, Rosetta." Della wasn't sure what to say. She knew she should persuade Rosetta to stay, but she clearly saw that the woman was worn out and fed up. "She's sick, you know. I'm not sure what it is, but it's serious."

Rosetta nodded and pointed to her head. "I do. It's something up here," she whispered again. "But Mr. Drew doesn't. Or he doesn't want to, anyway."

As the city bus pulled up at the corner, Rosetta adjusted her hat. "The school called and said the preacher volunteered to bring them home. I said okay, so they should be here soon." She turned toward the steps and then back to Della. "I pray they get things straightened out around here, but I can't be the one to do it."

Della reached out to give Rosetta a hug. "I understand, Rosetta. Thank you for all you've done. I'm sure no one will ever know how much."

Rosetta nodded. "Tell Miss Lish to mail me a check, all right?"

"Okay."

The older woman reached down and squeezed the baby's round foot. "God bless you, sweet girl." Then she hobbled down the steps toward her bus.

As Della watched Rosetta ride off in one of the front window seats of the big green bus, she spotted a young, barrel-chested man on the sidewalk in a dark suit and a collar, and she wondered which church he belonged to.

The children ran through the gate and toward Della where they both jumped into her arms. She hugged them back, and then Mary Jane pulled away and said, "Mama didn't pick us up today. We were the last ones on the playground, and they called Daddy's old office and nobody came." She pointed to the priest and a pretty little black-headed girl beside him. "Rose's daddy brought us home."

Della looked up at the priest and nodded. Anne had told her a few weeks ago that the priest at St. Michael's had been writing to her and that he had a little girl named Rose. Della said to the children, "I'm sorry you had to wait." She reached out and clasped both of their shoulders. "Your mama wasn't feeling well, kids. But she's going to be okay, in time."

Andrew stepped back and threw a rock he must have been holding all along. It hit the front steps and bounced down into the grass. Della came up behind him and leaned down toward his cheek. She kissed it. "I'm going to help y'all until she gets better. Don't worry, baby."

Then she smiled at the little girl named Rose and back to her niece and nephew and said, "Y'all take Rose in the house, and I'll fix you something sweet after I have a word with her father, okay?"

Andrew's eyes lit up. "Can we have a Popsicle?"

"Sure." Della patted his back. "Get you and the girls a Popsicle and eat it in the backyard."

"All right!" the little boy said. He ran toward the kitchen with Mary Jane and Rose scurrying behind him.

Della looked at the man. He had warm brown eyes with long dark lashes, and he looked a little uncomfortable in his suit and collar. Kind of like a weight lifter in a tuxedo one size too small.

"I'm Della Limehouse." She shook his hand. "Have you been corresponding with my cousin Anne?"

He smiled and nodded. "That's me. Roy Summerall. Call me Roy."

She put her hands on her hips and shook her

head. "Well, I can't believe it. Maybe Anne heard right after all."

"I'm sorry?" He had a confused look on his face.

She shook her head and waved him off. "Nothing, nothing. It's been a tough day, and I'm a little fuzzy right now."

"I hope everything is okay with Dr. Sutton," he said.

She looked up at him and though she had her frustrations with God, she sensed something in this man. Something larger and more pure than the life around her. And she knew it was safe to confide in him. "She tried to jump off the Cooper River Bridge this morning."

Roy leaned against the piazza railing as if to steady his large frame. He groaned.

"A security guard on his way to work pulled over and yanked her down before she got all the way over." Della bit her lip hard as the children giggled and carried on in the backyard. "Maybe there is a God, Roy Summerall."

Roy took a deep breath and regained his composure. He looked down to meet her eye. "There is, Della." He tugged at his collar. "What can I do to help?"

"Well, can you stay with these four children this afternoon while my husband and I go to Atlanta and tell Drew what's going on?"

"I'd be happy to," he said. "There's nothing I can't push back on the schedule for the next day or so."

"Thank you." Della felt a lump in her throat. She swallowed hard and said, "I'll get the bottles and some food ready. Come on in." As she held open the door, he insisted that she go first. And she turned back and said, "Oh, and call Anne, will you?"

"Okay." He pulled out his cell phone and hit the button for his contacts. "She gave me her number last week, but I've been too nervous to call her. The e-mail has been going so well."

Della nodded and couldn't help but smile. "Call her and tell her to come home, Roy."

When Della and Peter arrived in Atlanta, it didn't take them long to find the address of the Courtyard Marriott where the CDC was putting Drew up.

Della saw his Volvo sedan parked in front of one of the efficiency suites, so she and Peter walked up and knocked on the door.

"Room service. Hot dog!" they heard Drew's voice call from behind the door. When he opened it, he was in a thin white towel wrapped loosely around his waist. He looked at them, his unshaven jaw dropping slowly, as though they both had three heads.

"What?" a female voice called from the bathroom. The shower stopped and the voice called, "Can you bring me my hair brush, babe?" When he didn't respond, the bathroom door flew open, revealing a young woman draped in a towel. The wet tips of her long blonde hair dripped on the tile floor causing a little pool of water to form at her bare feet.

Della, still in the doorway, crossed her arms and narrowed her eyes at Drew. "This is not so sublime," she said.

The woman—Melanie from the carriage house—looked up, shrieked, and quickly closed herself back in the bathroom.

Drew raked the top of his salt-and-pepper curls with both of his hands. "What are you all doing here?"

Della cocked her head and stepped inside. She was grinding her teeth so hard that her head ached. "Well, we're not having as much fun as you."

Drew clenched his hands and leaned toward Della, who was balling her own little hands into tight fists. But before Drew realized what had hit him, Peter pinned him against the adjacent wall with force. A framed print of Stone Mountain just to the right of the two men fell to the carpeted floor.

"Watch yourself," Peter whispered sternly to Drew. Peter stood a head taller than Drew, his muscles taut, and ready to throw a serious punch if need be.

Della exhaled for the first time since she stepped into the room. Her temples were throbbing, and she felt her heart catch in her throat. *Thank God for Peter,* she thought. *Thank Roy Summerall's God.* She didn't deserve her husband, but she was overwhelmed by how much she cherished him—a man who understood right from wrong instinctively, a man who would protect her from the dangers of this world—including her own hot head and her likeliness to mishandle a just rage.

When Peter released him, Drew pushed him back. Then he quickly grabbed his towel which was coming untied. He pulled it tight around his waist.

"What are you two doing here?"

Della stepped in front of Drew, took a deep breath, and tried not to grind her teeth too hard. "Your wife is in trouble, and we came to tell you."

He wiped his nose with his forearm. "What do you mean?"

Della narrowed her eyes. "She tried to jump off the Cooper River Bridge today."

Drew looked away from them. His eyes were on the closed bathroom door, moving back and forth as a shadow crossed the threshold. He pulled at his hair and looked down at his bare feet.

"Why?" he shouted. "Why is she doing this!"

Della grabbed his arm firmly. "She's not *doing* this, you idiot." She pressed her fingernails into his skin, but she stopped herself from puncturing him good like every cell in her body wanted her to. "I'm no physician, but even I understand that." She shook his arm until he looked at her. "She's sick, Drew. She's contracted a disease, like cancer, only it's in her brain, and she needs serious help to get better."

He bit his lip. Something plastic toppled to the tile floor in the bathroom.

Della let go of his arm and met his gaze again. "You need to come home right away and take care of her."

"This can't be happening," he said, looking away and toward the window. Outside a bright yellow truck with a Domino's Pizza sign was pulling into a nearby space. "Not right now. We're just getting started. There's a weird flu in Mexico, and we're in charge of working with labs around the world to create a vaccine."

"It is happening," Peter said. His voice was deep and full, and it jolted Drew into looking at him. "It may not be convenient, but it's happening right now. And your wife needs you to man up."

Della nodded. She felt like she and Peter were of one mind and heart. Like they were in the same skin. It was an intimacy she treasured in this moment, and she vowed never to take it for granted.

Then she and her husband walked toward the door before she turned back. "She's on President Street. If I were you, I'd get there tonight."

Drew took a seat on the unmade bed and looked back at them. He was still clutching his towel. When he nodded, Peter closed the door. Then he and Della drove back down the highway home.

Chapter Twenty

Roy

Roy drove to the Charleston airport the next afternoon to pick up Anne. His mama had come in to take care of Rose so he could help with whatever Anne and her family might need.

Since they had been corresponding, he'd had this whole plan of how they would meet face-to-face again, and it involved a dozen red roses and a nice night out on the town at one of the fancy restaurants on East Bay Street.

But she was coming home to help take care of a very sick sister, and he'd have to put those plans on hold. However, he did get the roses. Roses were never ill-timed, and he stood by the security check point clutching the waxy paper in which they were wrapped as the passengers on the flight from Charlotte walked down the narrow hallway toward him.

He spotted Anne right away. Her height, her narrow shoulders, her long, wavy red hair. She was just as he had remembered, and he could see her smiling as she walked toward him, pulling her suitcase along behind her.

She stopped a foot from him, and he clutched the roses tighter. Then he jumped back when he realized a thorn had pricked his index finger.

"It's so good to see you." He nodded and sucked his finger for a moment. "Let me take your bag."

Then he handed her the roses and she smelled them and rested them in the crook of her arm. "Thank you."

He wanted to hug her for a lot of different reasons. They had exchanged dozens of letters over the last six weeks, but this was only the second time they had been face-to-face in their adult lives. What was the protocol for this sort of thing?

"I want to hug you," he blurted out as she looked up from her bouquet.

"I wish you would," she said, and he released her bag, grabbed the roses and set them carefully on top, then opened his arms wide and stepped forward and embraced her long, delicate frame.

Did she feel good? Oh, man! She smelled like honey and she felt like life itself. He breathed in as her hair tickled his nose, and he stepped back and smiled. "Wow."

She blushed and looked down at the ground for

a moment, then back up at him and nodded with an unhindered grin.

They stood like this for whole moments until a security guard came over, pointed to the bag, and said, "Does this belong to one of you?"

"Oh, yes," Roy said. He could feel the beads of perspiration forming on his head. He grabbed the bag and the bouquet and pointed toward the door. "I know you're eager to see your sister."

"I am," she said, and she walked beside him toward the electric doors. "But I was eager to see you, too, and I have a feeling you're going to be the joyful part of this trip."

It was strange to feel sad for someone whose loved one was suffering and yet feel so happy at the same time to be in their presence.

"I pray that there will be joy in all the parts of this trip," he said.

She looked at him as they stepped out into the balmy December afternoon. He watched her take in the familiar smell of low tide and salt air. "It's good to be home," she said.

When Roy pulled back into the St. Michael's parking lot late that afternoon, his bookkeeper, Gretchen, was standing by the commander with a worried look on her face.

"Y'all okay?" Roy said as he ambled toward them.

"No," the commander said. "Gretchen just

brought to my attention that none of the cash from last week's offering was deposited into the account."

Roy shook his head. "Who is the vestry member in charge this month?"

The commander narrowed his eyes. "Heyward."

Roy uttered a prayer for Heyward. He nodded toward the office building. "Let me try to get him on the phone, all right? I'm sure there's an explanation. Y'all go on home and I'll call you tonight if I find something out."

They didn't make a move toward their cars, but he turned away and headed toward the Broad Street building. Roy had been concerned about Heyward ever since he moved to Charleston, and he wanted to reach out to him and find out if something was wrong.

Heyward picked up his cell phone the third time Roy dialed it. "Hello?"

"Heyward," Roy said. "Do you think you could come over to the church office this evening and meet with me?"

He heard him slowly exhale on the other end of the phone. "Now's not a good time, Roy. Maybe sometime next week?"

"Heyward, the bookkeeper is concerned because the offering from last week has not yet been deposited. Do you know anything about that?"

There was a long pause.

"Heyward?"

"I'm on my way down there," the man said before he hung up the phone.

An hour later Heyward showed up. His bow tie was untied and his boyish face looked worn and ashen.

Roy pointed to the couch in his office. "Let's talk," he said.

Heyward took a seat and buried his hands in his head. "I'm broke. I haven't made any money in six months, and the bank is getting ready to foreclose on my home."

"I'm so sorry," Roy said. "What can I do to help?"

Heyward blew air out of his clenched teeth. "I borrowed the cash from the offertory so I could buy my kids something for Christmas." He looked up at Roy. "My wife said she'd leave me if there was nothing under the tree for the kids."

Heyward bit his lip. "I can't believe I did it, Roy. Took from my church. I've been waiting on a check from a client who owes me money. He assured me he'd pay me this week, and I was going to pay back the church account last Monday, the day after I took the cash, but my client won't answer my calls and now I'm in a heap of trouble. The commander will want to press charges. I guess I can't blame him."

"How much was it?" Roy sat back in his chair and rubbed his aching shoulder.

"Almost a thousand."

Roy turned to his computer, logged on to his personal account at Bank of America, and transferred $2,000 from his savings to his checking account. Then he wrote Heyward a check for $2,000. "Cash this and put $1,000 in the church account. Use the rest for whatever you need."

Heyward looked up and wrinkled his brow. "No, Roy. I know how much you make, and I don't know if or when I can pay you back."

"I'm your priest," Roy said. "You have to do what I say, right?" He leaned in. "Take the money, then ask your wife to come in with you for some marital counseling. I want to meet and pray with the two of you on a regular basis."

The man nodded and exhaled deeply. "Okay."

"God's got you," Roy said. "Even when things look the bleakest. Especially then."

As Heyward stood to shake Roy's hand, the commander knocked on the glass pane of the door. "Do I need to call the authorities?" he said in his gruff voice.

"No," Roy said. "It's all taken care of. Now go home like I asked you to and be at peace."

The man scowled at Heyward and turned and headed down the steps, then Roy walked Heyward to his car and watched him pull out onto Meeting Street.

When Roy looked up at the picturesque steeple trimmed in garland for the Advent season, he thought of the couple lying still in the dream he had last summer. Could it have been Heyward and his wife? He didn't know the answer to that question, but he did know that whoever the couple represented, the Lord had a plan to breathe life into their stone-like bodies.

Chapter Twenty-One

Lish

On the Monday before Christmas, Lish was released from the Institute of Psychiatry. As she sat in the lobby, watching the nurses walk up and down the hallway with little cups of medication, she thought of the bits and pieces of conversations she'd had with Drew and Della and Anne and Dr. Cussler since she'd been in the hospital.

Because Drew had to be in Atlanta until Christmas, Della and Anne were in charge of the safety plan. Lish knew she would be watched around the clock for the first several weeks, and once she felt strong enough, they would allow her to be alone for short periods of time.

Drew had come back twice to visit her. All she could remember of those visits were his eyes, jumpy and bloodshot, and him squeezing her hand saying, "I need you to pull it together, sweetheart."

* * *

She had sat quietly on her bed, kneading her sheets one afternoon as Drew explained to Dr. Cussler the enormous and highly stressful task ahead of him at the CDC. A rare flu had been recently identified in a Mexican village, and it could turn into a pandemic. It was up to his team to assess the virus and help create a vaccine.

"Lish's sister and cousin will be on site to take care of her through Christmas," he had told Dr. Cussler, who seemed nervous in front of Drew. Lish had noticed Dr. Cussler tapping the wrong side of his pen on his khaki pants, and she could see the little black lines forming across his thigh, but she couldn't find the words to tell him. "Then I want Lish to be able to move with our kids to Atlanta as soon as possible."

Dr. Cussler had gently poked the ball point of the pen into his leg and seemed to work up his courage. "I strongly advise against a move within the next twelve months." The psychiatrist turned to Lish, and she knew he expected her to weigh in. She had rubbed the edge of the sheet and did not respond.

"Look," Drew said. "Let us get through Christmas, then we'll see how she's doing." He stepped toward Dr. Cussler, who stepped back as if he wanted ample space between them.

Dr. Cussler cleared his throat, lifted his chin

toward Drew, and shook his head. "With all due respect, Dr. Sutton, it could be a mistake to rush a recovery."

Lish felt a light tap on her shoulder. She looked to her side and saw Anne and Della standing beside her, smiling tentatively. They took turns hugging her and then they each grabbed an elbow and gently lifted her up.

The Abilify, an antipsychotic medicine she'd been on since she arrived, made her dizzy, and they knew she liked to get up very slowly and feel her feet firmly under her before she took a step.

"We're so happy to see you," Della said. Lish noticed that Della had put lipstick on, and she was wearing the oval-shaped turquoise earrings Lish had bought her during a trip she took with Drew to Mexico several years ago.

Anne grinned and rubbed her sister's arm. "Ready to go home?" Lish turned to her sister, who looked better than ever. She held her shoulders back as if she was proud of her height, and her crimson hair glistened even beneath the stark fluorescent light of the Institute of Psychiatry. Lish didn't know the details, but she understood that Anne was dating the new priest at St. Michael's. Roy Summerall, a boy they had known as children. One of Elfrieda Summerall's nephews. She thought of Anne's revelation in the bell tower a few years ago. Maybe she had heard the voice of God after all.

"Yes." Lish turned toward the elevator. "I'm ready." She swallowed and waited for the burn, but it didn't follow. The Abilify had short-circuited the chemicals in her brain, and whatever made it hard for her to swallow was gone now. Sometimes she still felt the thump on the top of her head. It was very faint and usually came upon her when she'd overdone it or when she took a long, hot shower, but it usually subsided after a deep nap or a good night's sleep.

"Maybe it's just the memory of the thump..." Dr. Cussler suggested during their session a few days ago. He had been rubbing the heels of his hands together like he did sometimes when he was thinking hard.

She had nodded. "It could be."

Now as they drove up to 18 Legare Street, Lish grinned and pointed to the door, where Anne had made a beautiful wreath out of dozens of big waxy magnolia leaves from the tree in Mrs. Emerson's front yard. It was just like the ones Nana used to make. And someone had strung fresh garland along the piazza rails, and she could see through the big thick windows that there was a grand, brightly lit Christmas tree whose top must surely reach the high ceiling.

Della reached over to the passenger seat and rubbed her back. "Like it?"

Lish smiled and slowly blinked.

As she stepped out of the car, one foot finding the ground and positioning itself and then the next, the children scurried out with a long white banner that said, "Welcome Home, Mama." There was a red-and-green wreath on the banner made out of their handprints.

When Andrew and Mary Jane spotted their mother stepping slowly out of the car, they let go of the banner and ran to her. Andrew gently hugged her, and Mary Jane stood up on her tippy-toes, reached up her arms, and said, "Uhh, uhh." Lish didn't think she could lift her. She was still groggy and the pills made her lose her balance from time to time. Instead, she squatted down and took her daughter in her arms. She tried not to weep too hard when she felt the little girl's soft, full cheek against her own. She squeezed her tight and then rubbed her smooth dark hair, which smelled like baby shampoo and Frasier fir needles and maple syrup. Lish could stay this way for hours. She had missed her children, and she yearned to make up for the lost time.

When Mary Jane pulled back, she grabbed Lish's face and said, "I've been waiting for you, Mama."

"Me too," said Andrew. Lish reached out her

arm, and the little boy fell into it so hard that they all three plunked down on the ground. She hugged them both as tight as she could. She wanted to tell them how much she loved them, but the words were hard to find and string together. Both Andrew and Mary Jane pulled back and looked at her as if they were expecting her to say something.

"She's happy to be home," Della said as Cozy came over and leaned against her own mother. Mary Jane rested her head against her mother's chest and said, "We're happy to have her."

Then Anne helped to lift Lish up and Della came to the other side, and they walked her slowly up the stairs and into the house while Peter ran down the steps and picked both Mary Jane and Andrew up in his strong arms. He whispered to them, "Remember what we talked about, guys?" They nodded. "It's going to take a little while for your mama to get used to being home. She's getting well, but she's not all the way well."

"I remember," Andrew said, his arms crossed.

Peter kissed his forehead. "That's my man." Then he spun them around until they were both giggling and holding out their arms to feel the rush of cool air.

They had two quiet nights where they set their routine. Anne slept with Lish one night and then Della the next. Whoever was not with Lish took care of the baby, who still needed a bottle and a diaper change around four a.m.

Peter and Cozy entertained the children and Lish tried to meet her goals for the day: to get up by nine a.m., to take a shower, to get dressed, to eat a meal or two, to have a conversation with her children and watch them play in the garden for an hour or so.

On Christmas morning, Lish stood in her shower and stared into space for several minutes before she heard Anne's voice. "You're going to be okay," Anne said. Then Lish stepped slowly out of the shower and let her sister wrap a towel around her and pull her close. "It's slow going right now," Anne whispered. "But it won't be this way forever."

Lish's eyes filled with tears and she nodded her head. "Some Christmas, huh?" She wiped her cheek. "Is Drew here yet?"

"No." Anne squeezed her damp hair with the towel. "I'm sure he's on his way."

By noon on Christmas day, Drew pulled into the driveway in his new car, a big black Range Rover. The children ran out to greet him, and he opened the trunk and pulled out his extravagant gifts—a life-size, battery-operated Groovy Girl jeep for Mary Jane that she could drive around the yard, and a three-wheeled motorcycle of the same ilk for Andrew.

"Awesome!" Andrew shouted. He called Cozy over, and they all took turns circling the loquat tree and the rosebushes and the swimming pool over and over until Mary Jane fell out of the driver's seat on a sharp turn by the carriage house and scraped her shoulder on a stepping stone.

Drew had little to say to the adults. Della and Anne tried giving him as much space as possible. They pretended to be busy cooking the turkey and the dressing, and Peter spent most of the afternoon unpacking the toys that were so thoroughly wired into their packaging that he said he needed his blowtorch to extract them.

After a hectic lunch where Baby Cecilia fussed and Andrew popped Cozy so hard on the back with a spoon that she cried, the kids settled themselves in front of the Rudolph movie and the adults cleaned up—everyone but Lish and Drew, who walked slowly up to the third-floor piazza for a talk. Lish tried to keep her voice low in hopes that Drew would follow suit. She was counting on the hum of the dishwasher and the shrieks of the snow monster on the television to keep the others from hearing their conversation.

Drew didn't follow suit, and Lish imagined Della and Anne raising their eyebrows from two floors below as his voice rose and fell while he rationalized away his distance and detachment. Lish, too weary and weak to respond, listened and nodded and looked toward the carriage house where she had the faintest memory of watching Melanie rub Drew's back. She wondered if it was all a bad dream.

After the children were put to bed, Lish walked Drew down the stairs, where he shook Peter's hand and nodded to Della and Anne. "I've got to get back to Atlanta," he said.

Della rolled her eyes and opened her mouth to speak. But Peter quickly grabbed her arm, and she kept quiet.

"Let me walk you out," Peter said to Drew. The two men were out in the driveway for nearly thirty minutes. Lish knew Peter was trying to talk Drew into staying, but he wouldn't succeed. Then the rumble of Drew's huge motor sounded, and the bright beams of his headlights exposed a marsh rat in the garden. He pulled right out of the driveway and Lish could hear him, from their bedroom, as he pressed the gas and powered down the south end of Legare Street in his tall, dark cage of a car.

That night, as Lish sat in front of her vanity mirror examining her sagging jowls, Anne and Della came up together. "Time to get ready for bed." Anne handed Lish a pill and a glass of water.

"He's gone," Lish said as she swallowed the

little white tablet that made her dizzy and dull. She scanned their bedroom before viewing herself in the mirror again. "He doesn't want this… anymore."

"What do you mean?" Anne stood behind Lish. Three worry lines formed across the thin blue vein in the center of Anne's forehead.

Lish turned slowly around to face them. "I know Drew." She stood up and walked slowly to her bed, where she sat down and sucked her teeth. Then she rubbed the center of her head. *It's not the thump, just the memory of it*, she said to herself. "He wants a… new life."

Della crossed her arms. "Now *that's* insane."

Lish chuckled and shrugged her shoulder. Her voice was strong, but she parceled her words out one or two at a time, and it seemed like seconds before the next one followed. "There's probably…someone else. I don't…know." She placed her hand on the bed and looked up to Anne and Della. "But…this has gotten…too messy…for him. I know… Drew. He…wants out."

Anne breathed deeply, and she shook her head in disbelief. "How could he ever walk away from you and the children? That's just—" She cleared her throat. "Unconscionable."

Lish leaned back on the mound of pillows at the head of her bed and pulled the covers up to her neck. "It can all...come unraveled...so quickly, can't it?"

"It can't be someone else." Anne sat down beside her and took her hand.

Della was silent. She stood to hang up Lish's cream wool pants, and when she turned back, her eyes met Lish's. They locked for several seconds as Anne looked back and forth between the two women. Lish could tell that Della knew something, but whatever it was, it didn't need to be said. The reality was that while Drew's leaving wasn't right, it could certainly be what was happening. It could be exactly what Lish suspected.

Lish watched Della as she laid down next to her and gently sighed.

It was disconcerting when Della was quiet. Like a summer night without the hum of the crickets. Della took Lish's other hand and squeezed it. And they stayed this way for several minutes before Lish said, "Good night, y'all."

Chapter Twenty-Two

Roy
January 21, 2009

Roy had a spring in his step. It was a spring he hadn't had in a long, long time. Though it was January, the most depressing month of the year for some, he couldn't help but grin at any passerby as he stood under the church portico just before the weekday midday prayer service, inviting folks off the street to come in for prayer and a fifteen-minute respite.

Sometimes folks took him up on the offer. Quite often a tourist had the time to spare, and occasionally a lawyer or some other business person in a tailored suit would come on in and take a place in one of the box pews as a lay reader read the Scripture passage.

Anne was there most every day with Baby Cecilia bouncing on her knee. The baby girl had grown quite fond of him, and after the service he loved to carry her in his arms down Meeting Street to wherever Anne felt like having lunch.

Every other night, Anne was off the babysitting duty, and he would make sure they found some time to get together. If it was Alpha or vestry meeting night, she'd come by the house afterward and play Candy Land or Hi-Ho-Cheerio with him and Rose, and Roy thought Rose enjoyed it even more than him—if that were possible.

One Friday night after Rose said she wanted to go up to her room and play with her Barbies, Roy found himself next to Anne on the couch, just looking at her and smiling. They had very few moments when they were alone, and perhaps this was good. It was all he could do not to take her in his arms and profess his love for her, but he wanted to make sure they proceeded at a pace that was right with her and with God.

"I'm not going back to England," she said.

He wasn't sure how to respond. He knew the reason she had come home was to see about her sister, and Lish still needed a lot of help. But he was hoping that another one of the reasons that she wasn't going back was him.

She sighed her lovely sigh and tucked her hair behind her delicate shoulders. "My sister needs me."

"Yes, she does," he said. His heart was pounding so hard, he could feel it in his ears. "And so does someone else."

She met his brown eyes, and he pointed to his chest and then upstairs to the sound of Rose pitter-pattering in her room just above their heads.

Anne took another deep breath. He couldn't help himself. He wanted to know where she stood when it came to him.

"Anne, even if your sister had made a full recovery by now, I would have asked you not to go back."

He squeezed her hand. Her long, thin bones reminded him of the graceful herons he saw wading in the salt marsh. He pulled his hand away, not wanting to be too forward.

She blushed and then looked up to him. "Roy," she said. "If you would have asked me to stay, I would have said yes."

His heart seemed to pound even stronger in his chest, and his throat tightened. A few weeks ago he would have thought he was coming down with something, but he was familiar enough with the feeling by now to know just what it was. He was afraid to call it by its name just yet. But it filled his heart with an indescribable joy. He knew Anne was a gift from the Lord, and he said, *Thank you, Thank you* to his Maker as he leaned in to kiss her on the lips for the very first time.

"Yippee!" a voice called from the grand stairway. He looked over his shoulder to see the tail of Rose's fuzzy purple bathrobe as she ran quickly back up the stairs. Had she been watching all along?

"She's excited about where this might be going," he said.

Anne settled into the couch and took his heavy hand in hers. "She's not the only one."

Sometimes it's hard to focus when you're in love. But Roy had prayed for the Lord to continue to show him how to minister to his new flock. He asked them to fill out another prayer request card so he could pray for their specific needs during Lent. This go-round, everyone seemed more comfortable, and he received over 150 cards. This time folks were more honest too. It wasn't just "Pray for my Great Aunt So-and-So who is sick" kind of stuff. They wrote the things they were struggling with themselves: financial hardship, marriage problems, depression, chronic lust, envy, regret over a decision, unresolved conflict with a family member or old friend. Real-life stuff. But what struck him was the struggle that every fourth or fifth card seemed to name: anxiety. One-third of his flock had anxious thoughts or felt overwhelmed. Why? The needs of the Church of the Good Shepherd had been much more concrete and simpler to solve. But this anxiety—where did it come from? Nearly half the people who came and sat in his office were struggling with some form of fear or fretfulness. He started to pray for the troubled hearts and minds of each member of his congregation. He took the directory out and prayed for a page full of church members each day.

Then he asked some prayer ministers from a church he knew in Jacksonville to come over and lead a Saturday of healing prayer in February that focused on the verse "You will keep him in perfect peace, whose mind is stayed on You, because he trusts in You" (Isaiah 26:3). Over one hundred people signed up.

Chapter Twenty-Three

Della

One remarkably mild Saturday afternoon at the end of January, Della and Lish were watching the kids kick a soccer ball in the garden when an unfamiliar car pulled up and a young man stepped out with a certified letter that he asked Lish to sign.

Della helped Lish stand and steady herself by holding the rocking chair with her fingertips. Lish slowly nodded at the man and carefully signed the letter with his thick silver pen. Then she sat down and carefully broke the seal as the man backed out. Della watched her eyes move back and forth as she took in the words.

Then Lish handed the letter to Della, who read it quickly to herself as the children screamed with delight as the ball made its way into their makeshift goal, a cast net draped over two camellia bushes. Drew was filing for a separation. He admitted that he had committed adultery. He would provide for Lish and the kids. He would give them whatever they needed. He wanted to end their marriage as soon as possible.

"Lish." Della took her cousin's hand and squeezed it tight. She watched as Lish brought a teacup up to her lips, sipped, and swallowed before scooting back in her chair.

Then Lish settled the cup back in its saucer, placed it on the rail, and reached over to pat Della's arm as if she was the one who needed reassuring. "No...surprise."

"Mama!" Andrew called. "Look at this lizard we just found!" He lumbered up the piazza stairs, with his sister on his heels, and opened his hand to reveal a bright green lizard with a red, bloated throat. Mary Jane squealed as the lizard promptly leapt out and onto the old floorboards, darting between their feet. They all watched with wide eyes as the creature scurried off the side of the porch and onto a limb of the tea rose bush.

"Wow," Lish said unhurriedly. She forced a smile and nodded her head. "That's something."

One afternoon in February as Della was checking her e-mail during a planning period at school, she received a letter from the editor at her publishing house. She'd been waiting for him to respond to her novel for three months now. It had never taken this long.

Now she stared at the three-paragraph response to her three-hundred-page novel with disbelief. She read the heart of the letter several times:

While the writing is strong and the story, at times, is quite riveting, the ending fails on many levels. It doesn't ring true somehow. It's abrupt and incomplete. And it leaves the reader feeling both baffled and cheated. Yes, the murder is inevitable, but is that all there is to the story? I'm not sure why you chose to end it here, Della. What was your thinking?

As it stands now, the novel is unpublishable, and we simply can't accept it. In my mind, you have two options: 1. To rewrite the last third of the manuscript, contemplating what makes an ending that is both complete and resonant. 2. Take nine months and write something new.

Let me know what you want to do as soon as possible.

"Ugh." She leaned over her desk and rested her forehead on the heel of her hand. She didn't know whether to scream or cry. It was not too easy to write a novel when you taught six sections of middle school English every day, and you were caring for your cousin and her children every other night. And she needed that advance money something awful. Her old Honda had died two weeks ago on her way over to Legare Street, and she and Peter had picked out a used pickup on the lot at Marsden's Mitsubishi that they were going to buy as soon as the money came in.

"Bye-bye best seller," she said to herself as the students filed into her classroom, laughing and throwing a crumpled ball of notebook paper back and forth. She had tried to create a kind of commercial novel, a page-turner, and her editor had out-and-out rejected it. That hadn't happened to her in years.

She walked home in a daze with Cozy's hand in hers. The girl was chatting a mile a minute about a scuffle that occurred on the playground between two fourth-grade girls who were fighting over a swing. Her teacher had had to come between them and order them both to the lower school principal's office.

When they rounded the corner toward their crumbling, plum-colored duplex, Della saw Peter in the driveway putting a license plate on the truck they'd been eyeing.

Cozy ran ahead. "Daddy! Daddy!" He hugged her tight, and then he threw her high up in the air, her thin arms and legs spread and slightly bent at the joints as if she was a marionette or a sky diver in mid-fall.

"You bought the truck?" Della said. Her right hand was firmly on her hip, and she was trying to keep her composure.

He turned to her and grinned. "Remember the two shrimp I took out to that new art gallery on Kiawah Island a few weeks ago?"

"Yeah." She vaguely recalled him loading the sculptures in his father's truck early one morning.

He mimicked her by cocking his hip and slapping his hand on it. "They sold late yesterday to a couple from New York." He leaned forward and put his nose against hers. "Turns out this couple is pretty well-to-do, and they've asked me to sculpt three turtles for a home they have in Maine."

Then he straightened up and pulled a wad of cash out of his pocket. "I cashed the check, bought the truck, and I've got a dental appointment for Friday afternoon."

"You're kidding, right?" Della breathed deeply and let her hand fall to her side.

Peter shook his head as if to say no. "And there will be enough left over to put a few thousand bucks in the bank." He stuffed the cash back in his pocket, reached over and patted her backside. "How about them apples?"

She swung her arms around his hips and rested

her head against his chest as Cozy jumped up and down chanting, "Take us for a ride!"

"In a minute," Peter said as he pecked the top of Della's head. "So how was your day?"

She pulled back and looked up at him. "Not nearly as good as yours."

"You can tell me all about it over dinner at Rue de Jean."

"Rue?" she said. It was her favorite restaurant, but they hadn't been able to afford a meal out in months.

"Yep." He reached out and pulled Cozy into the center of their embrace. "Anne agreed to watch this little monkey along with the rest of the gang tonight." He rubbed the little girl's head with his knuckles, then leaned down and cupped his hand around her ear to whisper, "I'm taking Mama on a date."

"All right!" Cozy looked up at her mother and flashed a knowing grin. "Can I help you get dressed up, Mama?"

"You better." Della rubbed the child's cheek with the back of her hand.

That night after a bowl of the curry mussels, the duck special, and a choice glass of champagne, Peter and Della rode over in their newly purchased truck to 18 Legare to pick up Cozy, who they hoped was sound asleep in the lower bunk of Andrew's bed.

Lish was waiting for them on the piazza. She was rocking slowly back and forth in the dark in a flannel nightgown with two thick wool blankets draped around her shoulders.

"Hi."

Della jumped back, and Peter steadied her. She made out the figure of her cousin and said, "Sorry, Lish. You scared me."

Della hadn't seen her cousin in more than forty-eight hours, and it seemed like a long time now that she spent every other night at her home.

Lish looked up to them both. "How was…your date?" She tried to focus, to meet their eyes; Della knew it was hard for her this time of night, and she was not surprised when Lish looked away.

"Really nice." Peter leaned against the railing. "We were overdue for one of those."

"I'll say," Della chuckled.

They watched Lish for a moment as she grasped the edge of the chair and began to rock. They heard the heavy breathing of two late-night joggers, and in the distance the honk of a car horn.

Lish turned back to them. "Can I talk"—she swallowed with effort—"to you both?"

"Sure." Della took a seat next to Lish, and Peter leaned forward, giving Lish his full attention. "What's up?" he said.

Lish adjusted her posture. She examined the veins snaking their way across the tops of her hands and said, "I want y'all...to move in." She nodded across the garden. "To the carriage house."

Della looked to Peter, who crossed his arms and waited for more.

Lish's blue eyes glistened in the darkness. She licked her chapped lips and turned to Della. "I won't charge you...any rent." She wrung her hands. "Maybe you could...sell your place...or rent it out."

Then she peered up at the half moon hanging in the clear winter sky above them. "I...need you." She shook off a chill. "I need...your help."

Della cleared her throat. The thought hadn't crossed her mind, but she knew what Lish was trying to say. She might not get well this year or next year or the next after that. And they couldn't go on this way, spending every other night over here, living out of suitcases and Food Lion grocery store bags. Plus, Anne was in love for the first time ever, and she needed more time with Roy to see where things were leading.

Della reached out and took hold of Lish's shoulder. Her eyes were on Peter. "Let us talk about it, okay?"

Lish waited for a moment before she slowly nodded her head twice. "Okay." She stood and turned toward the grand front door. "Thank...you."

* * *

That night on their back porch, Peter patted his knee, and Della took a seat on it.

He squeezed her tight. "What do you think about your cousin's proposal?"

Della rested her head against his and looked up at the same half moon. "I don't know."

Ever since they drove away from 18 Legare, she'd been trying to decode a hidden message or another layer behind her cousin's request. She stared at the half face of the man on the moon. "I think she's trying to tell us she's not sure if she's going to get well." She sighed. "And that terrifies me."

He rubbed her back and pulled her even closer. "I think she was just asking for our help." He kissed her forehead. "Nothing more and nothing less."

"Maybe." Della sat up and turned back to him. "She's asking for help—indefinitely, I guess."

"Don't think of it like that." He rubbed her thin arms with his wide hands. "None of us can predict what's going to happen from one day to the next, you know?"

They both watched a thin layer of mist move across the moon. She felt his lips on her ear as he said, "I'm up for it if you are."

Two weeks later, Della and Peter got an offer on their half of the duplex. It was practically a miracle; nothing was selling on the peninsula as the economy continued to tank. But the parents of two college kids who had bought the upstairs unit a few years ago, when their twins enrolled at the College of Charleston, spotted the For Sale By Owner sign one Saturday morning, knocked on the door, and said: "We're interested."

"That's fantastic," Della had said as she stepped to the side and invited them in for coffee.

By the next week, they'd signed a contract, and by the end of March, Della and Peter and Cozy packed their little life into cardboard boxes and hauled it all over to the charming old two-bedroom carriage house behind the grand home at 18 Legare.

Chapter Twenty-Four

Della
April 9, 2009

In April, Dr. Cussler called a meeting with Della and Anne. He was not pleased with how slowly Lish still seemed to be moving—both mentally and physically. She walked like an old lady, hunched over and wobbly, and her energy level remained remarkably low. As for the depression, it had a strong hold on her. Three consecutive months of a high dose of Zoloft should be making a significant difference by this point, but wasn't. She was not the Lish they'd always known and loved—that much Della knew for certain. There were few flickers of the real her, and they were all concerned.

"There's a research project at MUSC," Dr. Cussler said. "It's new and fairly unconventional. But I think Lish could benefit from it."

"Tell us about it." Anne leaned forward on his big leather sofa. Her long legs squeaked against it.

Dr. Cussler raised his eyebrows and leaned in to meet them both from his chair opposite them. "It's called transcranial magnetic stimulation."

"I've heard of it." Della tapped her foot; then she nudged Anne on the knee. "Todd told me about it." She looked to Dr. Cussler. "It's like electroshock, but gentler, right?"

He nodded. "Precisely." He touched his fingertips to his head. "It uses a powerful electromagnet to bypass the skull with a magnetic field, and then the procedure is to induce weak electrical currents in the brain."

"Ugh." Anne rubbed her temples. "Does it hurt?"

"No." Dr. Cussler shook his head emphatically. "That's the beauty of it. It requires no anesthesia, unlike electroshock therapy, so it doesn't induce seizures or the side effects that come with them, like memory loss, headaches, and so forth."

The young doctor set his yellow legal pad on his knobby knee and looked back and forth between them. "This could jump-start the sluggish nerve cells that are maintaining Lish's severe depression." He shook his head. "Unfortunately, she hasn't responded to the antidepressants in the way

I hoped she would by now. I think this is worth
a try."

Della rubbed her knees. "Me too."

"How do you feel about it?" Della asked Lish
that afternoon as they walked at a snail's pace
down Meeting Street on their daily stroll with
Baby Cecilia.

"I'm...scared." Lish talked like a record in
slow motion and looked down at her feet; she put
one foot in front of the other. "But maybe..." She
stepped and stepped again. "It will help."

Della noticed the petals of a dogwood tree, fluttering down onto the sidewalk. She heard the *clip-
clop* of a horse pulling a carriage down Broad
Street and the *brush brush* of the custodian sweeping the entrance into St. Michael's Church. As she
watched the old city, still alive and thriving, she
pictured Lish as a ten-year-old, running down this
block in her tea-length dress on the way to dancing school at South Carolina Society Hall. She
envisioned her turning, looking back, and pulling
her arm toward her shoulder, gesturing for Della
to hurry up.

Now Della nodded as Baby Cecilia started to
protest. She was probably irritated by how slowly
they were moving. Della looked at her cousin, who
seemed oblivious to the protest and to the evoca-
tive streets and the beautiful spring blooming all

around them. She just watched her feet, one foot in front of the other. One foot in front of the other was all she could manage. Lish reminded Della of Papa in the afternoons, unable to face the world.

This is the hardest part, Della thought. *Having someone right beside you who is no longer really there. It's like you've lost someone and yet—there they are—breathing, walking, and every once in a while talking. But the personality and the voice and the vitality behind the voice are gone. How did Nana stand it?*

"Hey, you two!" a voice called from the cemetery. Della turned to see Roy bounding down the slate path toward the street. He was in purple shorts and a bright orange polo shirt. The unfortunate colors of Clemson University. (Anne would have to convince him to go with either purple or orange from now on, Della thought.)

He reached out to shake their hands, then he smiled at Baby Cecilia, who had settled down now that she saw his bright face. "I've been thinking about you all. Why don't you come on up to my office and let's catch up?"

Lish straightened up and turned to him. "Okay," she said. "Maybe…you can help us." She took a deep breath. "We're trying…to make a decision."

He nodded and smiled. "Absolutely." He gestured toward the Broad Street building where Della and her cousins had attended Sunday school and confirmation classes year after year when they were kids.

"There's nothing I'd rather do than catch up and pray for you." He turned to Della and patted her shoulder. "That's what it's all about, right?"

Della parked the stroller in the cemetery and lifted the baby out of her seat. They walked down the slate path toward the building and up a flight of stairs, where they found his office. It was a beautiful corner room, looking out over Broad Street. As Della stared at the bookshelves and the icons and the painted crosses from Honduras and Ecuador, she remembered the stained-glass one hanging in Nana's kitchen when she was a child. There were words above it—some sort of Scripture—but she couldn't recall them.

Della bounced Baby Cecilia on her knee as Lish slowly told Roy about the TMS treatment. (Anne had taken off for a bell ringing retreat in Richmond just after the meeting at Dr. Cussler's.)

Roy listened with soft eyes and a palpable empathy, and then he scooted his leather chair over toward the couch where they were sitting and took their hands in his. As he prayed for guidance, Della felt a kind of warmth radiating from his palms. She opened her eyes slightly, and as he closed with a heartfelt petition for Lish's complete recovery, she pictured the hands of a twelve-year-old boy, wrapping his shirt around Lish's bloody shin and then lifting her up into the paper basket on the front of his bike. Della could almost feel the hot air lifting up the strands of her hair as she chased behind the bike while he pedaled Lish home with remarkable speed.

When Roy said *Amen*, Della turned to watch Lish look up and attempt a smile. "I'm going... to do it," she said.

He nodded assuringly and took her hand again. "I think you should."

When they stood Della said, "What happened to your wife?" She knew from Anne that he was a widower, but she had not heard the particulars.

Roy turned back and met Della's gaze. "She passed away a couple of months after we had Rose."

Della couldn't help but put her hand over her mouth. "I'm so sorry."

He put one hand on his hip and shook his head. His eyes were warm, and he took the time to look at both of them. "She had a cancerous spot on her tongue, and we didn't discover it until she was six months pregnant."

Lish let out a sympathetic moan.

"It was tragic." He took a deep breath. "There's no other way to describe it." He gradually put his hands palm up and bit his lower lip. "But God's mercy somehow carried us through each day." He raised his eyebrows. "And the honest truth is, he still does." Looking back out the window, he added, "It's funny. Rose told me last night after Anne read her a bedtime story that she's never been happier. And I have to say I agree."

Suddenly Della remembered the words on the cross hanging in Nana's kitchen window. She never consciously memorized them, but the words came right to her mind. *"In all their affliction He was afflicted, and the Angel of His Presence saved them"* (Isaiah 63:9).

She felt a burning in her throat, and she wanted to both laugh and cry. Did she have that many bones to pick with God after all? Or did she have him to thank for all that was good in her life?

"So I'll call Dr. Cussler when we get home," Della said as they took a right turn off of Meeting onto Lamboll Street.

"All right." Lish swallowed and clenched her fists. "Thank you."

She's not completely gone, Della said to herself as she watched her cousin walk one laborious step at a time back toward her home as the birds twittered and the scent of the wisteria blossoms permeated the air with a syrupy sweetness. *At least the most essential part of her isn't, anyway.* Della looked through a hole in a crumbling brick wall and watched a blue jay dunk its head in a cracked birdbath. *Only Lish would endure this whole thing*

*without throwing a pity party or asking, time and
time again in an outraged tone, why?*

Two weeks later, Della drove Lish over to
MUSC for her first treatment. She would receive
four weeks of the daily forty-minute TMS sessions, and then Dr. Cussler and the neurologist
would examine her to see if there'd been a significant change.

Anne met them in the neurology unit, and
within moments Lish followed Todd Jervey, Dr.
Cussler, and Dr. Rand, the neurologist, beyond the
thick swinging doors and into the research ward.

Della and Anne stood still for whole minutes as
if paralyzed as they listened to the steady drone
of the machine on the other side of the wall. Della
had conducted her fair share of online research
about the effect of putting electricity on the brain.
Back around the turn of the century, doctors in
Italy noticed that their depressed patients with epi-
lepsy actually improved after a seizure, and since
then, they'd sought all sorts of ways to reboot the
mind with a jolt.

Eventually, Anne took a seat and Della started
to pace. She pointed to the stack of papers in her
seat. "I should be grading," she said. "But I can't
sit still."

Anne fingered a stack of magazines and pulled
out a *Newsweek* and started to read the lead story,

"Obama's First One Hundred Days" as Della's flats slapped the tile floor. "You're making me nervous."

"Sorry." Della sat down next to Anne and squeezed her wrist the way she used to when they were girls. "Man, I hope this works."

"Me too." Anne leaned her head on Della's shoulder. "I miss her."

Della put her face in her hands and let out a muffled, "I know." She rubbed her eyes. "I want her back." She looked at Anne head on. "All the way back."

Anne nodded her head in agreement. They had not said this to one another and it hurt to admit it. How far away the Lish they knew and loved seemed. Anne squeezed Della's wrist back.

Lish came out leaning on Dr. Cussler's arm. She was bleary-eyed and appeared even more exhausted than before she went in.

"There's a...tapping...in my head," she said to no one in particular. It was as if she was talking to the wall or the stack of magazines by Anne's chair.

"She needs to rest," Dr. Cussler said. Anne rushed over and took her by the arm.

"I'll pull the car around." Della fished in her pocketbook for her keys as she scurried down the hall toward the parking garage.

When they arrived home, Peter and Della

walked Lish up the stairs, one step at a time, to her room, and they didn't hear a peep out of her for the rest of the night.

During the next two weeks, Della and Anne took turns driving Lish to the late afternoon TMS sessions. Each time Lish came out seeming wearier than before, her arms limp and her shoulders hunched over. By the fourteenth session she could hardly lift her feet. She shuffled them now, like an old man. She didn't have the energy to lift them up.

"The treatment seems to be wearing her down," Della told Dr. Cussler, who called for a report on a day he couldn't be there. "She is worse than before."

He met Della and Anne at the hospital the next day and saw what they saw—an aged person, hunched over and shuffling, barely able to walk or string a few words into a sentence.

"I'm calling a meeting with the researchers," he said. He blinked several times and pulled at his little chin. "The last thing I want is to put her in a worse state than before."

The following week, Dr. Cussler discussed his concerns with the three research physicians before Monday's session. Then he met Della, Anne, and Lish in the waiting room at the usual appointment time and ushered them into a conference room.

"Dr. Jervey and Dr. Rand think we should keep

going," said Dr. Cussler. He looked to Lish, who was hunched over in a plastic chair, her back like an arc or a question mark. She reminded Della of their Great Aunt Bess, who had osteoporosis so bad that she spent the last decade of her life staring at her toes. "But I'm not sure."

He patted Lish's shoulder, and Della watched her slowly look up. Lish could barely meet his gaze, and after she tried she let her head flop back down. He gently touched her hand. "I don't want this to set you further back."

Lish slowly lifted her head once more to look him head-on. Her eyelids were still half closed as if they were weighted with lead, but she could make out his eyes. Just as Della was about to say, "Let's stop," Lish said, "Keep…going." Then she dropped her head again.

Della gnawed at the inside of her cheek, and she tapped her foot so strongly that the whole room seemed to be pulsing until Anne reached over and patted her leg.

"Are you sure?" Della pleaded.

Lish nodded in slow motion.

"Okay." Dr. Cussler scratched the top of his head as if he was nervous. "We'll proceed for another week, and then we'll meet again."

On the thirty-third session, on a late May afternoon, Lish slowly shuffled in with her eyes half closed as Della graded a pile of essays and Anne read the newspaper from front to back. Della was used to the steady drone by now, and it almost had a calming effect on her as she waited.

Anne had read two months' worth of all the magazines in the entire waiting room, so after she discarded the paper, she turned to a stack of brochures at the front desk and read them each twice. The first one was about headaches, the second was about depression, and the third was about the swine flu.

So much had changed in a year, Della thought as she lifted her head from her essays and stared at the back of the swine flu brochure. They practically all lived at 18 Legare taking care of Lish and her brood. Drew was gone. Lish was gone in a way too. But Della and Peter had never been tighter, and Anne was finally in love.

Baby Cecilia was about to turn one, and she was pulling up on the tables and putting everything in sight in her mouth. She only wanted Peter to hold her when he was around, and he made a fuss over her, kissing her and patting her in a way that filled Della's heart with a kind of joy and hope.

Lish's children were doing as well as they could despite the fact that their father rarely came to see them and their mother was here in body but not so much in spirit. Andrew could read the level two books, and Mary Jane just wanted to play dress-up with Cozy, who humored her most evenings by doing just about anything she wanted her to do.

This might be the way it is for years, Della thought to herself. She hadn't said this to Anne or even to Peter, but she had thought it for weeks now as the TMS wore them all down. Surely they had all thought it.

It is what it is, Nana used to say. And then Della thought of what the wise matriarch said to her one day when she didn't catch a second piece of candy from the Christmas parade. *You get what you get and don't throw a fit.* Words to live by, Della thought. She could feel her grandmother's love all around them still like a sturdy wall, a sturdy wall she leaned on quite often.

There were only four more treatments to go. Then what? *Don't ask that*, Della said to herself. *Just don't even wonder.*

Della was on her thirty-seventh essay comparing and contrasting *Number the Stars* by Lois Lowry to *Suzy and Leah* by Jane Yolen when she looked up to find Lish gazing back with her eyes a little wider and a look in them that seemed more alive somehow and remarkably familiar. It was the look of her cousin—the real one—and she watched as Lish blinked twice, held the front of her head, and said, "I feel a little better...this time."

Anne rushed over to her as Della stood and

studied her frame. Then Lish reached out as if she wanted to take both of their hands. Within moments, Della was on the other side of her, squeezing her warm, fleshy fingers. She narrowed her eyes. "You look better," she said tentatively.

"I agree." Anne nodded.

Lish smiled slowly. "Maybe," she said. "Maybe something's…happening."

Chapter Twenty-Five

Roy

The time came when Roy couldn't wait any longer. By mid-May, the spring in his step had turned into an out-and-out jump. One day, Ms. B. took him aside and said, "Shall we go look at some rings?"

"I want to," he said. "I just don't want it to be too fast for her."

"Look," Ms. B. said. She narrowed her little gray eyes. "I've known Anne Brumley all her life, and she's one of the finest young ladies in this city. I've known you a little while, but I have a real good feeling about you." She winked. "It's not too fast."

That night he had a sit-down with Rose about the matter. He took her out on the second-floor piazza with two glasses of milk and a plate full of Oreo cookies.

She was onto him immediately. "Why all the treats, Daddy?"

"Well," he said as they took a seat on the plastic lawn furniture at the edge of the piazza. "We need to talk about something."

"Okay," she said. She leaned forward in her chair and grabbed a cookie, which she dunked in the milk.

"Remember that day you got that invitation to the mother-daughter tea party, and you told me that you wanted me to meet someone?"

She nodded. "And you have."

"Yes, I have." He rolled his shoulder forward, then patted her knee. "I want to know... I guess I want to see how you feel about the idea of me asking Anne to marry me."

Rose's eyes grew wide and she nodded her head yes.

He held up his hand to slow her down. "Now, there's no guarantee that she's gonna say yes, Rosebud. I can't know anything for sure. We haven't known each other that long, so I don't want you to get your hopes up too high."

She went from nodding to bouncing in her chair. "Okay, but can't I be a little excited? I'm not sure if I can help it!"

"Of course you can." He looked out over the

rooftops and then back to her as she rose and fell on the seat of her chair. "So you like the idea of it? You'd like it if she said yes and came and made her home here with us?"

"Daddy." Rose gave an exasperated sigh. "You *know* I do. I've wanted this a lot longer than you have."

"Maybe she's the one." He felt his throat tighten. He wanted to protect his precious child, but he couldn't help but share in her excitement.

She crinkled her head. "Who else would there be?"

"All right then." He rubbed his calloused palms together. "Since I have your blessing, I'm going to do it."

Rose dunked her cookie in the milk a second time, took a soggy bite, and smiled a chocolate smile. "I knew it would happen," she said.

The next week, Ms. B. took him down to look at rings at Croghan's on King Street. They were awfully expensive but beautiful, and he settled on a single solitaire set in platinum that he thought would be just right for her. Ms. B. approved, and late in the afternoon on the last Tuesday in May, he grabbed Anne's hand after their usual lunch date and said, "Let's go to the top of the steeple. I heard you can see the Spoleto sculpture on top of the Exchange Building from there."

"Okay," she said and she led the way up the several flights of winding stairs to the utmost balcony at the tip-top of the 186-foot steeple. Once they were there, she looked down Broad Street toward the exhibit, and when she turned back around, he was down on his knees holding a little blue velvet box in his hands.

She cupped her freckled cheeks and her face turned bright red, and when she broke into a smile, he opened up the box and said, "Anne Brumley. Every good and perfect gift is from above. And I believe that you are a gift to me. I hope you will say yes and be my beloved partner on this earth for the rest of our days. Will you?"

She took a deep breath and reached down and took his strong, thick hands in hers. She pulled him up and looked him right in his eyes. "There is nothing I would love more."

"Whoo hoo!" he called. Then he took her in his arms, as her soft, sweet-smelling hair blanketed his face. They stood this way for a long time until he remembered the plan and stomped his foot four times on the balcony. It was the signal he had given to Ms. B., who had coordinated the bell ringers to ring a whole peal if she said yes, and the poor lady had been waiting on a rickety staircase for nearly a half hour before she got the sign.

Then as the rounds began and the steeple swayed the way it did when the bells were calling out to the city, he took the ring out of the box, slipped it on Anne's delicate finger, and embraced her beneath the beautiful arches as Rose and Mama looked on from the rectory window and clapped.

As he held his future wife in his arms, Roy looked down at the picturesque old city and then out to the harbor, where the sails of the boats twittered like moths on the water as the sun lit up the surface with little chips of light. He chuckled at how reluctant he had been to move to Charleston. God's plans were always better than ours. And he could feel a sermon forming in his mind about how we might miss the blessing if we don't acknowledge our shortsightedness, trust in his grace, and make ourselves downright pliable.

As the bells reverberated, filling the air with the sound of God's glory, Roy knew the Almighty had given him a gift he never thought he could have again. Roy loved the city, he had to admit it now, and the city, to his great surprise, loved him back. He had a new home, a very happy little girl, and a partner he could lean on until the end of their fleeting days of this earthly life.

Chapter Twenty-Six

Della
June 7, 2009

The TMS seemed to be the answer. Lish regained her strength little by little as the treatments continued, and by late May she was spending several nights by herself with the children. Della and Peter were right across the garden, and she called them whenever she needed help. But she hadn't called much lately.

At long last Anne was planning the wedding she always told Della she'd have, and as for Peter, he couldn't make crustaceans fast enough for the second-home owners with deep pockets out on Kiawah Island. His shrimp and turtles were all the rage, and the president of the College of Charleston had recently received an "English professor shrimp" as a gift from a wealthy alum. It was a shrimp with a goatee and horn-rimmed glasses reading Dante's *Inferno*. The president was so impressed that he asked Peter to teach a metal-sculpting class for Maymester and apply for a visiting instructor position in the Studio Art Department. And Peter loved what he was doing—sculpting and working with young people. It couldn't be a better fit.

One Sunday afternoon in June when the loquats had ripened and were falling off the trees, Della picked up the ringing phone with Lish's number flashing on the caller ID. She looked out the window and saw Lish, with the receiver to her ear, waving at her from the upstairs piazza.

"Wanna harvest some Japanese plums?" Lish pointed to the tree behind the big house.

"Yeah," Della said. "You bet we do."

Lish rubbed Mary Jane's head as Andrew flew an airplane around them. Then she looked Della in the eye across the yard and spoke into the receiver. "I'll call Anne and gather some buckets. Y'all meet us beneath the tree in half an hour."

"Yippee!" Cozy said from the den as Della told her the plan. The little girl was playing pick-up-sticks with Peter, and she held up her fistful of colorful wooden sticks. "Let's call it a game, Dad, okay?"

"No way." He pointed to his meager pile. "Give me one more turn."

"Oh, all right," she said.

When Cozy heard the rumble of Roy's truck and then the call of Mary Jane and Andrew who flew out of the back door of the main house, she abandoned the game and ran out to see everyone. Within minutes, the kids climbed up the tree, spread out in all directions, and snapped the loquats off of the limbs.

"Slow down!" Peter called as the kids tossed the fruit to the ground. He grabbed one of Nana's old metal buckets and held it beneath the center of the tree as the little orange plums rained down.

Then Roy stepped down from the porch with Baby Cecilia in his arms. She preferred the men—both Roy and Peter. But today she squiggled out and wanted to get down on the grass and stand up for herself.

Della stepped back to watch this scene. The kids in the trees, the Japanese plums falling, and then this—Lish squatting down and reaching her hands out to the baby, who reached back with a smile, saying, "Ma, ma, ma!" as Roy led her over to her mother.

Della laughed and brought her hands to her cheeks. The sun was on her face, and she looked up to Cozy, who plunked down on a limb near the center of the tree and began to peel back the skin and take a sweet bite.

Della thought about her editor's rejection of her murder manuscript and how she had decided to scrap the whole thing and start a new book, with Lish's blessing, about a young mother who battled a severe postpartum depression. As she contemplated the importance of endings, like she had so many times since her editor's response, she wondered what actually constituted not only a full and resonant ending but a happy one. She knew happy didn't mean perfect. It didn't mean all the loose ends tied up in a tight, tidy bow like the end of a fairy tale. (Does anyone actually believe that Cinderella and the prince never gained weight or uttered a harsh word to one another?) That wasn't real life, and she wanted her work to mirror reality. She suspected her readers wanted that too. Yet the ending had to have more than just a snapshot of our concrete existence. It needed that intangible something that buoyed us all this side of heaven. That feeling Della only could describe as hope. That undeniable mixture of joy and expectation that superseded the mess known as "real life."

Is this a happy ending? Della asked herself as she watched her daughter suck the meat of the loquat and reach for another. And then she turned to see Lish, who took Cecilia in her arms and kissed her cheek and neck before rocking her back and forth. Della watched her cousin's hands. They seemed sturdy and capable as they took hold of the toddler, as if to confirm through the sense of touch what every child longed to hear from their parent: "Yes, my little one. I am here for you."

Della took a deep breath as Lish lifted Cecilia up into the sky, the sun filtering through her plump little toes.

Yes, Della thought as Anne nudged her elbow and handed her a loquat. *This is.*

* * * * *

Dear Reader,

One theme which inevitably surfaces in each of my stories is the power of female friendships, and *Love, Charleston* is no exception. As one of three daughters raised in a Christian home, I was born into women's ministry, and I wholeheartedly believe that our sisters in Christ play a crucial role in building us up, allowing us opportunities to give and receive grace, and providing a good laugh when the tensions in life build.

Since we are fearfully and wonderfully made, it is no surprise that science backs this notion up. A recent landmark study from UCLA showed that female friendships counter stress. That is, when women get together the wonderful "bonding" hormone, oxytocin, is released which buffers the typical "fight or flight" response and produces an overall calming effect. And the famed Nurses' Health Study form Harvard Medical School found that the "more friends women had, the less likely they were to develop physical impairments as they aged, and the more likely they were to be leading a joyful life."

All this to say, I don't think it is a stretch to argue that attending a Women of Faith Conference will surely benefit any woman's spiritual, mental and physical well-being. You won't regret setting aside the time to come together with your fellow sisters for worship, teaching, laughter, fellowship, and if the science is on target, a little oxytocin too!

Warmest Regards,

Beth Webb Hart

Questions for Discussion

1. Why doesn't Roy want to move to Charleston? How does his view of Charleston society, particularly the parishioners of St. Michael's Episcopal Church, change over the course of the story?

2. Describe Roy's faith and his approach to ministering to his new flock. What makes his ministry effective?

3. The children play a crucial role in the three narratives of this story. How do both Rose and Cozy shed a new and hopeful light on the struggles of their parents?

4. When did you suspect that Drew's commitment to Lish was tenuous? Why didn't he stay and help her through her post-partum depression?

5. Do you think there are prejudices and misunderstandings about mental illness in our society? Discuss the story's treatment of Lish's post-partum depression. How do her loved ones react to her condition? How important is their reaction to her recovery?

6. Della's desire to provide for her daughter nearly justifies her potential infidelity. How has she come to view financial means as the ultimate source of both security and happiness? What is the danger in cultivating this kind of view?

7. What type of spouse is Peter? How do his actions prove his commitment to Della and their family?

8. This novel takes a close look at marriage. What are the typical conflicts and challenges husbands and wives face today? Are they any different than the struggles of previous generations? What does this novel say about the importance (and the deep-seated joy) of sticking together?

9. Della grapples with what makes a story ending both full and resonant. Is the ending to *Love, Charleston* a happy one? Why or why not?

10. By the end of the novel, Roy admits that God's plans are better than our own. How can we (in Roy's words) "acknowledge our short-sightedness, trust in His grace, and make ourselves downright pliable"?

About the Author

Beth Webb Hart, a South Carolina native, is the best-selling author of *Grace at Low Tide*, *Adelaide Piper*, and *The Wedding Machine*. She serves as a speaker and creative writing instructor at schools, libraries, and churches throughout the region, and she has received two national teaching awards from Scholastic, Inc. Hart lives with her husband, composer Edward Hart, and their family in Charleston.